F*CK marriage

Copyright © 2019 by tarryn fisher

All rights reserved.

Visit my website at www.tarrynfisher.com

Cover Designer: Maripili Menchaca

Editor: Lori Sabin

Proofread by Erica Russikoff

No part of this book may be reproduced or transmitted in any form or by any means, electronic or mechanical, including photocopying, recording, or by any information storage and retrieval system without the written permission of the author, except for the use of brief quotations in a book review.

This book is a work of fiction. Names, characters, places, and incidents either are products of the author's imagination or are used fictitiously. Any resemblance to actual persons, living or dead, events, or locales, is entirely coincidental.

All rights reserved.

ISBN-13: 978-1097105397

For Sarah Hoffman

PART I

CHAPTER ONE

BILLIE

The salon is warm, all west-facing windows. I stare out at the parking lot wishing for a fan, a breeze—anything to cool the heat on my skin. I watch as a mother chases her toddler across the cracked asphalt; he falls. Rolling onto his back, he screams, arms and legs flailing like a turned over beetle. When she picks him up, I see that her hair is stuck to her face in wet clumps. She's at her wits' end, either from the heat or the boy. I feel her. The entire state of Washington is an oven, and we are her bread.

With mother and boy tucked safely in their car and on the way, there is nothing to distract me from my current discomfort. My mind drifts to nicotine, my tongue curling around the imaginary flavor. I want a cigarette so badly I'm jittery. The bell to the door jingles, and one of the stylists walks in carrying two tabletop fans under her arms. She purses her lips to blow her bangs off her forehead, but they stay put.

"It's all they had left," she says to a different stylist.

They confer about where to put the fans, and in the end, they drag a table to the center of the room and make a fuss of arranging them. If I lean to the left, I can catch some of the breeze they're creating.

"Can you sit up straight?" my stylist asks, tapping me on the shoulder. "I thought you wanted to cut it." She stands over me, hands suspended, mid-action. They always seem so disappointed when you tell them you don't want to hack your hair off.

I can see the damp on her blouse just under her arms. She opens and closes her scissors for emphasis, drawing my eyes back to her face. I think of comparing her to *Edward Scissorhands*, but she's freshly twenty-five and I doubt she'd know who he is.

"Change of plans," I say. "I'm going home next week."

The word *home* is a sour word in my mouth. Even as I say it, my tongue curls back in protest. Home to me is a city, not a house, or a husband, or a family. Maybe because I don't really have those things anymore, or maybe because I'm not cut out to have those things.

"No one there has ever seen me with long hair," I explain, as if that's a good enough reason.

It's not entirely the truth. There's no one left to see me. My friends are gone. In my exodus from the city two years ago, I made the decision for them. For a while, they tried to stay in touch, but in my grief, I sent their efforts to voicemail. And just like that, they stopped trying. My ex was the one who stayed, so he inherited custody of our friends. It sounds silly to think that, but it's true. When there's a divorce, lines are drawn, sides taken.

I reach up, running my fingers through the length of it. It's past the middle of my back, hanging in sleek mermaid waves, thanks to Tina's grooming. I like the idea of them seeing me in my new body, with my new hair: I am thinner, longer, wiser…more jaded. I tell myself that being jaded gives me an edge. If Woods met me now, there'd be no way he'd call me trusting like he did all those years ago.

"Home, huh? I thought you grew up here in Port Townsend," Tina says.

She likes to make fun of my divided loyalty; though, if you put a gun to my head, I'd choose New York every time.

"Do you have a cigarette?" I ask.

"Nice try. You told me not to give you one no matter how much you beg."

"I just want to put it in my mouth."

"That's what she said," Tina jokes.

She rummages around in her bag and pulls one out: Marlboro. *Ew.* I stick it between my lips and close my eyes in pleasure.

"You're pathetic," she says when I hand it back to her.

"I know."

"—but beautiful."

"In New York I'm Billie, and here I'm plain ol' Wendy."

"Oh my dear," she says, spinning my seat around to face the mirror. "You're anything but plain."

I smile at my reflection. A lot has changed since I arrived home two years ago, my tail tucked between my legs. And Tina is right, partially right: I am no longer the plain girl I once was. Rejection is a fine motivator.

"When do you leave?" She unclips the robe from my neck, and I unfold myself from her chair. The breeze from the fan finds me and I close my eyes in pleasure.

"Tomorrow." I turn to face her.

"Will you see Woods?"

Tina's stylist chair doubled as a therapy chair my first year home. She probably knows more about my failed marriage than my own family.

"That's the plan," I say.

She frowns. "I hope you know what you're doing, Wendy. Be careful, okay?"

Careful? That's what I will not be this time. Careful is what got me into this mess in the first place.

"Sure," I say, and Tina frowns. "Wish me luck?"

"Luck? You don't need luck for revenge. You just need balls."

CHAPTER TWO

The guest house. It's seven hundred square feet with a wall of windows and an attic bedroom that faces a nature belt. Not a bad place to hide out when you're shamefaced with a broken heart. Other than a bed and a cracked leather sofa, I don't have a lot of furniture. The lack of space in New York taught me to be a minimalist. What I do have is exercise equipment. A treadmill, a rowing machine, weights, and a Pilates machine. It started with the treadmill a few months after I got back. I was in the middle of the second and third stages of grief: anger and bargaining. I looked at myself long and hard in the mirror (naked) and decided that my husband left me because I was fat. If I were thinner, fitter, more toned—I could surely lure him back. Prove my worth. I wasn't fat. But you can't deal with your big issues first, you have to gradually work your way up. If anything, I was curvy. Okay, maybe a little chubby. So, I bought a treadmill and a pair of running shoes and took out my anger on that human conveyor belt. As soon as I was sober enough to notice the results, I got addicted to exercising. Now, where there used to be layers of fat, there are layers of muscle. I'm not even sure I like being this ropey and hard, but when you lose control of your life, you seek to regain control in some other area, and so here I am. *Oh hey! You left me, but I can probably beat you up now. Oh sure, you have a younger woman, but can you bounce a quarter off her ass?*

I sell my equipment on Craigslist, and by the time I've packed up everything I've accumulated in Washington over the last two years, it fills one measly suitcase. I stand over the zipped and ready-to-go luggage feeling largely pathetic. My father finds me there, hands on my hips.

"This is it," I say. "I'm thirty years old and this is the sum of my life." I kick the side of it disparagingly.

I say it more to myself than to my father. Any type of emotional proclamations make my parents uncomfortable. As a result, I was a largely silent kid. My father chuckles like I've just delivered the punchline of a joke and then hauls my suitcase to the car without a word. Once he's gone, I give the place a final look over. I don't know that I'll miss it. It was a good place to rest...I enjoyed being naked without worrying someone could see me. I sigh deeply and head for the door.

"Bye, little house. See you."

I lost my virginity to Carter Benini when I was sixteen years old. This was after he handed me a melted Snickers bar and told me in that too-cool-for-school voice of his that he loved me. The truth is Carter and I had only been dating for a month, but he was captain of the football team and the type of guy who said, "Hey girl, you so fine," while biting his bottom lip. The biting of the lip thing had done me in; slimy attention was my favorite aphrodisiac. I was living in the moment, or at least I believed I was. Carter, unfortunately, had only lasted a moment before collapsing on top of me, and after we did the deed he pulled off the condom and proclaimed he was hungry, asking if he could have my Snickers. He took my virginity and he took my Snickers, and a week later he broke up with me. So cold. I found out I was part of a year-long commitment he had to de-virginize as many sophomore girls as he could. Talk about trust issues; I've always had them. I was devastated, of course. Teenagers can deliver lies but seldom have the stomach to take them. I took a whole year off from dating, dyed my hair black, and listened to my homegirls—Fiona, Meredith, Stevie, and Alanis—on repeat. I finally caved when Philip Von asked me to be his girlfriend my junior year. I told Philip that under no circumstances would I sleep with him before we'd been dating six months (the agreed amount of time my friends and I decided was appropriate to judge if a guy was a douche).

"It's cool," he'd said. I was worth the wait.

And he had me believing it until my best friend caught him at a Halloween party with a girl dressed as Vivian from *Pretty Woman*. It was a week shy of our six-month anniversary. Saved by the ho. It still hurt and I cried for two weeks. There was a string of relationships after that. I went through a brief slutty period in college when I slept with frat boys with R-letter names: Ryan, Ross, Rick, and Reid. And then during my senior year of college came Woods: sexy, unassuming, self-deprecating Woods. He always smelled like Juicy Fruit and he had a big head. It was impossible to find a hat to fit him. I loved holding his head between my hands, running my fingers through the thick brown curls. It was a solid head, you couldn't miss it in a crowd, and it was mine. Real talk: I'm the girl who always believes the newest set of words. Brandon's ... Philip's ... Woods'...

No matter how flimsy they are, if you dip them in some delicious lie, I'll gobble them up.

. . .

On my first date with Woods he told me that I was too trusting.

"What makes you say that?" I'd had a visceral reaction, jerking my head back before sluggishly feeling the weight of insecurity.

We'd closed down the restaurant where we had dinner. After mutually deciding we didn't want the date to end, we walked twelve blocks searching for a place still open to get another drink. We found a dive on First called American Trash, and I took off my shoes as soon as we sat down at the bar. My hair at the time was blonde, short and shaggy, and he'd reached up to tug on a piece near my cheek while the sleepy-eyed bartender mixed our drinks.

"Let me see your feet," he'd said.

Without question, I'd put my feet in his lap and he'd started rubbing them.

"See. You barely know me."

"They're just feet," I'd pointed out.

"If I'd asked for your wallet you would have handed me that too."

He was probably right. He talked about it like it was a novelty to find someone who wasn't jaded and so I believed myself special. At least to him. To the guy with the soft chocolate curls and the easy smile. That should have set off alarm bells in my head—a guy who was looking for a girl to trust him probably wasn't getting an A+ in the honesty department.

Turns out Woods got a big, fat F. When he said he was going to the gym, he was really having dinner with the lifestyle editor of our blog, a girl I'd hired myself. The perfume on his shirt that smelled like candy: hers, even though he claimed it belonged to our sixty-year-old client. He came home one evening just a month after we celebrated our third wedding anniversary and told me he wasn't happy and wanted a divorce. I laughed. Laughed, like he was pranking me. Life was pranking me, love was pranking me; Woods, he was completely fucking serious.

*A*nyway, we're divorced now. But for eight years, that man massaged my feet any time we were in a bar together. As it turns out, the most painful experience of my life was laying those eight years of a relationship into a grave I was forced to dig myself. The person doing the leaving hands you a shovel and you bury something you once lived to nurture.

That's the way it goes during the death of a marriage: the denial, the anger, the grieving, and then the inevitable purging of soul.

CHAPTER THREE

*N*ew York bulges in front of me, splitting her city seams across the horizon. Excitement crackles in my belly as I watch her come into view. I've been ridiculed for my love of this city back home, but I don't care. She's testy, ambitious; everything about her pulses lightning fast. She's easy on the eyes and hard on the nose. Warm wind blows through the open window and I crinkle my nose at the smell of exhaust fumes and piss. *Weak, Billie. You leave for two years and now you're wrinkling your nose like a tourist.* I smile, leaning my head against the back of the seat. It feels so good to be back.

I always feel most at home here because New York is me: my soul city. Neither of us knows how to sleep, for instance. And there is the fact that we make people from small towns feel uncomfortable.

I peer out the window as the cab veers left then right, swerving at the last minute to take the exit. It's the type of erratic cab driving that tourists bemoan for years after visiting. *Oh my God, you wouldn't believe how they drive in the city...*

In my expert opinion, you haven't truly experienced New York until you've thought you were going to die during a cab ride. My hair, a tangled mess after the red-eye I took, hits me in the face as the wind from the open window zigzags through the car. My cabbie is a nice man named Frank who has three snake tattoos. He stops in front of a building on Fifth Avenue and hooks his arm across the back of the seat to look at me.

"You gonna be okay? You're the color of my Aunt Bee's pea soup."

"Word," I say. "You should see what my insides look like."

"That bad, huh?"

I eye the cigarette propped behind his ear.

"Can I smell your cigarette?"

He plucks it from its resting spot and hands it to me without comment. Lifting it to my nose, I sniff.

"Okay," I say, handing it back. "Better."

When I step out, my entire body is tingling in anticipation. I flex my fingers and stare up at the building, while Frank retrieves my bag from the trunk. All of a sudden, I feel foolish for ever leaving New York. This is the place I love. Jules, my friend since college, has taken a job in Brazil for a year. She's letting me stay in her apartment until I get back on my feet. That means I have exactly a year to figure things out; if I can't reverse what I've done in a year, I'll gladly skulk back to Washington. The apartment is on the third floor, and after I pay my fare, I haul my meager suitcase up the stairs. The keyring Jules mailed me bites into my sweating palm. I know this city, I love this city, and yet my hands are trembling as I turn the key and push open the door. Relief kicks in as soon as I step inside. It's not the spacious one and a half bedrooms, or the hardwood floors, or even the impressive collection of thrifted furniture that I'm happy to see. It's the fact that I made it back, that I came back after what happened. I didn't let the hurt swallow me whole. Just thinking about the hurt makes me hurt, so I busy myself with looking around.

Jules had a cleaning company come in; I smell wood polish and bleach. I walk around the apartment touching the spines of her books, the carved wooden wings that sit on the coffee table, like an invisible angel ready to take off. I can't believe I'm here.

I spend my first morning back unpacking the few things I brought, examining the excellent light that trickles through the blinds making everything glow honey warm, and examining the contents of Jules' pantry— which is mostly empty except for a few cans of creamed corn and green beans. I find the coffee—a bag of somethin' somethin' from a shop uptown, the name of the beans handwritten in marker on the indigo blue bag. Jules has a very fancy coffee machine. She's taped instructions on how to use it on the counter. I stare at her instructions for a few minutes, my palms sweating at the responsibility. Espresso machines are for grown-ups, not girls like me who have never even owned a Keurig. In Port Townsend, I did the smart thing and walked to a coffee shop for my morning joe.

To my extreme delight, there are several coffee shops in the neighborhood. I try the closest one first, a place called Crunchy that has a cat sitting in the window. I smile wanly at the barista when he hands me my recycled cup, my new name scratched on the side in hot-pink Sharpie. *Yes! Yes! Yes!* That's me, Wendy from New York! I'm uptown, and I wear a size four, and no man would dare cheat on a woman with such magnificent mermaid hair.

I spend the afternoon shopping for supplies. Instead of a chain grocery store, I peruse a little sidewalk farmers market, plucking vegetables from baskets. In the evening, so as not to break the schedule I've been keeping, I pull on my Nikes and go for a run. And then, when the day is over, in the crisp sheets of someone else's bed, I curl up and cry. It's a very Billie thing to do, but oh well, no one can see me anyway. Tomorrow it's back to being Wendy.

The next morning I check my emails on my beat-up old laptop. It won't even turn on unless it's plugged in, and I tap my fingers on the counter while I wait for the screen to load. I'd given Woods a little consideration and sent him an email before I left Washington, informing him that I was moving back to the city. He'd responded right away, it was nice. He welcomed me back and asked if I'd be staying in our old loft. I never answered him. I'd put up an ad on Craigslist about the loft and had twenty messages within the first day. I'd chosen a guy in his thirties who was serious about his career and worked in finance. I figured he was less likely to have wild parties in the event that he would be working all the time. All that's left to do is pick up a box of things the cleaning company set aside and hand him his keys. In my rattiest jeans and an old Pearl Jam shirt, I set out for my favorite street in SoHo. It's nearly impossible to avoid painful memories in a city you spent ten years living in, but I try anyway, taking the long way around the places where my ex-husband and I spent a lot of our time. The gym, for example —I can't say I loved going, but Woods and I would trek there three times a week, holding hands, gym bags slung over our shoulders. It was part of our daily lives, a monotony that I appreciated at the time. I've found that the small moments hurt more than the big ones. The juice bar on Spring Street where we'd stop for breakfast on the way to the office, trying each other's drinks and laughing when we always liked the other person's better. The movie theater we went to on 181st, because it had the best popcorn and fizziest Diet Coke. All places that Woods and I shared the most intimate moments, moments that solidified my love for him and our life together. Seeing them ignites a hurt that I wrestle down to a smoldering level. Barely.

The loft is painfully empty when I step inside. My shoes echo on the wood floors; I like the sound because it reminds me of my hollow insides. Washed and scrubbed and dusted of our memories, the loft is barely recognizable. I choke out a laugh, because I laugh when I feel awkward, and I feel hella awkward in the home I shared with my first love. It smells the same and that's what makes me tremble. I try to shake it off, reminding myself that it's been two years. *Two!* I say forcefully to myself. When we'd moved in, Woods had commented on how it smelled like baby powder. I'd scrunched up my nose and agreed, hoping he wouldn't get any ideas. Babies were not on my radar ... yet. We never could figure out where the smell came from, though on several occasions our friends made mention of it too. I do a quick walk-through, trying to breathe through my mouth, my tennis shoes sweating on the freshly polished floors. Nights drinking red wine in front of our view; Saturday mornings scrambling eggs at the stove, Billie Holiday playing on the stereo. A fight we had about the bathroom paint color that ended in a smashed bottle of perfume and both of us laughing hysterically. Heavy, happy memories that make me swell and deflate at the same time. I thought he loved me, but I was wrong. By the time I make it back to the kitchen dragging the memories behind me like deflated balloons, my new tenant is buzzing through the intercom. I scoop up the box the cleaning people left for me and meet him at the door.

Farewell, goodbye, adios, fuck you! I think.

CHAPTER FOUR

*P*earl Lajolla is five years my junior. Five years; it doesn't feel like much, but it is. Five years means fewer wrinkles—probably right around the eyes and mouth—perkier tits, and more innocence. The innocence is the worst part. Men, especially Woods, are drawn to that shit. They act like they're not the ones who've made us jaded in the first place, and then punish us for having battle wounds by leaving us for someone they haven't fucked up yet. Pearl—was she truly innocent or just feigning? Who knows. There's a line Shakespeare wrote in *A Midsummer Night's Dream*: "Though she be but little, she is fierce." That was the first thing that came to mind when all five feet of her walked into the Rhubarb office the day I hired her on the spot. She was there in response to an ad I'd placed in the *New York Times*. I'd put the ad in the paper because I liked the old-fashioned quaintness of it. Woods made fun of me—*a hundred job sites on the Internet and you take an ad out in the paper!* Newsflash, Woods: *newspaper* is not a dirty word, it's just slightly antiquated.

The ad went like this: Open-minded blogger needed for an up-and-coming brand! Must love fashion, food, and fun!!

I cringe now at the wording, but my younger, untarnished self had been hopeful and apparently grandly enthusiastic.

Pearl had been wearing too much of everything when she walked through the doors for her interview: jewelry, makeup, perfume ... eagerness. But underneath the heavily made-up face and the heady smell of Chanel was a woman who never missed a thing. She was pretty except you didn't notice it right away. What you noticed first was the tiny-ness of her, and then the large expressive eyes that were always watching. Her pretty came secondary to her expressions, which were often comical. In that first meeting, she wore her hair pulled back in an impressively large bun. Her hair was a rich auburn that I imagined unfurled to her waist. Within two minutes, she confessed that she was a huge fan of the blog and hadn't happened upon the ad I'd put in the paper by chance. She'd been *waiting* for it, she said. Pearl had a friend at the *New York Times* who worked in classifieds. When she saw my ad, she called Pearl immediately. She told me all of this with the same lack of shame I'd seen on her face after I found out she was sleeping with my husband. Consequently, it was that very lack of apology that made me hire her in the first place. She was a go-getter and the no-excuse way she moved through life was her biggest asset. I'd shared a lot of myself with her that first year. She'd been eager to learn. An easy friend, she seemed to have had my back. But she only had it so she could stab it.

The bar where I'm meeting Woods is more of a dive than one of the trendy drinking spots in Manhattan. I hail a cab instead of walking the seven blocks and slide into the backseat, relieved that the cabbie is blasting the air conditioning. I have to start using the subway if I want my money to last. *Just this one time*, I tell myself. Small, dangerous luxuries. I call out the address as he almost kills us with his extra terrible driving.

"You're super bad at this," I call out to him.

But my voice is drowned out by the motorcycle that passes us. God, I love this city: I love this cab, and the subtle danger I'm always in just by living here. I lean my head against the seat and close my eyes. The cab jerks left and I'm thrown into the door. Outside the car is a cacophony of honking. I don't even bother to open my eyes. If I die, I die in New York. I'm okay with that. Ten minutes later, we make it to the bar and I slide out of the car, groggy. The cabbie calls after me—I forgot to pay him. Shoving a twenty in his hand I offer a meek apology. He speeds off without responding, and I walk unsteadily toward the bar. Woods used to accuse me of being too distracted with life to remember to do basic tasks like pay the cabbie or push the button in the elevator. He did those things, and I suppose I'm only getting worse at not doing them as I age. I push through the bar door and scan the room for a table. I need to be in just the right spot to hold the upper hand.

I lick the sweat from above my lip and shift in the stool, fanning myself with the sticky laminate menu. Woods is late. I expected as much, but as I glance nervously around the bar, I wish I'd planned to arrive late rather than trying to be here on time. Who knows when he'll actually show up. He has a knack for either being too early or embarrassingly late. Since he isn't here yet, I assume it will be the latter. When the bartender makes his way over, I order a lemon drop. My throat can already feel the vodka. I purse my lips and order two.

"So I don't have to bother you for another," I tell him.

"Another is our specialty," he says. "We're a bar not a gym."

I'm really soaking in that comeback when my phone pings. Woods telling me he's going to be late when he's already late.

I'm on my third drink, my tongue raw from the lemon, when the door opens and my ex-husband walks in. Something about Woods: he has the most sincere, expressive eyes. Brown and cozy like a cabin in the woods ... like a fire in the hearth when you're cold ... like sex when you're horny. He's everything, and I still know that. Cheating assholes shouldn't have such sincere faces. I'm past sober and well into buzzed as I watch him scan the room for me, hands in his pockets. That's what he does when he feels out of place—he buries his hands in his pockets. Funny how you can know a person so well while feeling like you don't know them at all. I thrill when his eyes pass right over me. Like Billie isn't even here. And she's not. Wendy raises a hand to beckon Woods over. Wendy smiles when he catches sight of her and raises his eyebrows in genuine surprise. Wendy holds but a shadow of Billie. My stomach is wobbly as I stand to greet the man who'd fucked me for almost a decade, then fucked me over.

"Wow," he says when he reaches the table. "I almost didn't recognize you."

I imagine he's just given me a compliment because his face is one-half awe, one-half shock. It's the face of a man who's just realized his grandma smokes pot.

"I thought people moved to Washington to grow out their pubic hair and drink Kombucha from recycled glass."

"Says the boy from Georgia who moved to New York to eat dollar pizza and considers himself edgy because he wears black."

"Hey now," he says. "Dollar pizza is good even when it's bad."

I smile because you can say whatever you like to Woods and he always lobs a comeback even if you're too dumb to get it.

He picks up my empty glass, tilting it toward his nose as he sniffs.

"Lemon drop," he announces like I don't already know.

He licks his lips and I get a flash of his head between my legs, tongue flicking while I scream.

The bartender appears, a new one this time. I'm grateful for the distraction, my cheeks are flushed.

Before Woods can order for himself, I say, "He's going to order an IPA, but he really wants a lemon drop."

He slides onto the stool across from me, an amused expression on his face. "She's right," he nods, "so just go ahead and bring the lemon drop."

The familiar banter is painful. God.

As soon as the bartender turns his back, Woods is smiling at me. The corners of his eyes crease and it doesn't make him look tired, or old, or haggard; if anything, he looks charming. Someone wanting to flatter him could say his wrinkles give him character. I don't want to flatter him.

"You look good." He always gets right to the point.

And I do look good. I've lost nearly forty pounds since the last time he saw me.

I get right to the point too because I don't trust myself.

"I'm renting out the loft," I say. "The cleaning company found these..." I slide the envelope across the table.

Woods tents the opening and peers inside. "My God, the missing social security card and birth certificate. We fought about this for three days. Where did they find them?"

"Under the fridge."

"Go figure," he says.

He sets the envelope on the table. A week ago, I'd emailed Woods to tell him I had some of his things that I would be happy to mail to him. He'd responded not ten minutes later, asking to meet instead.

"Where are you staying?" he asks.

I study the hairs on his forearms. "I rented an apartment."

"Why not just move back into the loft?"

"Been there, done that." I smile. And then I add, "Too many memories. If I'm back in the city I want to make new memories, not be reminded of all the old ones."

His lemon drop arrives and he touches his full glass to my empty one in a halfhearted *cheers*.

"Another?" the bartender asks.

I smile weakly. "I better not."

"I'll have another," Woods says, "and keep them coming." He unfolds a piece of Juicy Fruit onto his tongue.

"Still with the Juicy Fruit?" I ask.

Woods chewed Juicy Fruit like it was his security blanket.

"Always."

As soon as the bartender is out of earshot, he turns back to me. "Does Satcher know you're back?"

It's an odd question. I haven't spoken to Woods' best friend in years.

"No ... I was thinking about calling him."

Before our split, Woods and I had started our own business, a lifestyle blog called Rhubarb. The day I signed my divorce papers, I sold my share of the business to Woods' friend, Satcher Gable. All I'd wanted to do was go home to Washington. In retrospect, it was a stupid idea. The company had been my idea, my labor of love. It hurt to think that I handed it over to Satcher and my cheating ex-husband. I rub my forehead trying to recall what my therapist said I should do in times like these. I think I was supposed to repeat something over and over. Something about success ... forgiveness...

Screw it. I cuss under my breath instead, and then liking

the way it feels, I say it over and over like my forgotten mantra. *Fuck, shit, fuck, fuck, fuck, fuuuuuuck. Shit.*

"You okay, Billie?"

Woods suddenly looks like he really needs that next drink, so I decide to change the subject.

"I don't go by Billie anymore."

"Why not?"

"She was married to you."

He flinches but refrains from making a comment, the muscles in his forehead moving in emotion.

"Okay," he says. "So what do I call you now?"

"I'd imagine nothing. I'm your ex-wife. There's no reason to call me anything."

"Come on, Bil—"

"Royden—"

"Oh no, Billie, no. Why are you calling me that? That's tragic," he says, shaking his head.

I can't help the smile that pushes against my lips. I try to hide it with a frown, but he's noticed and he's looking at me with soft eyes. Eyes that have seen my best and my worst for nearly over a decade.

"It's a good name," I say. "You never liked it, but it's a good name."

He shakes his head like he's embarrassed, but I can tell he likes what I've said. When I first met him, we'd been introduced by mutual friends at a small mixer. He'd taken my hand and told me his name was Woods.

"That's not his name!" my friend Samantha called from across the room. She was drunk, and as she called out to us, her drink sloshed over the rim of her cup and onto the rug.

"Fuck," she said. "Fuck."

"What's your real name?" I'd asked, turning back to him. I

could hear Samantha behind me calling for a rag, her words slurring.

"My full name is Royden Lynwood Tarrow."

"Yikes," I said.

"Exactly." He'd then ducked his head, his mouth tucked in a smile, eyes still on my face, and I'd fallen. Fallen for him, fallen for that sexy embarrassment, fallen so hard I'd silently wondered if the two sips I'd had of my drink went straight to my head.

*N*ow I stare at the man who gave and took my joy, and I can't help but wonder if I'd allowed him to do it. Woods never asked me for anything. In our eight years of being together, he rarely made demands, and the less he'd needed, the more I'd felt obliged to give. It was a self-imposed pressure to meet his unspoken needs. And I think I'd gotten it all wrong in the end—we both had, which had led to our slow demise.

His phone vibrates on the table, spinning in a slow circle. We look at it at the same time. *Pearl* flashes on the screen. Woods scratches the back of his head, clearly embarrassed.

"I was supposed to be home ten minutes ago."

I raise my eyebrows, amused. "A curfew? The great Woods Tarrow has a curfew?"

"Stooooop," he says, laughing. "You know how it is..."

I didn't, in fact, *know*. When Woods and I were married I never told him when or where or how to be. I was the opposite of controlling, so much so that he once accused me of not caring about our marriage.

He suddenly grows serious. "You were never the controlling type."

I don't say anything. I don't need to.

Woods taps his fingers on the table, the fingers of his free hand kneading the back of his neck.

"What do you say we have one more drink, woman with no name?"

I look around the bar—the couples bent toward each other, mouths hovering close, hands pressing into the smalls of backs. There's anticipation in the air. Everyone is lapping up the night, their blood thrumming with alcohol. Woods and I stand under the apple juice glow of the bar lights and stare at each other.

"I can't," I say after a long pause.

To my delight his face falls. I stare in wonder: at his face and my effect on it. When you've been hurt as deeply as I have, it's the small triumphs that soothe the wound. When Woods told me he was leaving me I'd been hysterical—first bursting into tears, and then begging him to change his mind. His face had remained impassive throughout my tantrum. I'd thought that he'd been trying to hold it together, that he was equally as distraught about our failed marriage as I was, but when he moved in with Pearl the following day I realized his face had been a reflection of what he felt for me at the time: nothing.

I lift my bag to my shoulder, but he looks so distraught that I feel as if I need to give him something.

"Wendy," I say. "I go by Wendy now."

His face lights up. He's as much delighted as he is surprised. "You hate your middle name."

I shrug. "Not as much as I hate Billie Tarrow and everything she was," I say.

"Okay, Wendy," he says carefully. "See you."

"See you," I echo back.

I turn with purpose for the door and walk out, making sure I don't look back. On the sidewalk outside of the bar, a jogger nearly runs me over. I take my first deep breath of the night, the fumes of the city hitting the back of my throat. That went better than expected. At least I hadn't cried. *No*, I think. *Of course you didn't cry, you're not a crier anymore.* I think of Pearl—wherever she is—the phone pressed to her ear as she dialed Woods. There once was a time when I'd been phoning Woods and he'd been with her. How the tables have turned. Pearl stole a married man, and now I am going to make sure their marriage never happens. Woods is mine.

CHAPTER FIVE

"*B*illie!" I hear my name being called from somewhere behind me. I stop, scanning the crowd. There are throngs of people everywhere. I forgot how crowded the city is in the summer. It may not be me they were calling—Billie is a fairly common male name, especially in a huge city like New York. I feel silly for even stopping. Turning back around, I hear it again, and this time there's something about the tone that lets me know it's for me. It's through the middle of a cluster of teenage girls that a familiar face emerges: wide shoulders, hair pitch dark, and two dimples emerging from scruffy cheeks. My face immediately breaks into a smile.

"Satcher," I say.

He's slightly winded when he reaches me and I see that he's wearing running gear.

"I was on my run when I saw you two blocks up, had to sprint to catch up with you."

"My, my," I say, not even trying to suppress my grin. "I must be the first girl you've had to actually chase since middle school."

Satcher's grin is contagious as he embraces me. I notice that he doesn't even smell like sweat after a run in ninety-degree weather. I fan myself self-consciously when he lets me go.

"Did I get you wet?" he asks.

"Wha-what?" I clamp my thighs together.

"I'm sweaty." One corner of his mouth turns up in a loaded grin.

"I'm not wet," I say loudly.

Satcher laughs. "You're making me feel like a failure here, Billie."

"Oh God..."

"Wanna grab a beer? A really, really cold beer?"

I glance at him, flustered. I need something to cool me off, and it's not just the heat that has me sweating at this point. I hold up the small bag of groceries.

"We can drop it off on the way," he says, taking the bag from me. "How far are you from here?"

"Just a block."

He nods and we fall into step. I notice how many women stop what they're doing to glance at him. Their eyes are furtive, unsure of what they're seeing. Satcher has always garnered this type of female attention. He's not oblivious to it, but he doesn't seem to overly care about it either. One, because he's beautiful, but more so (and this is all personal opinion) it's his presence. I'm not into hippie mumbo jumbo despite inhabiting the Pacific Northwest for half my life, but if I believed in auras, I'd say Satcher has a really catching one: possibly made from moonlight, and champagne, and money—all things that make a woman feel warm, and fuzzy, and romantic.

"Woods mentioned you were back."

"What else did he mention?" I ask, casting him a sideways glance.

"That you look great."

"Really?" I inwardly berate myself for the way I perk up.

"Yes. Yes, though now that I'm seeing you myself, that was an understatement."

I feel the heat creep into my cheeks.

"Stop flirting with me, Satcher. I've blushed three times in the last five minutes."

"Look at that," he says. "I've made you wet and made you blush. Maybe I still have it."

I stop dead in my tracks to stare at him, and he laughs. When we start moving again I swat at him playfully and he dances away from me.

"Woods said you rented out the loft."

"Yup." I look at my feet.

"And that you need a job."

"Ugh. First of all, I don't need a job," I tell him. I pull to a stop in front of my building. "And furthermore, who the hell does he—"

"—He didn't really say that."

I stare at Satcher, who's grinning.

"I was hoping you'd need a job, and then I could talk you into coming back to Rhubarb."

I turn toward the door so he can't see my face. "Satcher, are you hearing what you're saying? You want me to come back to Rhubarb with both Woods and Pearl there?"

"Yes, why not? They're professionals. They can keep their feelings in check for the greater good of the blog."

I whip around, my keycard in the swiper. "Are you kidding me? They couldn't keep their feelings in check when they started fucking behind my back."

We step into the foyer of my building.

"Billie, I'm not going to lie to you. When you left, the blog took a blow. It's taken two years to build back our readership."

"So why do you need me? Sounds like you have things under control." I step through the door and Satcher follows behind me, holding my bag of groceries.

Satcher makes a face. "I'm an investor. I didn't buy the blog to work there for the rest of my life."

"So what? You want to hire me to run the blog for you?" I stop in front of the wall of mailboxes, resisting the urge to cross my arms over my chest.

"Exactly."

"And Pearl?"

"You'd be her boss."

I study his face. "Woods won't let that happen. They're engaged. He's part owner..."

Satcher is already shaking his head. "I'm sixty percent shareholder, Billie. Woods only retains forty percent of Rhubarb."

My mouth drops open. "You're kidding." I had no idea Woods sold out most of his percentage, but then I guess I never asked. I was too intent on hightailing it out of town so I could go lick my wounds.

"Why did he sell?" I ask. This is none of my business, and normally I keep my nose out of things that have nothing to do with me. But this was my company, the one I started, the one I felt forced to walk away from.

Satcher grins. It's the sort of wicked grin that says he has information I'll enjoy.

"Pearl wanted to buy a place in the Upper East Side. She was in competition with your loft, I think. I once heard them arguing about why you got the loft in the divorce. She wanted it."

That's right, I think—Pearl's obsession with my loft. Woods and I often had people over, especially in those early days when we'd just started Rhubarb. I remember glancing up from the pitcher of margaritas I was making in the kitchen to see Pearl with her phone out, taking pictures of various parts of my home. I'd convinced myself to be flattered, but I remember thinking there was definitely something strange about it too.

"So, what do you say?" Satcher asks. "You help me, I help you? You breathe life back into the blog for me, I help you irritate the shit out of Pearl."

My older neighbor, Mr. Morse, bustles through the door just then carrying his teacup Yorkie under his arm. I see that he's wearing the same mauve sweater vest he was when I first met him. No matter how hot it is outside, he always dresses like it's fall. Mr. Morse brought over a vegan casserole and a bottle of expensive tequila when I first moved in, telling me his partner had died six months earlier of cancer. I'd been charmed by his manicured hands and southern accent. We'd become fast friends in our mutual state of sadness.

His smile freezes when he spots Satcher, his eyes aligning with mine in interest.

"Hi, Mr. Morse," I say, reaching out to pet Bluffin.

"Wendy," he says in greeting.

"This is Satcher Gamble," I pause to look Satcher in the eye meaningfully, "—my new boss."

One corner of Satcher's mouth lifts in a smile, his dark eyes moving from mischief to laughter.

"Ahh," he says. "It's a good day to be alive."

Mr. Morse looks between us in amusement. "Well, it was nice meeting you," he says to Satcher. "I'll just be going up to give Bluffin his lunch."

We watch him go, climbing the stairs with the energy of a much younger man. Satcher turns back to me and I don't know if it's the air conditioning in the lobby or the way he's looking at me, but my arms erupt in gooseflesh. *Look at you*, I think. *Getting all worked up under the eyes of a handsome man.*

"Still want to get that beer?" He shifts my bag from one arm to another, and I blush in apology.

"Sorry, I got all preoccupied with my new job."

I lead him down the hall to the stairs. "I'm on the third floor," I say.

"Nice building." Satcher climbs the stairs beside me. "Why did Mr. Morse call you Wendy?"

"I'm subleasing it from a friend," I say. "And Wendy is what I go by now." We step into the hallway and I fumble with my keys, cursing under my breath. Satcher laughs behind me and I shoot him a look.

"Try that one," he says of my keychain.

Jules has a million keys on her ring; I've yet to separate the ones I actually need, which results in a ten-minute session every time I get home. I curse myself for my procrastination as I stick the key Satcher suggested into the keyhole, and miracle of miracles, it turns. The door swings open. I stand aside to let him through and he carries my bag to the kitchen without asking where it is. Oh, to be as comfortable in one's skin as Satcher Gable. I grin at the back of his head as he starts unpacking my groceries and setting them on the counter.

"You don't have to do that," I say.

"Are you kidding? I want to see what you bought."

I laugh, taking the bottle of amaretto cherries he hands me. "You soak them in whiskey," I say when he looks at me quizzically. "Delicious."

His only response is a slightly cocked eyebrow and the dip of his dimples.

"You know, I have beer here," I say, staring into the fridge. "Unless you're eager to be in that heat again."

Jules has three air-conditioning units in her cavernous

living room, which sets the apartment's temperature at a reasonable seventy-five degrees.

"I'm all about it." Satcher nods.

He stacks some cans in the pantry for me and then moves over to the living room. I set about making our drinks, grabbing supplies from Jules' teal fridge. Out of the corner of my eye, I see him standing at the window looking out over the street.

"How are things with you and Woods?" I call.

It's nosy, I know, but Woods was always a little jealous of Satcher, and with the uneven percentage of Rhubarb divvied among the two, it had to have caused some resentment on Woods' part. I slip out of my flats and walk the glass over to where he's moved to sit on one of Jules' beautiful chairs.

"This isn't a beer." He raises the glass to the light, examining its contents.

"No. It's a lemon drop," I admit. "I lied about having beer."

He raises his glass and I tap it with my own before sitting across from him. He takes a sip and makes a face.

"Woods and I are great. He bristled about things at first, but then he realized he liked making money without having to do anything."

My laughter bursts out like gunshots, and I press the back of my hand to my mouth to stifle it.

"It's nice to hear you laugh again."

"Does Pearl laugh?" I ask.

Satcher cracks a smile. "You're still not over him, huh?"

"I'm totally over him. So completely over him. No one could be more over a guy than I am over Woods."

"Right."

"What? Satcher, stop."

He shrugs like he doesn't know what I'm talking about.

"I'm worried about you, Billie," he says, standing up. "No

one should drink shit like this." He sets his empty glass down on the table and I roll my eyes. There's a fleck of sugar on his lip from the rim.

"Drank it all, I see," I smart back.

He heads for the door and I'm thrown by his abrupt need to exit.

"Monday," he throws over his shoulder. "I'll let you pick your office."

"So long as it's bigger than Pearl's," I call after him. "Night, Sasquatch!"

He lifts a hand above his head to tell me that he's heard me and then the door shuts and he's gone. I make myself another drink and head over to Jules' closet. Thank God for Satcher. Always, not just today in my divorced, sad condition. He's always shown up when I needed someone.

CHAPTER SIX

Why do people date? I asked that question in the blog chat room once, hoping for a deeper answer. The answer that made the most sense to everyone was that, as a whole, we were lonely. Except it never felt that way to me. I was never lonely in the way that other people described, not until Woods. He taught me love, and then inevitably, he taught me loss. When he left, I understood the concept of loneliness as it had been described by so many people. I was ashamed of the feeling: a weightless hollowness. Why couldn't I move on? Why didn't I want to shower, or eat, or think about the future anymore? My neediness embarrassed me. It was like a chipped tooth. I felt less because of it. Woods had given me gravity, planted my feet in New York, and my heart planted itself in him—his very existence. I was so young when we got together that my purpose became intertwined with his. They were joint vines that grew together: my marriage and my goals. Two things that had been acquired so early in life it was hard to separate the two.

That's why I left New York three days after my marriage ended, booking a one-way ticket to Seattle. Now looking back, it was a weak retreat. I'd been beaten, bested by a much younger, much thinner woman. I'd wanted to go back to the saddest place I knew to lick my wounds. Enter the weeping town I'd grown up in—perpetually damp, smelling of earth and salt. My parents, not knowing what to do with my hurt, gave me the keys to the guest house paired with furtive glances that I grew to hate. It's there that I camped out for the next two years, my behavior becoming rote with all the bitterness I felt. I had put on forty pounds before I lost it, drank vodka for breakfast, and smoked joints naked in the hot tub. Also, I fucked a guy named Keith Gus who cried whenever the Seahawks lost a game. Not my proudest years. It wasn't until the accident that everything changed. Everything, but mostly me.

The accident: a simple car crash, nothing fancy. It wasn't my fault (miraculously). The driver of the other car fell asleep at the wheel, and when he swerved into my lane, we collided like two Hot Wheels in toddler hands. He had to be taken out with the jaws of life. The scene was surreal as I watched them load him into the ambulance, shivering and wrapped in the coarse blanket a paramedic had handed me. The flashing reds and blues of the police cars tinted our skin. I'd walked away with a sprained wrist, a scratch to the forehead, and my life. He'd not been so lucky. I stalked him on Facebook after, wanting to know who he'd been before he lost his life to a nap at the wheel. He was twenty-six-year-old Angus Erwin. A mechanic from Port Ludlow. He had a one-year-old son, though he wasn't married. His people gathered at the site of the accident two weeks later, laying wreaths and letters against a handmade wooden cross. I parked across the street and watched, my windshield wipers lazy on the glass.

They brought candles too, but by then the rain had descended on Washington and the mist had snuffed them out. I sat there for what felt like hours, and after everyone left and the rain subsided, I hopped out of my car, running across the street to Angus' shrine. With the hood of my sweatshirt pulled over my hair, I pulled my lighter from the pocket of my jeans and lit Angus' candles one by one. They sputtered out after a few minutes, but I wanted to do something for him.

Afterward, I'd gone home, crawled into bed fully clothed and damp from the rain, and sobbed harder than I ever had in my life. I never told anyone about the accident, and at that point in my life there really wasn't anyone to tell. My parents were away to Rock Island for the week with friends, and by the time they got back I had a brand new car, no questions asked. Not even a: *Hey, daughter, I like your new ride.* Despite my parents' lackluster attitude, and despite the fact that I was pretending to be all right, the jarring impact of metal crashing into metal had nested something in my mind; a dark thought, edges tined in regret. I let it all go without fighting for it. My mind clenched onto the realization as if I were sober for the first time in two years. *Gone, gone, gone.* My love, my best friend, my beautiful life. Why? Because he'd come to me with his unhappiness and I'd plugged up my ears. I remember it now that there's some distance between me and the initial hurt. Woods wanting to take me to Aruba on our one-year anniversary and me saying no. The blog was new and doing fairly well and I hadn't felt like it was a good time to leave. He'd made reservations at the Ivy Room instead, but then I'd had to work late and completely forgot about dinner and our anniversary. After that, he was different. No matter how much I apologized, he never lost the hurt look in his eyes. And eventually, I grew bored with it. It's emotionally lazy to know you're hurting someone and try to forget the fact because it makes you uncomfortable. Marriage as a whole is uncomfortable. Two people from two different worlds trying to stuff all of their emotional belongings into one joined life. As it turns out, I was accustomed to being left alone, and Woods was accustomed to being smothered. One of us always annoyed and the other always hurt. That's the way we lived for a long time until I guess Woods did something about it.

I pull clothes from Jules' closet and lay them on the bed. She left ninety percent of her wardrobe behind when she left for her new job in Sao Paolo. For the first time in my life, I am her size: a four.

"*Wear it,*" she said before she left.

And so I will. I don't really have another option since the only clothes I brought with me from Washington are my flannels, ripped jeans, and rain boots. My bank account has dwindled down, only allowing me necessities for some time now. Jules' wardrobe is a blessing. I settle on an olive green sheath dress and nude heels. Woods is a leg guy and the nude heels will make my legs look longer. I'm ashamed by that thought but not so ashamed that I put away the dress. This is war and I am weaponizing every asset I have. It's why I came back and I am going to follow through. Woods isn't married yet. I have time.

CHAPTER SEVEN

Satcher's assistant shows me to his office on Monday morning. He introduces himself as Bilbo, and I have to ask him to repeat himself three times before he sighs deeply and tells me that his parents were huge fans of the Tolkien books.

"Bill-bow," he says, pinching the air with each syllable.

I note that most of the cubicles are unmanned and mention it as we walk the wide circle to where the main editorial staff have their offices.

"Satcher goes down to a skeleton crew in the summer. Everyone is due back this week."

Good idea. I never thought to do that. My payroll was always gargantuan.

"—Back-to-school posts," Bilbo finishes.

Bilbo is in the habit of singing the last word in every sentence. As he sings the word *posts* he makes big eyes to indicate the importance of the back-to-school frenzy. I remember all too well: posts about what to put in your child's lunches, where to shop for school supplies, and the best recipes for back-to-school cocktails for Mommy. Bilbo leaves me with a bottle of water and tells me that Satcher is on his way. With a smug smile, I settle into a velvet green chair that I'd bought for the office two years ago. He's kept things much how I left them, only replacing my slimline desk from Ikea with a much larger wooden desk. I raise my eyes at the three monitors, wondering how much Satcher has taken on, on top of Rhubarb. The door opens; I'm expecting Satcher but Pearl walks in instead. She's wearing her hair pulled back and twisted into a knot at the nape of her neck—her signature style. Loose pieces of hair frame her face in what's supposed to be an "effortless" look, but I know she spent thirty minutes perfecting it.

"Billie," she breathes, "I guess I should say welcome back." Pearl sets her coffee down on the desk, swiping a loose strand of hair behind her ear. She looks on edge, but maybe I'm searching.

"I guess you should," I echo. I don't, under any circumstances, feel the need to be polite to Pearl. "It's Wendy now, actually."

She raises an eyebrow, but before she can say anything, Satcher walks in carrying two coffees.

"Pearl." He looks surprised to see her. "I thought you were taking the morning off for your appointment."

Is it just me or does her face flush?

"It was canceled," she says quickly.

Satcher stares at her thoughtfully for a moment, eyes narrowed and lips pursed. Just as suddenly, he looks away. He's rifling through his desk when he says, "Coffee's for you, Bil—I mean, Wendy."

"Hey, thanks, Sasquatch," I say. "Is there anywhere in particular you'd like me to set up?"

"There's a cubicle open down the hall," Pearl offers. She's made herself at home in his office.

Satcher looks up from what he's doing. "Billie—"

"Wendy," I correct.

"Right. Wendy will be in the open office. Do you mind showing her where that is, Pearl?"

Pearl stares at him, her mouth slightly ajar. "Kimberly's old office?"

Satcher frowns, annoyed. "Yes."

"I thought we were keeping that office open for the senior content blogger."

"We were," says Satcher. "And now the position is filled. So since you're already here, see Wendy to her new office."

We turn to go, Pearl rigidly, when Satcher says, "Wendy—?"

"Yeah?"

"If you call me Sasquatch again, you're fired."

I wink at him.

Pearl, who refuses to wear pearls of any kind, flashes her giant bauble engagement ring as I trail behind her. I get it; I get the office, but she got the engagement ring. I follow her down the hall and a few heads pop up from their cubicles to look at me. There are only two familiar faces: Loren, who I hired to cover the food and beverage section of the blog, and Dave, the website guy. They both smile at me as I pass. Pearl would have urged Woods to replace some of the people who were loyal to me, and others would have left of their own volition when I sold. She turns a corner and stops in front of a door, blinking at me. Before she opens it, she turns around. Pearl, who is at least half a foot shorter than me, has no problem looking me in the eye. If I were her, I'd be ashamed, but I suppose she had the gumption to sleep with another woman's husband in the first place...

"I didn't even know you were back in town. Now Satcher is bringing you coffee, and you're in the corner office."

It takes me a moment to catch onto what she's insinuating. I stare at her, mortified.

"Not everyone has to fuck their way to the top, Pearl," I say.

"As far as I can see, you haven't done anything to earn this job."

That's when it hits me: Pearl wanted my position. She probably had a pretty good shot at it too before I came along.

"You mean like start this blog, turn a profit, and sell it for enough to live off the money for two years?"

Her dainty nostrils flare as she glares at me. She's on the verge of shooting some word poison at me, I can tell by the way her whole body is wound up like a little dog defending its territory. *Hackles,* I think. *She has her hackles bared.*

"You had no reason to come back," she says. "There's nothing left for you here."

I cock my head to the side. "Isn't there?"

To my enjoyment, the corners of Pearl's mouth tuck in her frown, dulling her eyes.

"You look a lot older," she says, tilting her head to the side. "Divorce took a toll on you." And then she marches off before I can say anything else.

Older and wiser, Pearl, I think as I let myself into my new office. *Older, wiser, and meaner.*

There's a lot to be said for spiteful pettiness. It's underrated by those moral do-gooders who jive to the beat of karma. I make a show of hanging my new nameplate next to the door, and then for good measure, I buy everyone in the office lunch even though my bank account is dwindling dangerously low. *She'll get hers*, they told me. But when I look at Pearl, who is trying her best to pretend I don't exist, I decide that she definitely did not *"get hers"* as everyone told me she would. Calling the shots in the company I started, riding Woods' giant dick every night. I figure karma must be a cool bitch, but she's too busy for me. In which case, I've decided to *be* karma.

Satcher comes to see how I'm settling in and offers to give my furniture back.

"I've been trying to unload that green chair on someone for two years," he says.

"Stop it. That chair is beautiful and it cost me a thousand bucks."

He grins like he knows it.

"It looks good in your office," I say. "I'll start with a clean slate if you don't mind."

He sets down a bottle of Champagne and two glasses on the windowsill.

"How was Pearl?" Even as he asks, he rolls up his sleeves and gets to work on assembling my new desk.

"Flustered."

"You know, Billie, you could just move on. Forget about this vendetta you have against both of them. I can set you up with some of New York's most eligible men."

"It's Wendy," I say. "And what vendetta? New York is as much my home as it is theirs."

"I'm not arguing that," says Satcher. "But if you think I don't recognize that look in your eyes, you're mistaken."

I place a hand over my heart, and fluttering my eyes innocently, I say, "Satcher Gable. You always think the worst of me."

He grins from where he's sitting on the ground sorting planks and screws into organized piles.

"By the way, I saw those three monitors in your office. How much have you taken on exactly? I mean, it's no secret that you're a workaholic, but, Satch…"

"It's nothing," he says. "I don't have a family. I have to

keep myself busy, and I might as well keep busy making money."

"True that," I say.

"Why don't you pop the bubbly? I like to drink while I work."

We're both sitting on the floor sipping from our glasses and laughing at something I've said when the door opens and Woods walks in.

"Way to knock," I say, tossing back the rest of my drink.

He's wearing a denim jacket over his white V-neck, which makes him look like the type of douchebag who buys his girlfriend a new set of tits and drinks vodka cocktails while wearing a pinky ring—oh wait! That is him.

His eyes travel between the two of us and then land on the desk Satcher is assembling. I'm lightheaded from the Champagne, slouched against the wall, but Woods barely glances at me; his eyes are trained on Satcher. I try to hide my smirk behind my newly refilled glass. This was exactly the type of subterfuge I was hoping for, wasn't it? To get under my ex-husband's skin as thoroughly as possible.

"Taking a little break, Satch?" Woods says. "We can hardly drag you away from your office, and here you are drinking Champagne and assembling furniture like a newlywed."

I see a muscle in Satcher's jaw jump. He drops his screwdriver and rights the desk to standing, examining his work.

"Speaking of newlyweds, when is your wedding date, Woods? Should be coming up soon." I kick my shoes off and stare at him pointedly.

"October, actually," he says, not taking his eyes off Satcher. "Of next year..."

"Lovely! When everything starts to die," I say.

Woods smirks, he can't help it. I've caught his attention now. His warm eyes roll over me like hands and goose bumps erupt on my arms. While the rest of the world clamored for pumpkin-flavored things and oohed and ahhed over the leaves changing color, Woods always bitterly called fall the death of summer.

"I don't suppose I get an invitation, do I?"

Woods doesn't bite. He acts like he hasn't heard me, but Satcher does.

"You can always be my plus one." Satcher looks up from where he's lifting my computer monitor onto the desk, his eyes bright with mischief.

I stare at my ex-husband, who excels in confrontational avoidance. He's flustered; we're ganging up on him and he hates it.

Satcher winks at me. "All done!" he says, standing up. He takes a step back to admire his work. All three of us are checking out my desk when Pearl rushes in, a constipated look on her face.

"It's been fun, Billie," says Satcher. "I'll have Claire come over to brief you on our fall schedule; we still have some slots to fill." He's halfway out the door when his broad shoulders turn. "Also, you're going to need to hire a new fashion editor. Marie is pregnant."

Marie not Pearl, thank God.

I give him the thumbs up and then he's gone, leaving a pissed-looking Pearl and a stressed-looking Woods in his wake.

"Is there something I can help you two with?" I start carrying things over to the desk: the stacks of paperwork I need to look over, a cup of pens...

I don't have a photo—everyone else has photos of loved ones propped where they can see them ... I try to think of who I could put a picture of on my desk and sadly come up empty-handed.

"I was just collecting Woods," Pearl says.

Collecting! Her voice is like ice. I look up from what I'm doing, half amused, and see them both staring at me. Did they need a dismissal?

"Collect away..." I wave them off and I'm relieved when they head for the door, Woods looking like he still has something to say to me. *Too bad*, I think. *You've been collected.*

Five minutes later, Loren pops her head around the doorway.

"Welcome back." She grins. "I'd have brought you a cactus for your desk, but ... um ... Satcher didn't tell us you were coming back."

"It's okay, it kind of all happened at the last minute. It's good to be back."

Loren glances over her shoulder and then slips through the door, closing it quietly behind her.

"Pearl's pissed."

"Oh yeah?" I lean back in my chair, trying to keep the smile off my face. Loren and I have been nothing more than Facebook friends for two years, but it feels natural to have our old office camaraderie back. I rest my palms on the desk and push up so I'm standing.

"She's—" Her words are cut short when my office door opens again and Satcher walks in.

"She's pissed," he says, shutting the door behind him.

Loren props herself on the arm of the nearest chair while Satcher sits inside of it.

"What's she doing?"

"Reaming Woods out." Loren sniffs.

"For what?"

"For letting you happen."

"She should be pissed at Satcher then," I say, shrugging it off. I must be really bad at hiding my delight because Satcher raises an eyebrow and smiles knowingly.

Loren heads for the door. "Everyone put on your seatbelts. It's going to be a bumpy ride," she says before slipping out.

"Ride from hell." He looks at me squarely and I shrug.

"Don't care. I've already been on life's ride from hell. I know all the turns."

He grimaces and then stands up, heading for the door. He stops at the last minute to say, "Let's not make Rhubarb a ride, yeah?"

"Get out of here, Sasquatch," I say without looking up. "I need to work."

"Tomorrow, the rest of the staff are back," Satcher warns. "Best behavior."

CHAPTER EIGHT

The vibe in the office the next morning is somewhat like the first day of school. Refreshed and ready, the employees of Rhubarb gather in the common area, popping pods in the coffee machine and discussing where they went on vacation. I listen outside the door, anxiety clawing its way up my throat. There are familiar voices: Dee, who attended my wedding. I hired her part-time after her baby was born to cover the Crunchy Mom section of the blog. She probably tried the hardest after I left, sending me update texts even when I didn't answer. I hear Pearl too, she's updating them on her wedding planning while they *ooh and ahh* like good minions. I'm nearly hyperventilating when Satcher appears through the front door, a drink carrier in his hand. *Shoot. Shit.* I was supposed to get coffee. His eyebrow quirks up when he sees my face.

"It was my turn," I say when he hands me a cup.

"I knew you'd forget," he says.

Our eyes meet and I suddenly feel hot under Jules' Rebecca Minkoff dress. The room has suddenly gone quiet.

They've heard our voices. I squeeze my eyes shut, but Satcher pushes me forward, forcing me into the open doorway.

"Dammit, you fucker," I say under my breath.

"Morning." He flashes a smile around the room, his dimples making a few of their eyes glaze over: men and women.

I smile, smile, smile! So big and so genuine, at least to their eyes. Suddenly, there are arms around my neck, exclamations of surprise. Janelle, our photographer, Dee, Loren ... and Eric, who runs a column called Pretty Gay. Pearl's smile is frozen on her face like a mannequin. I see that a couple of them glance back to gauge her reaction to my presence. After a few minutes of questions from all of them, Dee goes to the fridge and pulls out the bottle of Champagne, the smile pressed so sincerely to her lips, my chest tightens. The Champagne is a tradition I started when we moved into the building. We always kept a bottle chilled in the fridge ready to celebrate. Now Dee pops the cork at eight o'clock in the morning and everyone holds out their plastic flutes for a swallow. Everyone except Pearl, who demurely declines, saying she's watching her weight for the wedding.

"It's just a sip," Loren presses. "To welcome our Billie back."

Pearl's face is strained as she accepts the glass, clutched between her fingers like some dirty object she'd rather not be touching.

"Where's Woods?" someone calls. "Go get him."

One of the employees I don't recognize scurries out. I wait, tensed, the flute sweating between my fingers. I switch hands and rub my open palm down my dress. When Woods follows the girl back into the room, the air stills. He meets my eyes and my stomach does a rebellious flip. *Quit it*, I want to say.

"You guys are always looking for a reason to drink," he teases.

Loren makes the toast: "To the best damn editor and blogger that ever was," she says, raising her glass. "Welcome back!"

There are cheers of *Hear! Hear!* and then everyone's tossing back their early morning bubbly. I notice that Pearl has only pretended to sip hers. Her eyes are on the floor near Woods' shoes. Alert and hard as graphite, they follow him when he walks toward me. He's opening his mouth to say something when Satcher steps in front of him, blocking his direct route.

"You've been coming into the office a lot. I thought the plan was to back out slowly."

"I didn't know I needed to ask permission to come into my office," Woods replies.

There's something about their exchange that is off. Normally, Woods and Satcher keep up a steady stream of banter; their relationship hinges on their shared sense of humor. But Satcher's shoulders are tense and Woods' face is stormy. They both look like they are about to explode. Everyone is either watching them or looking away uncomfortably.

"Do you know the best thing to do in a situation like this?" I ask. Now I'm the center of attention, or at least I should say the center of a tense, ticking silence. "Whip out your dicks and measure..."

There's a pause and then the laughter erupts. The new people look relieved (the new boss isn't so bad) and the old people raise their empty glasses grinning like it's good to have me back. Tension is broken. Even Satcher is smiling and Woods is looking at me with a sort of endearing expectancy. He's used to my sense of humor; eight years in a relationship will do that. Everyone dissipates after that, plastic flutes hitting the trash, and the common room emptying out as people make their way to their desks. Loren pats me on the shoulder as she leaves, a smug smile on her face.

"You've been sorely missed. Welcome back."

I grin back at her, feeling a sense of belonging. Yes, it's good to be back. This is my stride, this is what I've missed. And that's when it hits me: it's not just a man I came back for. I want it all ... every last thing.

After my first day back, Woods initially comes into the office every other day, but by the end of the second week he's there from nine-to-five like the rest of us. I deduct that he's either there to keep an eye on me or Pearl. Aside from the hard looks we give each other when we cross paths in the office, Pearl and I give each other a wide berth. If she's noticed that Woods is in the office more she doesn't let on; though, every time he comes into my office for anything, she follows within a few minutes, finding some reason or another to drag him away. It was like this before, I think, when we were married. I have memories of Pearl always needing to pull him away for this or that.

"So obvious," I say to Loren after Pearl interrupts Woods and me to tell him her printer is jammed. A jammed printer, an emergency at their apartment, trouble with their wedding venue—and all in one week. Her creativity at making up issues to get him away from me is impressive.

"You should schedule a lunch with just the two of you to see what she comes up with to get him out of it," Loren suggests.

I laugh, but the truth is that spending any time with Woods affects me deeply. Being around him has the opposite effect that it used to. Where his presence used to energize me, it now makes me feel drained and tired. I tell Loren this and she nods like she understands.

"It's because you never got closure," she says. "The fighting it out. The trying one last time. The heartbreaking honesty—those are all things you need to experience to move on."

She's right, but lack of closure is hardly Woods' fault. I left town without a fight.

"There's still hurt," Loren says.

"No," I argue. "It's been years. I'm over it."

"Sure." She shrugs, like she doesn't want to argue. "You know yourself." She doesn't believe me. I don't believe me either.

Sometimes I think I am over Woods. Sometimes when I am really honest with myself, I can acknowledge that the person who knows me best in this world isn't my mother or father—they hardly know me at all, or my friends who only get to see the best side of me, but Woods. Woods, who I spent eight years with. He saw me from every emotionally unflattering angle, in every bare moment of honesty and ... without my makeup. The fact that no one knows me as well as my ex-husband, who left me for another woman, is both devastating and frightening like I'm not worthy of being known fully. There were no warning signs, no moment when I knew our bond frayed and severed, no months of impending doom. I was blindsided.

In early September I interview candidates to fill Marie's position. Marie, who is in her last month of pregnancy, and who looks like she's uncomfortable every minute of every day, sits in on the interviews. I gauge her facial expressions to see how much she likes each applicant. I learn that when she frowns she's doubting their experience, and when she smiles she's already written them off. We interview a younger woman named Zoe, who has long red hair and comes in wearing a velvet head wrap. Marie compliments the color, a bright cobalt blue. It's the first time I've heard her compliment an applicant, and halfway through the interview she interrupts my questions to ask her own. When Zoe leaves, Marie informs me that she's the one. *The one!* Like we're marrying her. I agree, however. Satcher, who meets her briefly in the hall outside his office, seems to like her as well.

It's not until Marie has had her last day and is sent off on permanent maternity leave, that I realize I've been conned. Zoe has moved into her cubicle, unpacked her matching marble pencil holder and stapler. We welcome her with a Champagne toast, doughnuts, and a name plaque for her desk. All is well until I'm walking home from work one evening. I'm in the best of moods. Since I've been back at Rhubarb readership has grown by twenty percent, I've hired two new employees, and approached Satcher with a plan for growth and expansion. I'm going over what I'm going to speak about in the next staff meeting when I spot Zoe sitting in a popular bar up the street. I pause on the sidewalk wondering if I should go in and say hi, maybe have a drink, when I see Pearl walk toward her from the rear of the bar. Their greeting is familiar: Zoe jumps up, wrapping her arms around Pearl's neck in a hug, and I realize that they're celebrating. Because they know each other. I wonder if they're old college buddies, and if Pearl was the one who encouraged her to apply for the job. I have a sinking feeling in my stomach for the rest of the walk home.

When I get back to the apartment I toss my keys on the counter and pull out my phone. It rings three times before Marie's brusque "Hello" sounds in my ear.

"Marie, it's Wendy," I say. There's a pause before her voice comes back, this time softer ... more cautious.

"Hi," she says. "What can I help you with?"

"Did you know that Pearl and Zoe know each other?"

She sighs. "Yes."

"So you were in on their plan?"

"Look, I have to go. What happens at Rhubarb isn't my concern anymore."

I laugh. "In a few years, when you want to go back to work because you're sick of being a stay-at-home mom, it'll be your concern. Don't forget, I'm the one who'll have to give you a reference."

She's quiet and I think she's hung up when she says, "They grew up together. Pearl didn't think you'd hire her if you knew..."

The line goes dead; she's hung up. I set the phone down and walk over to the window. Watching the traffic always helps me think. I suppose it could be as simple as Pearl wanting to work alongside her friend, but nothing is ever as simple as it seems with her. Pearl always has a plan, and a backup plan, and a backup to her backup plan. I'll have to keep a close eye on things.

On Monday I find Zoe in the office early, working at her desk. Pearl has yet to show up for the day, so I have a few uninterrupted minutes to talk to her.

"You settling in okay?"

She's beaming when she swivels around to face me.

"Yeah, I'm super excited."

Super: a word used in copious amounts by anyone under the age of twenty-seven. *That's super great*, I want to say. *Super awesome*.

"Well, I'll let you get back to work."

She smiles without teeth and turns back to her computer.

. . .

At lunch I find myself in the common room heating up leftovers from the night before and listening to a woman named Diane give explicit details about her C-section. Diane is one of Pearl's friends, and for this reason, she never makes eye contact. I've gone to extraordinary lengths to test my theory, once stepping in her way so she'd bump into me, knocking my water bottle out of my hand. She'd picked up the water bottle and mumbled, "Sorry," before rushing off to her desk. No eye contact.

She ends her story with "and he fainted." I take the *he* as being her husband, Victor. She glances at me before reaching across the table to pat Pearl's hand. "Don't worry. Woods will do great. He's so into taking care of your every need. Vic is such a baby."

Something flares in my chest: shock, panic, pain. And then Pearl quickly announces to the room that she's not pregnant and Diane is referencing "the future." Their laughter trills like the barking of a tiny, angry dog.

Needless to say, several sets of eyes flicker to my face, gauging my response. I try to hide what I'm feeling, but I'm afraid I'm not fast enough. Woods having a baby with someone who isn't me. Why does it still feel like he's cheating on me? Diane looks pleased with herself. I can tell by the way she smirks at Pearl. Woods hadn't wanted children. We both loved kids, but he was deathly afraid of messing his own up. Clearly, his opinions have changed. Or maybe he wants them with Pearl. Pearl knew Woods and I hadn't planned on having kids; we had a discussion about it way back when.

"We can't wait to start a family," she asserts. "Woods wants kids really bad." I turn my back to the microwave so they can't see my face.

As they start discussing baby names, I think about how I

can leave without looking obvious, until Peter the computer guy makes the most awkward statement of the day.

"Won't it be weird that your child with Woods will have the same last name as Billie?"

Play it cool. I raise my eyebrows and pin my gaze on Pearl, waiting to see what she'll say.

She's been thwarted, by Peter of all people. She blinks rapidly, obviously annoyed.

"We can't blame Billie," she says finally. "Tarrow is a desirable surname, while her maiden name ... what was it again, Billie? Bolster...?"

"Yes, Bolster." I nod.

"Right," says Pearl. "Billie Bolster..." She snickers. "I'd want to keep Tarrow too."

"It would be Wendy Bolster," I say, dumbly.

"Changed your first name and not your last," she says. "Interesting."

It's a small victory for Pearl, who wiggled her way out of embarrassment by embarrassing me. I smile wanly and stir my tea with the tiny red straw. *Okay, Pearl,* I think. *If you want to play it like that...*

"Hey, Diane," I say. "You should write a piece about your C-section for the blog. I'd love to publish it."

Diane looks stricken. She's never been asked to write anything, but I know that's what she wants to do. I pulled her application last week; she wrote *journalism* under her interest section.

"Really?" She stumbles. "I mean, I think I could do a great job if you're being serious..."

"I am." I smile. "If you could email it to me before the end of the month..."

"On it." She's trying to play it cool, but her hands are shaking. The moment she's been waiting for. I don't look at Pearl before I walk out, but I can feel her annoyance radiating from her body. Diane belongs to her and I've just crossed a line.

As soon as I'm back in my office, I cradle my arms on my desk and drop my head into them. I thought that for the most part the hurt had receded, but hearing Pearl talk about having children with Woods has scratched open a long-closed wound. How is one man able to want different things depending on who he is with? I'm not very maternal, maybe that's why he didn't want children with me. I'm work-obsessed, extremely driven, and often tense and snappy, and that was especially true in the last year of our marriage. There's the rapping of knuckles on my door and I straighten up quickly.

"Come in," I call. Why do people always choose my lowest moments to pay me an office visit? Pearl walks in carrying the proposal she owes me. Her timing, I feel, is planned.

"Thank you," I say curtly when she sets it on my desk. She studies my face and I wonder if she's looking for the tears I was so ready to shed a minute ago.

"Do I let you or Satcher know what my vacation days are?"

I'm caught off guard by her question.

"Um ... I guess you can give the dates to me," I say. I pull a notepad toward me so I can write them down.

"October tenth through the twentieth," she tells me. And then she adds, "We'll be in Portugal for eight days."

Portugal. My stomach turns. Woods and I had always planned on going to Portugal together. It was our thing. I swallow the lump in my throat and say, "The tenth to twentieth. Got it."

She hesitates. I wonder if she wants me to comment on their vacation.

"Um ... well, I've got the dates. Anything else?"

"No. That's all." She reluctantly heads for the door.

"Pearl..."

She turns expectantly.

"Why Portugal?"

The self-satisfied look on her face informs me that I've asked the question she's been wanting to answer.

"Woods said he's always wanted to take the love of his life there." Now that she's dropped her bomb, the rest of her steps out of my office have more spring.

CHAPTER NINE

"Why are you avoiding me?"

I look up from my computer, surprised. I hadn't heard Woods come in.

"Because I have a super big crush on you and you're already engaged." I meant it as a joke, but when I look up his expression says he doesn't know that.

"Is this uncomfortable for you?" he asks. "Are you all right?"

"Woods..." I push away from my desk and cross my legs ceremoniously. My sigh echoes around the room. "First of all, I was joking. And don't try to act all concerned about me now, not after what you did."

He nods slowly, absorbing what I said. "I just ... this is..."

"Hard..." I finish for him.

"Yeah."

I scratch my head. "It'll get less so as we move along," I say. I don't believe that for a second, but Woods seems encouraged. I uncross my legs and slide my chair back toward my desk, hoping he'll leave. I wonder why I can still separate the smell of his skin from everything else in the room, why it's still so familiar after all this time.

"Is Pearl being weird with you?"

My fingers hover over the keyboard. I think of Zoe, and Portugal, and the baby discussion in the break room.

"No," I say. "She's being a bitch."

He laughs. I lean back, stretching my arms over my head.

"I'll talk to her..."

"Don't bother. Honestly, Woods..."

"Billie, you don't deserve that. Not after ... what we did. So, I'll talk to her. And I'm sorry."

I'm shocked into silence, during which time Woods heads for the door. I watch his retreating back. He sounded ... genuine. An almost apology, I think.

I understand that he's moved on with his life, and that I'm supposed to too, but the fact that he's taking Pearl to Portugal feels like one of the sharpest blows since the divorce. Portugal? *Really, you piece of shit?* The place we had an entire folder dedicated to? We'd both add articles, restaurant reviews, and the occasional hundred-dollar bill for spending money. Portugal was ours, along with our plans for a sheltie puppy that we were going to name Annie, and the house we'd build with a winding metal staircase that led to our bedroom. We'd made plans that had been specific and special to us as a couple, or at least I thought so. What I am now realizing is that those plans had been Woods' all along, they weren't for me specifically. He made me feel special, but I hadn't been. I was an enhancement to the life he wanted, not the partner with whom he wanted to weather any storm in life; a side dish rather than the entrée.

. . .

My jealousy is consuming; I'm ashamed to say that it's eating at me. Woods notices the difference. He's always watching me, and I know he's wondering what's going on in my head. When he finally asks about it I'm leaving the office for the day. He catches me near the elevator. I can smell him before I see him; the familiar cologne and Woods' smell, tinged around the edges with the faint sweetness of Juicy Fruit. I roll my eyes, mainly because I know I'm cornered.

"Billie." He tries to make his voice sound surprised. Like he ran into me rather than chasing me down.

"Oh hey," I say casually. A yawn arrives at the perfect time and I make a show of covering it up.

"How've you been?" he asks as soon as we're both in the elevator. "I feel like you're a million miles away."

"I'm a million miles away from you," I say without looking at him.

"Ouch. What did I do now?"

I sigh. I really don't want to get into it. It's been a long week. We're reaching our quarterly deadline, and the work to get everything up and ready has nearly wiped me out. Rhubarb is three times the size of what it used to be and I'm not even working for myself anymore. It feels a little like I'm putting quarters in Woods' and Satcher's piggy bank, but unless you own your own company that's generally what the workforce is like.

"It's fine, Woods. Nothing new."

He's quiet until the doors to the elevator slide open, and right as I'm about to step out, he speaks. "I'm sorry. For whatever it is."

I turn and glare at him sharply. Apologies are annoying when you *want* to be mad.

"No, you're not. That's the worst part."

"God, Billie. I'm a fuck-up, but that doesn't mean I enjoy hurting people."

One corner of my mouth lifts into my cheek. I was so sure of my anger, but Woods' specialty has always been making me feel like shit for thinking he's shit.

I'm bubbling on the inside, and not in the good full-of-joy way; all of my negative emotions are at a boil. I'm a pot of anger, resentment, jealousy, and bitterness, and I'm coming precariously close to all of those things boiling over the top, burning anyone near. He follows me out of the elevator and onto the street. We emerge into rush hour like two toddlers, teetering and dodging the stream of stony-faced New Yorkers. Somehow, we're headed in the same direction even though I know Pearl and Woods share an apartment five blocks heading the other way.

"Where are you going?" I ask suspiciously. I don't want to talk to him, but no matter how fast I walk he's keeping up. At this rate, I'm going to have to run out into traffic to lose him.

"I'm walking you home," he says.

I stop in the middle of the sidewalk and someone slams into my right shoulder.

"You've never walked me home. Not even when we were married."

"Well, I should have," he says. He says it with so much conviction I blink at him, shocked.

"What?" I say this dumbly, like my mouth and brain are stuffed with cotton.

"I should have walked you home. And I should have paid more attention to what you loved, not what I thought you should love. And I should have treated you like you needed protecting even if you didn't."

I look around trying to discern if I'm dreaming or if this is really happening. To my left is a Subway restaurant and across the street is an Urban Outfitters; neither of these things would ever make it into my dreams.

Woods' face is undeniably sincere. *He has a sincere face*, I remind myself. It's not necessarily that he's being sincere. Woods is a golden retriever; even if a golden retriever has rabies you'd be tempted to reach out and pet it because—hellooo—golden retriever. My boil calms to a simmer. I let him walk me home. We don't speak much because it's hard to have a serious conversation when you're walking through the mass noise of New York. When we arrive outside of Jules' building, he bends down to give me a kiss on the cheek, and then he just walks away.

I swipe at my cheek every few minutes, but the spot he kissed stings for over an hour. I call Jules, who answers on the third ring, her voice sleepy.

"Sup?" she slurs.

I can hear her checking the time. She's only a few hours ahead, but in college we called her the nap queen.

"Jules," I say. And it's all I have to say. She knows.

"Fuck Woods," she says before I can get anything else out. "Fuck him to hell and back."

That isn't a bad idea. Woods was a good fuck. I don't say this out loud—she'd freak out on me. I keep my lips shut against sexual confessions and wait for her rant to be over. As soon as she's finished, I launch into my story and tell her what's been happening at Rhubarb: Pearl, Diane ... and then eventually my walk home with Woods.

"Whatever, Billie," she says. "You're back and he's kicking himself for ever leaving. Don't get sucked into his dangerous remorse. I'd like to tell him off for walking you home. So slimy."

I smile into the receiver. A man walking a woman home is slimy now.

"It's harder than I thought. I still feel things."

"Of course you do..." Her tone is softer this time. And I marvel at her ability to always make me feel validated. "Unless there are no feelings, you can't just jump back into your ex's life. That's nuts."

I agree about how nuts it is while quietly squirming on my end of the line. Maybe it was a stupid idea to take the job. I didn't really think it over before I accepted Satcher's proposal. The idea of being that close to Woods and Pearl was too enticing. A train wreck you couldn't look away from, except I wanted to be *on* the train.

"It was stupid," I say. "But I needed the job..." My voice wavers on the last part. In truth, I could have found a job somewhere else. I probably *should* have found a job somewhere else.

"How does Satcher seem?" she asks. Her question is odd. Satcher seems like ... Satcher.

"Fine. I mean, he's Satcher. He had his shit together when he was in diapers."

She laughs. We've all been fringe friends since college. Jules is my best friend and Satcher is Woods'. There has been a lot of social crossover over the years, though the two of them were never particularly close.

"He seems fine," I assure her. "He likes to come to my office to gossip about Pearl."

She laughs, but then she has to go. We hang up and I feel better right away. I touch the spot on my cheek where Woods kissed me. I don't feel anything. Perfect.

CHAPTER TEN

*I*t's the last week of our fall-to-Christmas catalog, which means everyone is under a deadline to present at least four holiday post ideas as well as the photos that will accompany them for our winter spread. They don't have to be entirely done, but the ideas need to be there and be fairly cohesive with our theme. During weeks like this everyone stays late working overtime, so I'm surprised when Pearl comes into the office and announces she's leaving early.

"Early?" I say without looking up from what I'm doing.

Satcher, who is standing by my desk waiting for me to finish up signing some papers, asks the inevitable follow-up question.

"What's so important that you're missing our quarterly overtime?" He's wearing his glasses today on account of itchy eyes, and he dips his head to look at her over the top of them. It's incredibly sexy and I'm still staring at him when she says—

"We have dinner tonight with our parents."

I don't miss the possessive note in her voice when she says *our parents*. Which I assume means hers and Woods'. As in …

my former in-laws. I feel possessive too. I had a good relationship with them—great even.

"Ah well, then I'll let you two get to it," I say dismissively. Better they both get out of here, they dampen the mood anyway. But apparently Satcher isn't done with her.

"It's important that you be here for this," he says. I stare at him wondering why he's being such a hard ass.

She opens and closes her mouth, and I can see the mountain of excuses she's ready to give him. But arguing with Satcher is like arguing with your parents. He makes you feel stupid just by the way he looks at you. Pearl must know this because she clamps her mouth closed and mumbles something about moving the time.

"Why'd you do that?" I ask him when Pearl's out of earshot.

"Why not?" he says, nonchalant. "She takes a lot of liberties because of Woods. We have work to do."

"Okay," I say. "You're kind of scary sometimes, you know."

"I know," he says.

I pinch his cheek and he swats me away with a frown.

"Somehow, I'm never able to scare you though," he says.

"I've known you for too long, Sasquatch."

"Say, you wouldn't know what restaurant they're going to tonight, would you?" I ask.

"I know," Loren says, walking into my office and dropping a stack of fabric samples on my desk.

"You wouldn't." Satcher raises an eyebrow.

"I would," I say, looking expectantly at Loren.

"They're dining at The Modern." She winks at me and I grin as she leaves, a smug smile on her face.

"What are you doing tonight, Satch?"

"I presume going to The Modern with you...?"

"I'm glad we're on the same page. Now work your magic and get us a reservation."

Since Satcher has slept with most of the eligible women in New York, he has no problem getting us a reservation.

For the sake of time, I agree to meet him in front of the restaurant at seven. I arrive five minutes early and stand awkwardly on the sidewalk, my lower back sweating under Jules' designer dress. I'd chosen a black dress with a collared neckline and left the buttons open low to show some cleavage. The waist of the dress is cinched and the skirt is flared and short. I had to use my own shoes since Jules' feet are bigger than mine, and settled on a pair of black heels that wrap around my ankles. I'm nervous, my conscience as knotted as my insides. This is a shady, shitty thing to do. *But you came back to New York to be shady and shitty,* I remind myself. Two women stand a few feet away from me, smoking. I inch closer to them, sniffing desperately at their air.

"Billie."

Satcher comes up behind me and I spin around.

"It's Wen—"

"Nice dress," he says.

His eyes linger on my cleavage. I blush, struggling to keep my mouth in a neutral line. In high school, Brett Galloway told me I had nice legs despite the fact that I had braces, glasses, and a unibrow. I'd said *thank you* and then proceeded to trip over my own feet, skinning my knee in the process. Satcher's compliment has a similar effect. I stumble slightly over a crack in the sidewalk and thank God he doesn't seem to notice.

"I wish I could say I missed the conservative Martha Stewart dresses," he says.

"I did not dress like Martha Stewart," I say, aggravated. But even as the words leave my mouth I know he's right. I donated most of them to Goodwill when I moved back to Washington, trading my career-girl wardrobe for practical jeans and fleeces.

I want to tell Satcher that the dress I'm wearing belongs to Jules, but his compliment made me so warm I don't want to ruin it by admitting I'm not as stylish.

"So what's the goal tonight?" he asks, holding the door open for me.

"The goal?"

"Pearl ... Woods..."

"Oh." I frown. I'd almost forgotten we were here for that. I have a fleeting thought that it would be nice to have dinner with Satcher without anything else on the agenda. Satcher smells like a grown-up: spicy and expensive. I think about the cologne Woods uses; half of the men in Manhattan smell like Woods. I used to catch whiffs of it everywhere.

"I'd like to make them uncomfortable," I say. "Woods' parents loved me." I lower my voice. "I guess that's all—I just want to make them uncomfortable."

"Puts Pearl at a disadvantage," he says.

"Exactly." It's not until we're being led to our table that I realize he meant a disadvantage, as if we are competing for the same man. I'm frowning when I hear my name being called. I look up, suddenly pinning a smile onto my face. Of course. That's why I'm here! Look happy!

Denise Tarrow is a tall, willowy woman, elegant in all the right ways. She graduated from Yale and spent a few years teaching at the University of Georgia before quitting to start a family. When Woods moved to New York, his parents sold their house and followed. Currently, she teaches Art History at NYU and my favorite thing about her: she's a Taylor Swift groupie. She stands when she sees me, her face lit with emotion. It's automatic, me walking toward her outstretched arms. I let myself be pulled into her embrace and breathe in the familiar scent of her perfume.

"Billie, Billie!" she exclaims. "I didn't know you were back in the city ... my God, did you know, Woods?" She turns accusingly toward her son who looks like he's swallowed a goldfish.

I beam at Denise, noting how her eyes are more crinkled at the corners.

"I've only been back a few weeks," I say. "I haven't really had time to contact anyone."

"Of course," she says. "Well, you were missed, my dear girl." She holds me firmly by my upper arms, looking at my face like she's trying to see the last two years of hurt. I stare into her grey eyes, my emotions trembling under the surface. I'd loved Woods' family, it had been easy to love them. From the moment we met, his mother treated me like I was the daughter she'd waited for her whole life. It had been the biggest rush of my life since her son treated me like the woman he'd waited for his whole life.

Denise looks over my shoulder and gets an eye full of Satcher. Her expression goes from surprise to realization. She releases me, her eyes pinned on my face, the sound of his name jarring everyone at the table to look away from us and at my dinner date. With everyone distracted, I'm able to get a look at their expressions. I scan the table, my eyes roving over six faces, trying to take everything in. Woods is staring at Satcher, a shocked expression on his face, while Pearl looks like she wants to throw up.

I'm jarred from my thoughts by Denise, who once again is saying my name.

"Why don't you two join us?"

I'm already shaking my head even as she says it. To my enjoyment, Pearl's face is frozen in mortification. I hear myself saying, "Thank you, but Satcher and I have some things we need to go over for Rhubarb."

Denise looks disappointed. "Lunch then. Next week."

"I'd love to." I smile.

We leave in a flurry of goodbyes. Satcher places his hand on the small of my back as he steers me away from the table. I feel their eyes hot on my back. *Small victories*, I think.

"Well, that was ... awkward," Satcher says, sipping his drink a few minutes later.

"You think?" I'm still riding the high of Pearl's expression.

"Your ex-husband's mother asked you to lunch."

I take a sip of my lemon drop. "I'm aware."

He looks incredulous. "How far are you going to take this revenge thing, Billie?"

"Wendy," I correct him. "And it's not revenge to have lunch with your ex-mother-in-law. We were a part of each other's lives for years."

"You could have called her if you wanted to see her."

"Okay, fine," I hiss. "I wanted to fucking hurt Pearl. Are you happy?"

Satcher's head jerks back. "The real question is: are you?"

I down the rest of my drink and stare at him.

"Fuck you, Satcher. You have no idea what I went through."

"Don't I?"

We're interrupted by our server who comes to take our order. As he scribbles things down on his pad, I consider my options. I could just ask Satcher what he means. Or I could ignore the comment. He's probably just goading me anyway. My curiosity wins out.

"How do you know?"

It's the first time I've seen his dimples tonight. "What—you think you're the only one who's had a broken heart?"

I should have known. A man as unattainable as Satcher Gamble must have been hurt somewhere along the way. Hit in a way that left him raw enough to never have a serious relationship again.

"I'm the only one who has had my kind of broken heart."

"Fair enough," Satcher says. "My kind was named Gretchen."

"Oh God," I say. "That name didn't give you a hint?"

"At least she stuck with the name she was given..."

We're both still laughing when our second drink arrives. I happen to look over at that moment and see Woods watching me from across the restaurant. I give him a weak smile before turning back to Satcher. I miss Woods. I miss him so much.

*A*fter dinner, I excuse myself to use the bathroom. I'm washing my hands in a bowl sink with flowers trapped in the plexiglass when Pearl empties from a stall behind me. She falters when she catches sight of me and then proceeds to the sink next to mine like a woman approaching a snake. I eye her in the mirror expecting her to say something, but she simply finishes washing her hands, shakes them over the sink, and leaves the bathroom without a word. It throws me off, her lack of reaction. I was prepared for something sharper than cold indifference. I finish up in the bathroom, drying my hands. When I walk out of the door, I almost collide with Woods.

"Hey," I say.

"Hey yourself..." There's an awkward pause before Woods says—"So you guys just talking about business or is there something more?"

"Excuse me?"

He bounces on his heels, hands in his pockets.

"Just give it to me straight, Billie."

"Like you gave it to me straight when you started fucking Pearl?"

He runs a hand through his hair. "I didn't mean to hurt you."

"But you did."

He drops his gaze, the muscles in his jaw working. He takes a step closer to me so someone can pass behind him. We're at lover's distance, our air mingling. I look at his lips and he looks at mine. When we used to kiss I'd feel drunk. He was just that good. His voice is low when he says, "I know you, Billie. It feels like you've come back to make trouble."

I smirk, raising an eyebrow. "Does it now?"

"Woods?" Pearl rounds the corner. When she sees me, her face pales.

Woods' eyes don't leave mine. "I'll be right there," he says.

I hold his gaze, my chest heaving. "Go," I say firmly.

His nostrils flare as he holds my gaze for five more seconds, then he turns abruptly and follows Pearl back to their table. I go back into the bathroom to calm down. I'm shaking. I'm a snotty mess when the door to the bathroom swings open. I try to hide my face, embarrassed by my sloppy emotion, but then I see Satcher standing in the doorway. He points to a stall and we both cram in.

"What happened?"

"Nothing. Why? What do you think happened?"

"You're crying."

"Am I? No, I'm not. I don't cry."

We're practically pressed together, our chests touching.

"Goddammit, Billie..." I smell beer on his breath. I used to love it when Woods' breath smelled like beer.

It's like the finest hairline crack suddenly expands into the Grand Canyon. I start sobbing, my fists pressed against my eyes like a child. Satcher has to wedge his arms up around me, and I cry harder because the backs of my calves are touching the toilet and it's so gross.

"Satch," I heave. "Why ... did ... I ... come ... back?"

"Billie..." he says it like *Billeee*. "This is where you belong. You can't let anyone chase you from where you belong."

Satcher is right. I had a friend in Washington whose husband slept with her neighbor. Creepy situation, the woman only bought the house next door to them because she was obsessed with the family. There was some stalking involved. When the entire situation imploded, my friend refused to leave even though she'd have to always see the woman who'd broken her family apart.

"I already did," I say.

He bends down to rip a piece of toilet paper from the roll. Bunching it up, he dabs at my cheeks and nose. I feel pathetic. He's technically my boss, and I'm having a nervous breakdown in a toilet stall in front of him.

"But you won't again. Never again. No one has a right to your happiness. It's a private thing and you have the right to defend it."

I nod, mostly because I don't know what to say to that. Satcher is a fairy godmother when it comes to words. It's probably why the blog has done so well without me. I straighten my shoulders, determined to salvage what is left of my pride.

"I'm going to clean myself up a little."

He looks at me hard before reaching behind his back to slide the latch open. As he does so, his arm brushes against my breast and I catch my breath. Luckily, Satcher doesn't notice my reaction. I hear him greet someone as he leaves the stall and I smile despite how rotten I feel.

. . .

F*CK MARRIAGE

When I emerge from the bathroom ten minutes later, Satcher is handing his credit card to the server.

"This was supposed to be on me," I say.

He lifts the last of his drink to his lips. "Welcome back to New York," he says dryly.

I glance over at Woods' table and see that they're gone. A server is setting the table for the next reservation. I'm disappointed.

"Want to get another drink at the bar?" I'm looking toward the bar to see if there are any available seats.

"No."

My head jerks back around. Satcher is signing his receipt, scribbling in the tip amount. He won't look at me.

"Why not?"

"Because I did my good deed for the night," he says. "You needed me for whatever this was and now we're done."

"Satch..." I say. "It's not like that."

"Yeah, it is." He stands up, tucking his money clip back into his pocket. I want to reach out, grab him, tell him he means so much to me, but instead I just stand there dumbly.

"Night, Wendy." His lips meet my cheek and then he's gone.

I feel it. My selfishness is growing inside of me like a mass. It's starting to pool out. I look at my feet where all my ugly should be in a puddle; instead, there's only concrete floors and my cheap heels.

I leave The Modern, my dinner sitting heavy in my stomach. I'm making a mess of everything. Satcher is currently my only friend and he's angry with me. And can I even blame him? I used him tonight, and no matter how aloof and detached I view him to be, he is a human being with feelings. I remember where he lives and decide to rush him with my apology. I head there now, still a little buzzed from my last drink. I've always been impressed by his apartment.

While the rest of his friends (me) were bottom-feeding, Satcher had already bought his first place. Always two grown-up steps ahead of the rest of us. And it isn't that he comes from money—he claims he was at the right place at the right time, which happened to be New York City before the financial crash. He'd gotten out just in time, his bank account lush, and his heart set on buying his first start-up company.

Satcher is smart and he can turn things to gold simply by investing in them, which is why I'd sold him my half of Rhubarb. If I was going to walk away from my beloved blog it would be to sell it to someone with the Midas touch.

The sidewalk outside of his building is empty, aside from a cab idling against the curb. I wonder if it's waiting for Satcher, but then the door swings open and a pair of long legs unfold onto the asphalt.

"Woods," I breathe.

He doesn't see me right away. His eyes are trained on Satcher's building, a strange expression on his face. I come up behind him not knowing exactly what to do. Do I call out to him? Tap him on the shoulder? What is he doing here anyway? I decide to wait until he notices me. I flit up the sidewalk behind him, dodging an overturned paper cup spilling neon blue slushy. Satcher has a doorman and he eyes us both as we approach. Woods senses someone behind him and turns. I process his look of shock, which turns to appreciation as he eyes my legs.

"What are you doing here?" he asks.

I wouldn't exactly call his voice cold, but it is definitely suspicious.

"Fuck off. What are *you* doing here?"

My switcharoo works. He looks flustered.

"I need to talk to Satch," he says.

He waits for me to announce why I'm here, but I set my jaw to let him know it's not going to happen. We breeze past the doorman and into the foyer and then we freeze, awkward.

"Where's Pearl?" I ask.

"Home."

"Did you fight?"

He frowns, looking annoyed. "How did you know that?"

"I know you," I say. "Like the back of my hand."

He purses his lips and nods.

"So," he says. "Want to skip this place and go get a drink?"

I glance at the elevators, unsure. I really need to talk to Satch. Make sure we're okay.

"And be the girl you left me for? Not a chance."

I'm so proud of myself I don't even notice Satcher stepping off the elevator. Not right away at least. His eyes widen when he sees us both standing in his lobby, and reluctantly, he heads over, a frown marring his face.

"Satcher," I say before he can speak. "I came to apologize. And ask if you'll get a drink with me."

Satcher raises an eyebrow and looks at Woods.

"I wanted to get a drink too," he says.

"We came separately," I explain, glancing at Woods out of the corner of my eye.

"I was actually just heading out." Satcher glances at his watch.

"I'll walk with you..." I offer.

Satcher looks annoyed. "It's a date," he says. "I have a date."

"So you two aren't a thing?" Woods motions between us.

"Are you fucking kidding me, Woods? That's why you came here? To ask him *that?*" My hands find their way to my hips.

"He's my best friend. I have a right to know what his intentions are with you."

"No. No, you don't have a right." My chest is heaving and tears are burning my eyes. I can't believe that after everything he did, he feels like he has any right to my life. I look at Satcher, my gut rolling. "Can we get out of here? Please."

He only hesitates for a second before nodding. And in that moment, I feel like he's made a choice between his best friend and his best friend's ex-wife.

He nods at Woods and I grab onto his arm, walking quickly to keep in stride. I don't look back. If I look back I'll turn back.

CHAPTER ELEVEN

He stops abruptly once we're out of sight and I teeter forward on my heels. Satcher reaches out a hand to steady me. His fingers brush the underside of my breasts and I hear myself suck in my breath.

"I'm sorry," I say. "I'm an asshole. I shouldn't put you in the middle of ... whatever this is."

"Revenge," he offers.

My bottom lip pushes out when I nod.

"Forget it," Satcher says. His eyes scan the street; he's already dismissed me. I feel awkward. Clearly Satcher doesn't want to talk about it and I didn't have a plan past apologizing. I'm about to fall back so that I'm not trailing behind him like a lost puppy when he throws me a bone.

"Though I don't know how I feel about being a key player in my best friend's demise."

I bite my lip. "I didn't mean to put you in that position ... I was being selfish." And then I ask, "Are you guys still ... close?"

He isn't looking at me when he answers; his head is turned toward traffic. "Not really."

"Why not? What happened?" My interest is genuine, but I can tell Satcher is annoyed.

"I really do have a date."

"Of course, yeah. Do you need a cab?" I ask feebly.

He glances at his watch. "We can walk it."

I'm empowered by the word *we* as we set off, the autumn air just a hair too cold to be without a jacket. Glancing at him out of the corner of my eye, I notice that he's changed into more casual clothes: jeans, and a polo shirt that fits tight across his chest. I don't know where we're headed and I'm too afraid to ask—Satcher looks like a storm cloud waiting to burst. I want to reach out and touch him. Press my fingers into his skin to gauge his anger. I also don't want him to be angry with me.

"Who's the girl?" I ask finally.

When he turns his head it's like he's shocked to see me walking next to him.

"What?"

"Your date ... who is she?"

"Just some girl. It's not our first date."

"Oh," I say. "Do you like her a lot?"

"I like her enough."

We walk in silence for a few minutes, the city burning her energy around us. Satcher holds out an arm, stopping me from stepping into the street, and a motor bike whizzes by a second later.

"Sorry," I say, embarrassed. "I'm just..."

"Distracted?" he offers. His smile doesn't reach his eyes and that bothers me. I've always been really good at making serious, professional Satcher smile—from the eyes. "Can I ask you a question?"

"Yeah," I say. Though I don't mean it. Satcher asks raw questions, the kind that make you think uncomfortable thoughts.

"Would you take Woods back, if he really wanted to be with you again?"

I have to talk around the lump in my throat. "I don't know. Is it okay that I don't know?" I frown. I've thought about it a million times, haven't I? Fantasized about the possibility of Woods realizing he still wants to be with me, but I never know if it is because I really want it or because I've been wronged.

"I don't know," Satcher says, looking at me. "Is it?"

"He was my first love," I say. "There's something that ties you to your first love, don't you think? Something that won't let go."

He looks at me strangely.

"You'll find someone and you'll feel that way about her," I say.

Satcher looks amused. "Will I now?"

"Yeah. Maybe you're spending tonight with her. You never know..."

He laughs. "God, I hope so."

I sneak a look at him, his beautiful jawline shaded by stubble, dimples at full moon. She's lucky, whoever she is. Satcher has eclectic taste in women. I can't even imagine who is waiting for him. It could be anyone from a supermodel to a math genius, both of which he's brought to our dinner parties.

Five minutes later, we stop outside of a trendy bar on Second and shuffle our feet like two teenagers who don't know what to say to each other.

"Well," I announce comically, looking around his shoulder into the fancy hipster bar where he's meeting his date. "It's no Pimbilly's Pub..."

For a minute I think he doesn't remember, the joke flying over his head like the football two teens are tossing back and forth on the sidewalk. But then he laughs—nothing crazy. It's just a tiny little laugh. The real joy is in his eyes, which are lit up as he looks over the memory.

"Pimbilly's Pub," he repeats.

Back when the group of us were broke and in college, we'd meet up at Pimbilly's every Friday night to celebrate surviving another week of the semester with three-dollar drafts. It was a hole-in-the-wall dive, situated in the same building as a laundromat and one of those nameless food marts that charged five dollars for a half gallon of milk. Outside was one of those giant bins that sold bags of ice bearing an even bigger sign that said: DON'T FORGET THE ICE. We'd shut down the bar and then the group of us would stumble out yelling, "Don't forget the ice!" as we marched back to the dorms through the snow, or rain, or an especially muggy summer.

"Don't forget the ice," Satcher says quietly.

I smile, my foot lifted to take the first step away. I don't want to leave ... or maybe I don't want to leave *him*.

But, then he says, "Do you think it's still there?"

"Pimbilly's?"

"Yeah," he says.

"I don't know. I haven't been out that way in ages."

He pulls out his phone and I watch as his fingers move quickly across the screen.

"It's still there," he says, pocketing his phone. He seems comforted by this fact. "Hey, thanks for walking me to my date."

I've been dismissed. Our nice moment, short-lived, pops like a soap bubble.

"Chivalry is alive." I position my hand for a fist bump, but he laughs at me and pulls me into a hug instead.

"See you tomorrow at work," I say.

Satcher hesitates. He hasn't let go of me, and I stand frozen to the spot unsure of what to do. If you've just apologized for something, it is in bad taste to pull away from the person, even if it's to allow them to be on their way.

"You sure you're up for this, Billie? Working at Rhubarb ... seeing them every day?"

I'm not. I may be in over my head. I *am* in over my head. But it would take me weeks and maybe months to find another job, and there is something comforting about being back at the blog I created. It reminds me of who I can be if I try.

"Yes," I say confidently. "One hundred percent."

He lets me go and nods, slowly looking toward the bar. "All right then."

"I can handle it."

He looks less than sure, but I pin on my most dazzling smile.

"I'll bring the coffee tomorrow," I say for good measure.

I hear someone say his name and we both turn toward the voice. Walking toward us on the sidewalk is the type of woman who induces fear into other women. It's a given she wasn't born that way, I can tell by the slight way her lips stick out, pumped full by a doctor with a ready needle. But her tits are real—small—and her hair is thick, hanging almost to her waist.

"A blonde," I say to Satcher.

The last woman he dated was a Brazilian fitness model.

"Red, yellow, black, brown—what difference does it make?"

"Clearly none to you. The man who doesn't have a type."

She's almost on us now.

"Oh, I have a type," Satcher says. "My type has a type. That's the problem."

I don't have time to ask what he means because she's kissing Satcher on the cheek and looking at me with unveiled curiosity.

"This is Willa," he says to me. And to Willa he says, "Billie, the friend I was telling you about..."

"Oh, right, Billie." She looks relieved. "Welcome back to the city. How are you settling in?"

"Oh, you know, it's an adjustment being back. I still have a layer of moss growing on my back from Washington."

She laughs, a graceful and polite tinkering. *Ha ha, you're so funny. Why are you crashing my date?*

"I better get going," I say. Willa's eyes tell me that's exactly what I should do.

I'm suddenly exhausted, wanting to slink away to my apartment far from these two beautiful people who have their shit together and are probably in the process of falling in love. Willa waves and then latches onto Satcher's arm as they head for the door. Between his broad shoulders and her narrow waist, they make the most beautiful couple. Right before they walk through, Satcher turns back. I pause, unsure of what's happening. Did he catch me staring? Am I being weird?

"Billie!" he says it loud enough that everyone in the near vicinity turns to look. "Don't forget the ice!" And then he's gone.

I stand on the sidewalk feeling out of place with my huge grin and inhaling someone's cigarette smoke. I'm New York debris—a paper cup, an empty chip bag, the stub of a cigarette—empty, salty, and stubbed out. A fixture and yet a nuisance.

CHAPTER TWELVE

I drink too much, not just recently ... probably always. I drink about as much as I feel sorry for myself. My self-pity has the personality of a toddler: loud, demanding, erratic. Your husband cheats on you and suddenly you're blaming the downfall of your marriage on your thick thighs, you know? Or maybe your double chins—of course he cheated with someone who has fewer chins. But once I lost the weight, I blamed my boring personality, my oppressive personality, my demanding personality. I'm still stuck there, trying to prove to everyone that I've changed. Trying to prove to myself that I have.

I get ready for work slowly, my head throbbing. I have to stop drinking, but the thought makes me depressed. Some days are harder than others, though hard is the new normal. I remember a different version of myself: slightly shallow ... busy—so, so busy. I was the type of woman who didn't slow down because if I did I'd have to think. Thinking was for philosophy majors, depressed people, and activists. I was a lifestyle blogger who liked to juice my meals and never commented on politics. The articles I wrote: *The Best Tennis Shoes for Your Buck!* And *Cheese Dip Recipes That Will Have Your Friends Swooning!* Divorce cured me of some of that. When your perfect world crumbles there's nothing left to do but think.

"I want to take Rhubarb in a new direction," I say in the staff meeting on Monday morning. I look around at their faces and clear my throat as eyebrows raise. Pearl's face, however, remains stoic even when Zoe shoots her a look. "When I started the blog four years ago, I wanted to be relatable, but now looking back, the only type of woman I wanted to relate to was the upper middle class white woman." Several people glance at each other, shifting in their seats, uncomfortable. "We tell women how to shop, how to cook, how to organize their pantries, but what we've failed to do is be honest."

Satcher appears in the doorway; he leans against the frame, arms crossed, eyes roving over their reactions. I'd discussed this with him yesterday and he'd showed neither disapproval nor enthusiasm.

"This is your baby," he said. *"Do what you think is best."*

"Will you be in the meeting to support me?"

"Nope. You're their boss now. I don't need to micromanage."

His answer made me nervous—it was his money hinging on the success of the blog, not mine. When I said as much, he laughed at me.

"Billie, this was always your thing. You built it from nothing by being shallow. If you want to rebrand and be deep then go ahead. Trust your instinct."

I want to remind Satcher that I'd trusted my husband and look how that turned out for me.

I prepared a PowerPoint the night before, working through four glasses of wine while I worked.

Now, with all of their eyes on me, I touch the mouse and the overhead screen jumps to life.

"We are going to expand past our very narrow demographic by adding several new features to the blog..."

Woods appears behind Satcher, his eyes narrowing around the room. I know he's wondering why no one told him there was a staff meeting. *Because you don't really work here anymore*, I want to explain. *And soon your bride-to-be won't either.*

I click the mouse and the next page of the presentation appears. There's a list of new topics the blog will cover.

Loren lifts her finger to say something. I nod at her.

"Who will be writing the Life After Divorce column?" There's a little smile on her lips; it's evident she knows exactly who that'll be.

"Me."

Woods pales.

Pearl speaks next, her voice tinny in the large conference room. "Isn't that a little classless?"

"Which part?" I try to keep my voice even, but I can feel the vein on the side of my head throbbing.

"You writing about divorce when your ex-husband still owns the blog..."

I stare at her face: sharp chin, sharp nose, sharp cheekbones. Pearl is all angles, both in appearance and life.

"About as classy as his former mistress running the Health and Wellness section of the blog." *Goddammit!* I have no self-control.

Satcher facepalms from the doorway. I ignore Pearl's red face and the snickers and move on to the next slide. My hands are shaking.

"Because we're making room for new areas, there will be some shifting around in assignments." I look directly at Pearl when I say this. "I've hired Kerri Water to come in and take over Health and Wellness."

I see one of her friends reach out to squeeze her hand. Pearl angrily bats her hand away and glares at me.

"No one discussed this with me. You can't just move me mid-year..."

"I can," I say calmly. "Your contract says you were hired to be an editorial writer and you'll still be one, just in an area you're more qualified for."

"And what is that?" she asks sharply.

"Accessories," I say.

There are a few snickers. Pearl's head jerks around as she looks for the culprit.

Kerri Water is a fitness sensation. She has over two million followers on Instagram and recently signed a deal to design a sneaker line for a popular brand.

"As a longtime reader of Rhubarb, Kerri is excited to team up with us."

There is excited whispering all around. What I don't tell them is that Satcher and Kerri were fuck buddies a few years ago, and she still carries a flame for him. He barely had to twist her arm when I asked him to approach her about it.

"We're also bringing on two more fashion bloggers that will be more conducive to diversity."

"What does that mean?" Pearl asks.

"They aren't white," I say. "Or straight."

Loren claps. I grin at her before continuing.

"Our rebranding will include a section for single mothers, the LGBTQ community, and every week we'll feature a small homegrown business so that we can give a step up to start-up companies. And, this year we'll be attending the Blogstyle conference in San Francisco."

There's excited clapping all around. During Rhubarb's first two years it hadn't been in the budget to take everyone to the conference. Satcher and I had discussed it and decided it was important for the brand to go.

When I look up again, Satcher is gone and the only one left in the doorway is Woods, who is still frowning.

As soon as I've covered the budget, and the meeting is over, he heads to where I'm closing down my laptop.

"You never told me." His tone is accusatory.

"I didn't know I had to." I avoid his eyes as I grab the last of my things and head for the door.

"You still have to answer to—"

"To whom?" I interrupt, jerking upright. He doesn't say anything. "I answer to Satcher, who hired me to do exactly what I'm doing. Now, if you'll excuse me…" I push past him out into the hallway, where I almost bump into a livid Pearl.

"What do you think you're doing?" As she speaks, she rotates her body sideways, blocking my path to my office.

I'm surprised by her gall. Not only am I her boss, but I'm twice her size. *This little bitch thinks she's invincible*, I think. How long was she waiting out here to confront me, out of earshot of the rest of the staff?

I sigh. Cornered by the treachery twins. I look over my shoulder to see Woods still behind me. I'm surprised by his expression: narrowed eyes, taut mouth stretched into a line of tight disapproval. But he's not looking at me; his eyes are on Pearl. I wonder if this is an *I can talk shit about my ex-wife but you can't* situation.

When I look back at Pearl, I manage to keep my face neutral. "My job," I say, answering her question.

"You think you can come in here and uproot everything we've been working hard at for years after you abandoned Rhubarb—"

"Whoa! Are you kidding me right now?" I've stopped

trying to walk past her. My arms are full and I wish I had a place to dump everything for this titillating confrontation, but with Woods behind me and Pearl in front, I'm cornered.

She crosses her arms over her chest.

"Pearl, I left Rhubarb because you were sleeping with my husband," I say it very matter-of-factly, but the moment the words are out of my mouth, all color drains from Pearl's face.

"That's in the past," she says.

"Well, isn't that convenient for you." I try to push past her, but she squares her shoulders, standing her ground.

"I'm not moving departments," she says. "You'll have to find someone else—"

"Can you put that in an email?"

"What?" She looks dazed at my interruption.

"An email," I repeat. "I need everything documented for when I fire you for breaking your contract..."

She opens and closes her mouth and then looks hard over my shoulder at who I presume is Woods.

"Billie..." I hear him say my name very quietly from behind me.

"It's Wendy," I say this loud enough for everyone to hear.

"You can't fire me." Pearl's voice is getting louder, more shrill.

She's probably right, considering she's shacked up with a shareholder. But right now I don't care; all I want is to get out of this toxic sandwich I'm cornered in.

"Why not?"

She's caused enough of a commotion that people are starting to listen.

I hear Woods say my name again, this time with more urgency. And then the unexpected happens: Pearl clutches her stomach just as red blossoms across her white pants. She screams at the same time I drop everything I'm holding to catch her.

CHAPTER THIRTEEN

The trip to the emergency room is one of the longest I've ever made. My cab gets stuck behind two accidents, and by the time I walk into the hospital, Pearl has lost her baby. Satcher texted to tell me. I find Satcher already in the waiting room seated next to a green-faced Woods. Woods is staring into a paper cup of cold coffee like he wishes he could drown himself in it. I take it from him and throw it in the trash, then I walk down to the cafeteria and get him a green tea. Woods isn't a coffee drinker. As the healthier eater of the two of us, he was always trying to get me to make the switch from coffee to green tea. I put the paper cup of tea in his hand. He blinks at me hard like he's trying not to cry. I can feel Satcher's eyes on me, but I don't look over. I'm embarrassed ... ashamed. I antagonized Pearl and she lost their baby. I am the worst person in the world.

"Thank you," Woods says. He says it sincerely like he means it and I offer a weak smile.

I know he doesn't blame me for what happened to Pearl, he's not like that. In all the years I accused him of things, he never accused me back. I think that made me angrier—that while I ranted and bitched, he never lowered himself to my level of petty anger.

I take the seat next to him and stare at my hands.

"How is she?" I ask.

"They're checking her now," he says.

I want to ask why he isn't in there with her, but I keep my mouth shut. Plenty of women are private about that sort of thing.

We sit like that for twenty minutes before the doctor comes out to get Woods. He looks at me before he stands up.

"Thank you," he says. "For the love."

I nod, tears burning my eyes. He follows the doctor down a hallway. That's when I finally look at Satcher.

"For the love?" Satcher's eyebrow is raised in question.

I squirm in my seat pressing my lips together. When we were still married and things were getting rough, we took the love language test at the suggestion of one of our friends. With a bottle of wine and an attitude of resolve, we settled on the couch with our laptops to take the quiz. It was a good idea, but a lazy half-assed attempt to improve our communication. We needed more than a quiz at that point. Woods got a tie between Acts of Service and Quality Time. I got Physical Touch.

"It's self-defeating," I'd said staring at our results. "I don't have enough time to dedicate to what you need, and you don't want to touch me unless we're in a good place and I'm meeting your needs."

"It doesn't have to be that cut-and-dried," he'd argued.

My brain couldn't accept that. "Yes, it does. We're too different to love each other in the right way." I'd stood up, teetering sideways from the wine.

"We obviously had enough in common to get married," he'd said. He was still sitting, his feet propped on the coffee table, laptop balanced on his lap. I remember staring down at him and thinking how clueless he was. Life just wasn't that simple. People changed, their likes and dislikes evolving with time and experience. What we'd had in common wasn't there anymore.

"I'm not asking you to give up your dreams..." He'd sounded frustrated and my walls went up right away. I was defensive ... wrong.

"Then what exactly are you asking for?" I'd snapped.

Woods looked hurt. I was the one yelling, while he was calmly sitting on the couch trying to talk things out.

"Interest, consideration—a relationship, Billie. That's why you get married, to have a relationship with someone..."

"We have a damn relationship," I'd argued.

"You don't even know that I hate coffee, Billie. I don't drink coffee anymore..."

"What the fuck are you even talking about, Woods?" He was being petty ... needy. I'd loomed over him, my voice and face wrought with anger.

"Green tea," he'd said slowly. "I switched to green tea about six months ago..."

Guilt. So much, but instead of acknowledging what my husband had just said I acted like it was ridiculous.

"This is so stupid."

That was it for me. I'd stormed out of the room, slamming our bedroom door, and crawling into the bed to wallow in self-righteousness. What did he want from me, for God's sake? I was chin-deep in Rhubarb, trying to get it off the ground so that we could live comfortably without worries. I barely slept, and my doctor had just put me on anxiety meds. When we'd started the business we'd both been on the same track, but somewhere along the way, Rhubarb had stopped being something that brought us together and instead started ripping us apart.

"He just means for the tea," I answer Satcher.

I can tell Satcher doesn't buy it, but thankfully he doesn't say anything else.

"I should go." I stand up.

"Yeah," Satcher says.

I don't know why, but his tone makes me angry. I glare at him one more time before snatching up my purse and marching for the elevators. I don't say goodbye. The last thing I need is Satcher's goody two-shoes judgment. I thought I'd changed, grown up, but in moments like these, I know I'm still the same defensive fuck-up I've always been.

*P*earl takes two weeks off of work. During the time she's gone, Rhubarb feels lighter, more joyful. The employees who normally steer clear of me due to their loyalty to Pearl, warm up, chatting with me in the common room and even once inviting me to happy hour with them after work. I feel guilty for how much I enjoy her absence. Especially since I'm the reason she miscarried. Satcher avoids me, never making eye contact, and only talking to me if it's to respond to a question I ask, or to deal with Rhubarb business. Woods comes into the office twice to pick up some things for Pearl. We collide in the hallway, his arms full of paperwork, and mine full of the props I just went to get from the storage room.

"Hey," I say.

"Hey yourself."

"How is she?"

His face immediately clouds over. "I don't know. She doesn't want to talk about it. She's ... shut down."

I nod. Women deal with things differently than men. We want them to meet our emotional needs without us having to spell it out for them. It's an *if you love me, you should know what I need* type of thing.

"She's grieving. Hold her. Order the food she likes and fuss over her," I say. "She just needs her pain acknowledged and to be taken care of."

He nods. "Thank you."

We stand there for another thirty seconds, Woods just staring at me like he wants to say something else. But I never give him the chance.

"I'll see you," I say, stepping around him.

I haven't gotten five steps when he calls after me. "Wendy..."

I turn. The wooden sign I'm holding digs painfully into my waist and I shift feet to alleviate the pressure.

"It wasn't your fault," he says.

It feels like someone has just shoved me sideways. I feel unbalanced ... panicked.

"I know you're blaming yourself." He pauses as someone walks by to get to the bathroom.

Woods lowers his voice when he says, "The doctor said it was an ectopic pregnancy..."

I nod, tears filling my eyes. Somehow that should make me feel better, but it doesn't. I was raised Catholic, I'm good at guilt.

"Well, look at us comforting each other," I say.

Woods grins. "We've come a long way."

But is it the right way? I want to ask. Because it doesn't feel right. None of this does. Mayhap I am the bitter, jealous ex-wife. Yes, that is probably it. Even if there aren't feelings involved, it would bother me that my ex-husband was trying to procreate with someone else. It's just ... awkward ... uncomfortable. Like our life before didn't matter. Divorce isn't supposed to happen, but it does, and no one really knows how to deal with it. It frees you of one thing while imprisoning you with a thousand others. Life isn't even remotely fair.

"Okay, well, I better go," I say, suddenly feeling the full force of awkwardness.

My palms are sweating. When I get back to my office, I lock the door and lie down on the carpet with my palms flat on the ground, staring up at the ceiling.

I'm close to dozing off when my phone pings from my pocket. I think about ignoring it, but eventually I raise my hips, reaching to slide it out of my back pocket. I sit up right away.

CHAPTER FOURTEEN

*D*enise Tarrow never beats around the bush. The very first time she met me, she said, "*So, are you going to give me grandkids, or are you one of those career types?*"

I'd been too shocked to respond, and by the time I'd found my voice, Woods had chastised her and the conversation had moved on to something else. I liked her despite her lack of filter and general inclination to meddle in other people's business. Once you got used to her personality, it was hard not to appreciate the care behind her actions.

I'd almost forgotten about her mentioning us getting lunch until she texts to ask if I want to meet at Gramercy Tavern on Tuesday.

I stare at that text for a long time debating what to do. Having lunch with Woods' mother feels like I am stepping over a line. And while that's exactly what I came back to New York to do, doing it so soon after Pearl's miscarriage feels wrong.

It is tacky, no doubt.

Almost as if she's reading my mind, she sends a follow-up text.

Pearl doesn't have to know...

I can't suppress my smile. That seals the deal because I text back and tell her I'd love to meet. We decide on an early dinner, and I set down my phone with a sinking dread. This is what I had wanted just a few months ago. To prove to Woods that marrying someone else is a terrible idea. But now that my plan is unraveling in just the way I wanted it to, it feels ... dirty.

On Tuesday I'm heading out of the office an hour earlier than usual to meet up with Denise when I bump into Woods on the stairwell. I don't normally take the stairs, but there is an Out of Order sign on the elevator doors.

"Still have that shirt, huh?" I eye the T-shirt he's wearing. The lettering is faded, but you can still make out the words.

"It's my favorite."

"Band or shirt?" I ask.

"Both."

I bought the shirt for Woods at a concert we went to on one of our first dates. I can still remember the way his skin smelled when he leaned in to kiss me, the beer on his breath and the way his thumbs rubbed circles on my lower back as his tongue made its way into my mouth.

"Want to grab something to eat?" he asks.

There is scruff on his face and the tender skin around his eyes looks grey, like he hasn't slept in a week. I imagine this is all taking a toll on him.

"Can't." I smile. "Maybe another time..."

"Come on," he says. "I need you."

At first his words hit me in that sore, insecure place where I keep the things that I pretend not to care about: Daddy issues, Mommy issues, Woods' issues...

I need you. He used to say that to me while his lips kissed a line down my neck, fingers roving over my body. I feel heat climb to my face at the memory.

I think about all the times I needed him, like when our marriage was on the rocks and I was stretched as thin as membrane, and he stuck his dick in someone else instead of keeping his vows to me.

"Not today, Woods," I say glibly. I take two more steps, cursing the broken elevator.

"Why not?"

I hesitate. Should I just tell him? I don't want to be cruel when his life is already hard, but he'll find out about it eventually.

"I'm on my way to see your mom."

He squeezes one eye closed while scratching the back of his head. "That's awkward."

"No more than you asking me to lunch when your fiancée is at home recovering from a miscarriage."

He grins. "What a pair we are."

"Were," I say, trotting down the stairs. "What a pair we were."

"Pessimist!" he calls after me. His voice echoes.

It feels good to walk away from him. I wonder if this is how things started with Pearl: the occasional flirtatious exchange in the stairwell, trips out to lunch when I was too busy to notice.

I don't have time to think about it; I'm already late.

Denise has just returned from a cruise. When I hug her, I swear I can still smell suntan lotion on her skin. She holds on to me for a few extra seconds.

"You're glowing," I tell her when she lets me go.

"Oh. You don't glow at my age. I just got a little sun, that's all." She takes her seat delicately, folding her napkin across her lap.

But she is, she's glowing.

"Robert cheated on me," she says.

The server who was just approaching the table hears her comment and makes a wide arc to give us some time.

I smile at him apologetically before I turn to Denise and say—"What?"

"Don't look so surprised. Where do you think Woods learned his bad behavior?"

"I figured it was from his dick."

"Touché..."

I shake my head, trying to take it all in. Woods is already an established cheater. I decide to start the questions with my ex-father-in-law. "He's done it before?"

"Yes. Started our third year of marriage, and it's been on and off since. Sometimes we have a good five years with no cheating, but he always starts it up again."

"And you ... stay with him?"

Denise lifts her menu, pursing her lips; I watch her eyes scan something before she sets it down on the table and slides it away. I've always viewed Denise as a feminist: independent, nonplussed by opinions, taker of no shit. Reconciling what she is saying with the woman I always thought she was leaves a lump in my throat. I wait for her to speak since I don't know what to say anyway.

"He's always so sorry. He comes back, he cries, we take a vacation, he upgrades my ring."

Over the eight years Woods and I were together, I recall Denise getting a new ring every few years, the diamond growing in size. I glance at her finger now, feeling ill. Why is she telling me this?

"You're wondering why I'm telling you all this now?"

"Yes, actually."

She folds her hands on the table, her upper body leaning toward me. She's so willowy she reminds me of a branch bending in the wind.

"My son is still very much in love with you," she says. It's like someone just stuck my finger in a light socket; every part of me lights up in shock. "This thing with Pearl," she makes a dismissive sweep with her hand, "it's not real, nor is it sustainable."

I'm shocked. Shook. Shocked and shook by her words. "I'm sorry about your situation, Denise, but in my less-than-expert opinion on love, I think that if a man is in love with you he shouldn't throw himself into the arms of another woman."

"Don't be condescending, Billie. You haven't lived long enough to know that. Men don't cheat because they're not in love, they cheat because they don't feel loved."

"He didn't just cheat. He came home one day and told me he was leaving me for someone else."

"A cry for help," she says. "They want to be worshipped. They want a woman who thinks they're the greatest, strongest, most virile."

"And I didn't?"

"You were busy."

"Denise, you're telling me that my husband cheated on me because I didn't stroke his ego hard enough?"

She looks at me hard.

"All right," I say. I close my eyes. "Say what you're saying is true. Why does Robert cheat on you? You're practically the perfect wife."

"Oh, my dear, things aren't always what they seem. You know that."

I can't imagine what she's talking about. Everything about their lives and marriage has always represented perfection. I feel as if I'm six years old and just found out Santa Claus isn't real.

"It's become a cycle we're unfortunately comfortable with. The longer you stay in an unhealthy relationship, the more druglike it becomes. You're willing to deal with the side effects because they're predictable. You can trust the bad in a way you can't trust the unknown."

We're cut off by the server who's made his way over, a look of apprehension on his face. Once we've ordered and he's retreated from the table, there's a pregnant silence between us.

"I take it you don't like Pearl." It whooshes out of me. If there were only a way to suck words back in like spaghetti.

"Oh, she's fine. Basic. Woods was just trying to find the best parts of you in someone else. It won't last. Thank God the miscarriage happened."

Wow. Whoa. It is one thing not wanting them together, and an entirely other thing to be glad she miscarried. But then there is also the matter of what she is saying about Woods and Pearl. Could she be right? I'd thought that Woods couldn't find any good parts of me anymore, and that's why he'd left. I frown down at my drink.

"I don't know, Denise. They seem to be pretty happy."

"You thought you were happy too, remember?" She pats my hand. "You have time. Wedding's not for another year. And hopefully she doesn't get herself knocked up again."

For the next week I can't stop thinking about my lunch with Denise Tarrow. On my twenty-third birthday, Woods presented me with a portable DVD player, while Satcher showed up at my party with a first edition copy of my favorite children's book. Where my reaction to the DVD player had been tepid, fabricated excitement, my reaction to the book Satcher presented had been childlike glee. I'd seen the hurt on Woods' face and felt terrible. It was a small incident, neither of them would remember it now, but it stuck with me because in the eight years we were together, Woods never quite got the gift thing right. Over the years, he gave me a beach chair, a set of pots and pans, a guitar, guitar lessons—things I didn't have time for. He was either trying to send me a message or he didn't know me at all. I summed it up as the latter. And if my own partner didn't know me, perhaps I was unknowable.

There's a wrapped gift on my desk one morning when I get into the office. I sit down, eyeing it warily. It's the size of a ring box and wrapped professionally in gilded silver paper with a satin ribbon. I poke it with my finger and it slides across my desk. I don't trust gifts. There is always a motive behind them.

"What's that?" Loren walks in, a Styrofoam Cup Noodles in her hand. She sits down in the empty chair, crossing her legs, and begins wrapping noodles around her fork.

"I don't know. It was just sitting here."

"Well, open it," she says. A noodle hits her chin and she pulls a napkin from her bra to dab at the splash.

I pick up the box, turning it over in my hand. There's no card. Gingerly, I tuck my finger into the space between the tape and the paper and separate it. Underneath the wrapping is a velvet box. I crack the lid. When Loren sees my face, she sets down her Cup Noodles and rounds my chair to get a look at what I'm holding.

"Geeeezus," she says. She reaches for her noodles without taking her eyes off the box.

Inside, resting on a black pillow, is a silver pendant in the shape of a hand. Instead of an extended middle finger, the ring finger is propped up and empty.

"What does it mean?" I ask.

"Fuck marriage," Loren says. "And a cry for help."

"You think Woods left this?" I think of what his mother said.

Loren shrugs. "Could have been anyone, I guess. They certainly hit the mark though, didn't they?"

I spread both hands on my desk. A little piece of jewelry has triggered an idea. I stare at my hands as I think, the ideas rushing faster than my hand would if it were holding a pen. "This is it, Lo," I say.

"What?"

"The header for the blog: I'll call it Fuck Marriage. Brand it with the empty ring finger."

Lo nods slowly. "Seems a bit aggressive, but it may work."

"Of course it will work," I say, standing up. "That's what we are after our relationships end; we're angry. Do you know how many times I wished there was someone—someplace I could go for help? I bought the self-help books, I went to a counselor. None of it was what I needed. I wanted a community, I wanted a friend. And that's exactly what this column can be: the friend women wish they had. Get Dave in here so we can brand this."

I pull the pendant out of the box. Unclasping my necklace, I slide the pendant onto the chain and return it to my neck.

This is exactly what the blog needs: a dose of hardcore reality. Fuck Marriage could be my unofficial apology letter to Woods. To my marriage. And who knows, maybe blogging about my broken heart will help heal it.

CHAPTER FIFTEEN

A membership to the East Side gym costs $150 a month. Steep change for communal fitness. The chain gym two blocks over offers their monthly membership on bright neon flyers for $49. But the East Side gym is where Woods works out five days a week, so I shell out the cash and follow Rocket, the overeager meathead whose face resembles Ernie from *Sesame Street*, while he gives me a tour.

"Rocket, that's an interesting name," I say as he shows me where the dirty towels go.

"I named myself. My parents gave me a bad name so I just changed it."

"Cool," I say. "What was your name before?"

"Simon." He makes a face.

"Simon says: change your name," I joke.

But Rocket is too young to get the reference. He leaves me at the elliptical machines where five women are already sweating through their designer workout gear. I make my way over to the weight machines, where I know Woods will go first.

"Well, well, well..."

I spin around and find myself facing Satcher, a smug smile turning up the corners of his lips.

"Now why would Billie Tarrow get a membership at a gym that's in the opposite direction of her apartment when there is a perfectly good gym across the street from where she lives?"

I can feel my face turn red. I turn away, my only response a noise I make in the back of my throat. Satcher, undeterred, follows me.

"Could it be that a certain ex-husband has a membership here?"

I claim an open rowing machine a few feet away from the mats and get to work, still ignoring Satcher. I don't want to row, I want to pretend to work out while I wait for Woods to arrive. Satcher stands over me, his white Nikes perfectly clean, not a single scuff.

"Why are you even here?" I snap. "It's Friday. Shouldn't you be fucking a supermodel?"

He takes the machine next to mine when the girl next to me gets up and starts rowing. "We're on the rocks," he says.

I glance over to check his face, which reveals nothing. "Why?"

"Why not?" He shrugs.

"You have commitment issues." I push back harder than I mean to and my neck jerks forward painfully. Every few minutes I glance at the door to see if Woods has arrived.

"Yes," Satcher says simply.

I stop rowing and stare at him. "So do something about it."

Satcher glances at me out of the corner of his eye. "Like what?" he asks, amused.

"I don't know," I say, watching the way the muscles in his arms flex every time he pulls back. "Counseling, forcing yourself to stay in a relationship until your fears go away..."

"Is that what you did?"

"Seriously, Satcher..." I swipe at my hair, pushing it out of my face. "Are you trying to pick a fight with me?"

"Maybe."

I didn't expect that. I wipe my palms on my pants not knowing what to say.

Luckily, he's the one to speak first. "You have this perception of me. I don't know where it came from, but it's wrong."

"Okay," I say. "So you're not a womanizing, shallow, rich dude who likes beautiful women?"

He grunts. "Whoa! Wait just a damn minute. *Shallow?*"

I laugh, which Satcher seems to enjoy.

"Does any insult faze you, Sasquatch?"

"Only the true ones."

"Must be nice to be that confident." I sigh.

"Must be nice to be so beautiful," he says.

I look around to see who he's talking about; there are women everywhere. "Where?"

When I look back at Satcher he's staring right at me. I'm frozen, heat climbing my neck as I try to understand if he's messing with me. I blink and force myself to focus.

"Um..." As my discomfort increases so do Satcher's dimples. "Honest to God, Satcher. You always do this to me. You love to make me uncomfortable and confused."

Satcher, who seems to be immensely enjoying this, places a hand over his heart and frowns. "Billie—"

"Uh-uh..."

"Wendy," he corrects. "I assure you that it's not my intention to make you feel uncomfortable or confused. But you should definitely explore why it is exactly that I make you feel confused and uncomfortable. Sounds like a personal issue."

I open and close my mouth. There haven't been many moments in my life where the cat has actually gotten my tongue. I don't like how out of control I currently feel, or how his eyebrows are lifted practically to his hairline as he messes with me.

"Are you flirting with me?"

He doesn't say anything, but his smile is enough to send every pathetic girl feeling I have into overdrive. I stand firm against the butterflies and try to look unfazed. For lack of anything better to do with my hands, I take a sip of water from the bottle I brought and spill half of it down the front of my shirt.

"Shit..." I'm brushing off water, hot with embarrassment, when I hear Woods' voice.

"So you guys are gym partners now?"

My eyes don't immediately leave Satcher's face, they linger on the smug set of his lips before I turn my head to look at my former husband.

"Hello to you too," I say.

Woods is annoyed; his eyes always get really small when he's annoyed. He has a wad of Juicy Fruit in his cheek, and he holds it there while he stares between Satcher and me like we're two teenagers coming home late from prom. I hold my shirt away from my skin, feeling awkward. I don't know how the two of them got to this place, but there's a palpable tension between them.

"I'll see you, Billie." Satcher winks at me before moving away, never actually acknowledging Woods' presence.

I watch him go, disappointed. We'd been having fun, even if he was teasing me. I'm not the only one staring at him; half of the female gym in the vicinity turn their heads as he passes by.

"That's something I never expected," Woods says.

"What?" I'm still watching Satcher's back.

"My best friend and my ex-wife..."

My attention snaps back to Woods and I want to laugh—I

do. I am so far from Satcher's type it is upsetting to think about. I almost correct him and then think better of it. Let Woods think there is something going on between me and Sasquatch. I raise my eyebrows in a what-in-the-world way.

Woods sighs. "I better get to work."

I start to walk away and he calls after me.

"Hey, Billie!"

"Yeah."

"You look ... great."

I suppress my smile. "Thanks. You too." And then it takes everything in me to walk away. I can feel his eyes roving ... roving, but I keep walking. Slow and steady wins the race.

CHAPTER SIXTEEN

I catch the red-eye to San Francisco alone. Everyone else flew out yesterday, but we are launching the newly branded F*ck Marriage next week, and I still have to finalize a lot of the details with Dave, who stayed behind to keep things running. Now with an hour to go before the luncheon, the first of the events, I have clothes strewn all over the hotel bed and zit cream on my chin. What are the chances I have a huge event and get a zit for the first time in two years? I glance at my outfit options for the day.

I selectively packed things from Jules' closet, knowing I'd have to wear them since they were all I brought. Now, looking down at the tight black pants with a sheen that makes them look oil-slicked, I feel a wave of apprehension. Maybe this isn't me. I pull them on anyway, despite my loud inner protesting, and put on the emerald green halter top I brought to pair it with. I look good. Really good. But not like me.

Something about having your heart broken and getting divorced gives you a raw sort of edge. I feel like Sandy in *Grease* when she dons her leather pants and fuck-me heels and goes to reclaim Danny with her new attitude. This is who I am on the inside, and it will just take a little practice to get comfortable expressing it with my (Jules') wardrobe.

An hour later when I walk into the luncheon, I know I've made the right decision. The vendors greet me with happy surprise and several of the other bloggers run up to welcome me back and to tell me I look great. I'm riding high on all of the affirmation when I grab my first mimosa from a serving tray and make my way over to one of my old blogger friends, Annalise. She yells in excitement when she sees me. We remove ourselves from the bustle to talk, standing next to the drink table where I pluck another mimosa from the tray.

"It wasn't the same when you left. Satcher did a great job holding things together, but I assume he brought you back for a reason." This from Annalise; she started the Fab, Fit, Five blog around the same time I launched Rhubarb. She has five kids, all of them blonde and blue-eyed, and her blog is basically a recipe for depression if you're not a size two, don't breastfeed for a year, and throw peanut butter and jelly into a paper sack instead of making healthy gourmet school lunches.

"I assume so too," I say, noting that Annalise has a new, upgraded engagement ring on her finger. Goodbye to humble beginnings. Her husband, Ned, is a developer. He recently built them a new mansion, which Annalise posts regularly on the blog's decorating section. Despite my stint with depression when I was in Washington, I always kept up with what Fab, Fit, Five was doing; there's something endearing about Annalise, right down to the way her finger and toenails always match her lipstick.

Once we're done covering business, she lowers her voice considerably and asks, "So how has it been working with Pearl?"

If Annalise ever swore, I imagine the offensive word would be said in the same tone she says Pearl's name.

We both look up at the same time to where Pearl is arm in arm with Woods, talking to a vendor. She has chosen a white ensemble—probably to remind everyone of her upcoming wedding— with teal heels and a chunky gold chain around her neck. Her diamond ring can be seen clear across the room.

"Ow-ow," Annalise says. "Her bling is blinding me." Annalise's ring can rival Pearl's, but I appreciate the support.

"You don't need a ring like that when you start out," she says. "You earn the larger carats by being married and having to put up with their bullshit."

I laugh. "You cussed!"

She blushes. "Yeah, sorry. I just get worked up sometimes. And there's always been something about you that makes me feel free to say what I want."

"Ha!"

"He still loves you, you know." She looks at me sideways, a slight brightening of her eyes. "See, there I go again..."

"Woods?" I ask, surprised.

"Who else, dummy? He can't keep his eyes off of you."

I follow Annalise's gaze to where Woods and Pearl are, and true enough, his eyes are trained on me. It both thrills and mortifies me—him being with Pearl and watching me so blatantly.

"He's a cheater," I say. "Maybe he's bored with Pearl and remembers how flexible I am."

Annalise lets out a chortling laugh that draws the eyes of several bystanders. She covers her ruby red lips with a hand and makes surprised eyes at me. I laugh because her eyes are already *so* big.

"You know not every man who cheats is a cheater."

"The fuck, Annalise?" I say. "Did you read that in the Positive Southerner handbook?"

She swats me playfully on the arm. "It's the same for

women. And I wouldn't be lying if I said that when I was mad with Ned when he was working all the time, I didn't consider finding me a twenty-two-year-old with a six-pack."

"Of beer or muscle?"

"Girl, don't be dumb. Beer."

I shake my head. Wherever I go, women have different opinions of cheating and how it should be dealt with. I have a feeling Annalise would sweep it under the rug as long as Ned bought her a new bauble.

"For real though, Billie. Woods always looked at you like you were a cold glass of something he wanted to put his mouth on. You were just too busy to notice."

I immediately deflate. She's not saying anything I haven't thought myself. I have a tendency to have tunnel vision, and back then I was solely focused on Rhubarb—aka myself.

"He's gonna flirt with you tonight," she says. "Mark my words. In those liquid sex pants of yours. You'll see. If he mentions the pants, you'll know his mind is in them."

I open my mouth to say something, but Annalise's expression changes. "Shh-shhh." Annalise grabs my arm and squeezes. I watch in fascination as her features rearrange to resemble an entirely different woman.

Pearl and Woods are walking toward us. Woods, I notice, is staring straight at me. Annalise greets them first in her southern drawl, which is heavier than it was just five seconds ago. I'm preparing for her to "bless their hearts," which causes me to giggle nervously.

"Hey, y'all. So glad you decided to come out this year. I was wondering when I'd see you again." I'm inordinately grateful for her in this moment, the ease with which she glides through the awkward situation.

Pearl is trying to act normal, but I see the way she eyes me when I'm not looking, cataloging my hair, my outfit, my demeanor. I know her well enough to know that when she's insecure, her eyes grow even wider than normal, and she stops making eye contact. We chat about the blogosphere for a few minutes, and they catch me up on some of the drama: the bloggers who've sold, the ones who are making twice as much as what they used to. While Pearl and Annalise splinter off into their own conversation, Woods turns to me.

"Pants," he says.

My mouth wants to drop open, but I keep it smugly turned up; an indifferent grin.

"The way they look on or taking them off?" I ask.

Now it's his turn to look shocked.

"I suppose one thing leads to the other..."

I can't help but laugh. Still the same charming, flirtatious Woods.

Pearl is struggling to stay focused on what Annalise is saying while also trying to eavesdrop on us. I remember this about her from the old days: we'd go to an event and she'd come back with gossip from almost everyone who was there.

"How do you know all of this?" I'd ask her.

"I'm always involved in five conversations at once, even if people don't know I am."

I wonder if Woods knows this little detail about his soon-to-be bride.

"You going to be around tonight to get a drink?" he asks under his breath.

I lift my eyebrows in surprise. Is he really asking me to get a drink with his fiancée right there?

Is it me or does her whole body stiffen?

I lick my lips before I speak, trying to buy time to formulate a good answer. "I ... uh ... no. I'm having drinks with Annalise and a couple of the girls."

His disappointment is palatable. "Where?"

I glance at Pearl. "Are you shitting me right now, Woods?" I hiss.

"Where?" he asks again.

I sigh. "The Viable Vine. Woods...?"

"Hush," he says. "I wasn't asking permission." His voice is low, but there's something in his eyes that causes me to bob my head in a brief nod.

I am fairly good at reading my ex-husband. Two years has done little to change the slight tells in his body language. And by the look in his eyes, the slight puckering of his full lips like he's just licked a lemon, I know something is up. I can't use it to my advantage if I don't know what it is.

At lunch, Rhubarb shares a table with Chic Creek (we call it Shit Creek for laughs). We all congregate around the table, holding our cocktails and asking polite questions. When we're told lunch is being served, we sit, and I somehow end up between Woods and Courtney, Shit Creek's founder and main gal. Courtney used to look like the girl next door, but Shit Creek made a shit ton of money and now she looks like a woman who's made a ton of money and put it all in her face. She has lipstick on her teeth when she smiles at me.

"Back so soon?" She has a country twang even heavier than Annalise's. I flinch, but halfway through I try to redirect it and end up twitching like I have a goddamn tic.

"I hardly think two years is *soon*," I say.

"Well, I thought you'd settle down in the PNW. Find a lumberjack and have a few babies..."

Pearl, who's listening from across the table says, "Don't be silly, Court, her taste is Woods. Definitely not a lumberjack."

Court? Of course they are friends now. Pearl is marrying Woods, which gets her an invitation into the blogger wife club. I distinctly remember her bitching about being shunned by Courtney just a few years ago. She'd suggested making a burn book, *Mean Girls'* style, and featuring *Court*.

They've planned this—I see the exchange they make with their eyes.

"I think we all have the same taste in men, actually," I say. I look at Courtney innocently. "Remember when you made a pass at Woods when you were getting divorced?"

The rule is that you can be as mean as you like without being direct. Cut, but with underhanded sugar. When someone like me comes along wielding the truth as a knife everyone is up in arms. There is a stunned silence around the table. Woods looks like he needs another drink. Pearl looks away, a disgusted look on her face.

"I'm sure you're mistaken." Courtney smiles tightly. "You always seemed to think Woods was cheating on you. Honestly, it's probably your insecurity that drove him away."

I gasp. I open my mouth and palm at the same time. I'm about to give Shit Creek Courtney a lashing with tongue and hand when I hear Satcher's voice behind me.

"Sorry I'm late. Billie, there's a problem back at the office. Can I borrow you for a minute?"

When I turn around, he's smiling obliviously at me. Every woman at the table flutters their eyelashes at him. I'm annoyed. Shit was about to go down and now Satcher is pulling me away.

I scoot my chair back, and excusing myself, I snatch my drink from the table to follow Satcher out of the banquet hall and through the open doors of the patio.

"You okay, Billie?"

"Is Wendy okay? Hell, no. Is it just me or was the bitch level high in there?"

"Ehhh... " He scratches the back of his head, squinting at me. "It was what was expected."

I round on him. "You're Team Pearl now?"

"I'm on your team; that's why I'm out here. You've been gone a long time. Pearl's worked hard at that relationship."

"Yeah, well, I never had Courtney's loyalty anyway. Bitch."

"From what I heard, you were equal parts bitchy."

"Whose side are you even on?" I have to set my drink down to throw my hands on my hips. Satcher eyes me, amused. "Listen to yourself. A few years ago no one messed with you, you know why?"

I shake my head.

"Because you didn't engage with petty. You were the queen and you never stooped to their level."

He's right. I was a chubby queen but still the queen.

"Well, the queen has fallen on hard times. And now I'm here to play bitch ball."

Satcher rolls his eyes. Eye-rolling is something he doesn't typically stoop to, so now I feel extra childish.

"You're hypersensitive, and you think everyone's out to get you."

"They are."

"Exactly."

I fold my arms across my chest, looking closely at him for the first time. He smells like a bucket of hundred-dollar bills soaked in cedar wood and whiskey. He's for real wearing a navy blue waistcoat under his tailored blazer. I get the fuss, I do, but he's annoying the shit out of me with his hoity-toity attitude.

"Nothing works out for me."

"Nothing ... really? Woods encompasses everything? Because I can think of plenty that works out for you when you actually try."

He's looking out at the water now, elbows resting on the railing. No sign of the dimples; he's frustrated with me. Maybe I *am* being a brat. Maybe.

I move to stand next to him, both of us admiring the water in silence.

"My glass is almost empty," I say, holding it up. "Literally and figuratively." That gets me half a smile, a flash of dimple.

"I hate to say this, Billie, but this whole feel-sorry-for-myself thing is getting old."

I roll my eyes. Only Satcher could say something like that to me without me getting raging angry. I still pout.

"Your marriage ended. Lots of marriages end on account of a cheating asshole—"

I shrug.

"You've had your time to grieve, you deserved that after what happened. But now you're back, and it's time to live. If you don't live now, then when?"

"I don't remember how to," I admit. I'm ashamed of how sulky my voice sounds. "Living after a broken heart isn't like riding a bike. You genuinely forget how to go about doing it."

"I respect that. But it's do or die, isn't it? And you're too spiteful to let Pearl and Woods kill you."

Satcher rubs his hands across his face. He looks tired. I'm a bad friend.

He's beautiful. He's my ex-husband's best friend, but he's beautiful.

"You okay?" I ask. I know from experience that we often mistake put-together people for happy and emotionally healthy, when it is all a guise.

He's still leaning against the railing, but he turns his head to study me like he's truly surprised I'm asking. I make a mental note to not be so damn self-centered all the time.

"Tell me," I urge.

He hesitates for a moment and then says, "They found a mass in my mother's right breast. She finds out her biopsy results today."

"And you're not there..." I nod in understanding.

Satcher is a family guy. He doesn't have one of his own yet, but I remember how close he used to be with his sisters.

"Yeah..." he says, flatly.

I'm not sure what to do. I don't want to tell him I'm sorry even though I am; it feels like a weak word.

"Go."

"What?"

"Go to New York. Go home and be with her. You shouldn't be here."

He looks surprised at my suggestion, and I wonder if he even considered it or if he felt that obligated to be here.

"This is my business. I should—"

I grab both of his hands and force him to look at me. "It may be your business, but it's my blog," I interrupt. "I'll take care of everything as if I still own it. Promise."

He purses his lips. We're facing each other, holding hands. I imagine we must look like a couple having a romantic moment on the terrace.

"Are you sure?" Satcher's brow is creased, and without thinking, I reach up to smooth it, thinking of the day he spotted me on the street and came running after me to offer me a job. He always shows up when I need help.

"I'm a hundred percent sure." I feel puffed up about this ... good. Being able to do something for the man who is always doing something for me.

What I do next I blame on the Champagne.

Leaning up on my tiptoes, I aim for his mouth. By the time I see the look in his eyes it's too late. He turns his head and my mouth meets the stubble on his cheek, startling my lips. It's a sharp rejection, and I take an immediate step back. I spot the pity on Satcher's face, and I'm suddenly sober. I look away quickly. Paired with what went down inside I feel pathetic. A fool.

Embarrassment burning my throat, I touch Satcher's hand, which still rests on the railing.

"I'm so sorry, Satch. Go home, okay?" And then I do the only self-respectable thing left to do: I run.

I don't know if I'm running from Satcher, my embarrassment, Woods and Pearl, or myself—down the stairs that lead to the boardwalk, checking my watch as I head toward the pier. Lunch will just be letting out. I don't need to be anywhere for another few hours, which gives me some time to lick my wounds and compose myself.

Ugh, Billie.

My self-hate revs into overdrive as I dodge tourists, licking my lips where the salt from my tears is gathering. Really fucking pathetic. And the worst part is I'm hungry. I wish I'd been an idiot *after* I ate. I look around for something to eat and see a hot dog stand and ice cream cart back-to-back. I linger at the hot dogs for a minute and then round the cart to join the ice cream line. If I can't be at home with a pint of Ben & Jerry's, I'll eat my way through as many scoops as they'll give me here.

My plan is to walk back to the hotel, but ten minutes into my walk I realize that I have no idea where I am. I merge with the tourists looking for a landmark I recognize when I hear my name being called. Satcher pulls up beside me in what I presume is a rental. Rolling his window down, he calls my name again.

"Billie!" and when I don't respond—"Wendy!"

"I'm fine, Satcher," I say without looking at him. "I just need some time..."

I keep walking and he drives slowly beside me. Cars pull up behind him and honk, but Satcher doesn't pay attention to them even when they speed around him, yelling out the window.

"Let me drive you back to the hotel." There's an onslaught of traffic as cars race by, and I don't hear the rest of what he says.

"No. I'm fine," I say again. A gust of wind lifts my hair and whips it into my ice cream.

"You're upset..."

No, I'm embarrassed. I lift my chin a little, crush my lips together. I wish he'd just leave me alone, leave me to my embarrassment.

"If I did what you wanted me to do, I'd be just like him," Satcher says.

It takes a minute to realize who *him* is. I feel dizzy and sick; I'm crashing down from a pretty great buzz.

"Ugh," is my only response. I'd not considered Willa in all of this. Willa and her perfect body. Willa and her symmetrical face. I suppose that was selfish of me, that the girl he's seeing didn't even come to mind when I tried to drunk-kiss her boyfriend.

"Billie—"

"It's Wendy," I bite back. "Wen-dee."

"Will you drop this fucking Wendy shit already?"

I'm so startled by his tone that I stop walking and stare. The light has changed again and there's a fresh round of honking as Satcher blocks an entire lane of traffic.

"Why?"

"Because you don't become a different person by changing your name. You're still the same spiteful, childish, ridiculous woman you were."

"Fine," I spit. I am sick of Wendy anyway, always so fucking put together. I lob my ice cream cone at his car and it connects with a wet thud.

"Seriously, Billie?" He shakes his head, a look of utter bewilderment on his face.

"Wendy was the mature one!"

He peels off and I stare at the melting puddle of mint chocolate chip wistfully.

CHAPTER SEVENTEEN

I'm somber that night at The Viable Vine, my fight with Satcher hanging heavily on my heart. I pick at the appetizers they order and only half listen to their conversation. There are five of us, nix Courtney who claims she doesn't drink but always carries a bottle of water around that I've long suspected is vodka. The girls are giggling, already on their third drink and getting sloppy. I'm toying with the stem of my glass, my lemon drop tepid, and wondering if Woods is actually going to show up. I've had a headache for the better part of four hours, one I feel like I deserve, which is probably why I haven't taken the Tylenol in my purse. At nine thirty they stand up, looking at me expectantly.

"Billie," Annalise says. "Earth to Billie..."

"What? Oh. Sorry."

"We're heading back to the hotel, you comin'?"

"I'm going to stay a bit. You go ahead."

Annalise looks unsure, but then her phone starts ringing and she walks out with it pressed to her ear, waving at me. I throw back my lemon drop and order another.

I'm getting ready to close my tab and head out when Woods saunters in. He's already buzzed and I realize he must have been out with Pearl before this. Where did he tell her he was going? Surely not to meet with me.

"Hey." He slides into the seat Annalise had occupied not thirty minutes ago.

"Hey, yourself."

He takes a sip of my lemon drop. "Like candy." He grins.

"So," I say casually, "what's up?"

"What do you mean?"

I stare at him. "You said you needed to talk to me about something."

"Oh, right," he says. "Let's just visit for a minute."

Visit. I forgot that he used to say things like: *Let's visit.* It's painful when you remember good things about the person who broke your heart. It's better to remember the things you hated, if only to keep the anger stronger than the sadness. He asks about how my parents are and if I dated while in Washington. I tell him about Keith Gus.

"You dated a guy named Keith Gus? Wow. Tell me the part about the crying again..."

I roll my eyes. "He used to sob when the Seahawks lost. One time he was so depressed, he wandered drunk into the woods in his boxers and didn't come out till the next morning."

"And where were his boxers?"

"Oh my God, Woods." I can't help but smile. "They were gone."

He doubles over at the waist he's laughing so hard. When he comes back up, there's a curl hanging over his eye and I have to stop myself from touching it.

"Wow," he says. "I forgot how fun you are." His eyes are glowing warm like honey.

"You're drunk." I shake my head, pressing my smile into a tight, disapproving grin.

"Keith Gus..." He shakes his head.

"So," I say. "You and Pearl..."

He pulls out his pack of Juicy Fruit and offers me one. "Had to go and kill the mood..."

"That's not *happy in love* speak," I say. "What gives?"

Woods grimaces. "She's not happy you're back."

"I don't imagine so."

He rubs his forehead. "She wants me to talk to Satcher. Ask him to let you go."

Heat rises to my face and I feel a tightness in my chest. "Are you fucking kidding me? Rhubarb is my—"

"—was," Woods says. "It *was* yours. You sold it."

"I only sold because you fucking cheated on me. You and I both know I never would have left if I didn't have to." I'm practically standing now, ready to storm out.

He holds up his hands in surrender. "You didn't have to go. I took your trust away, not your business."

I'm so angry my vision blurs. "Do you have any idea what that did to me? You just pulled the rug out from under me. I had no idea there was even something wrong between us."

"That's exactly right, Billie. Because you were too busy to notice."

"You're not going to put this on me," I fume.

But despite my anger, a familiar prickle of guilt works through me. Something I've already considered. Something he probably told our friends and family. *Always working ... neglectful wife ... doesn't want to start a family. Career-obsessed.* I snatch my clutch from the table.

"You can tell Pearl I'm not going anywhere," I say. I pause, a lie brewing in my mind. "I'm fucking Satcher, he's not going to fire me."

I enjoy the way the shock hits him, fills his eyes first with disbelief then anger. It's so satisfying that I wish I'd recorded it on my phone's camera so I could watch it again and again. I start marching for the door then remember my lemon drop, the one that just arrived at the table. I circle back to the table and drink it in three large gulps with Woods watching.

"Thanks for the drinks," I say.

I go straight to Satcher's room when I get back to the hotel. He opens the door on my fifth pound, wearing only jersey pajama pants. I stare, I do. His chest is the eighth wonder of the world.

"We have to have sex," I say, pushing past him into the room.

"Say what?"

"It's freezing in here." I stop at the thermostat and see that he's set it on sixty.

"I like cold."

I walk over to the window rubbing my arms.

"Woods met me for drinks. He told me that Pearl wants me gone. He's supposed to talk to you about it."

Satcher frowns. "Ah. So why are we having sex?"

"I told Woods we were fucking and I couldn't be fired."

Still holding the door open, Satcher shuts it. He takes a moment to close his eyes and sigh. "Billie..."

"I know, I know. I'm sorry, all right? I just didn't want him to think he could sway you."

"And what makes you think he could?"

I purse my lips and pull uncomfortably at the neck of my shirt. "Could he?"

"No."

"Can we say we're sleeping together then?"

He tilts his head back and squints at the ceiling. "Are you really asking me that?"

"Absolutely. A hundred percent."

A whisk of a smile. Satcher is amused.

"We won't tell your girlfriend," I say. "It'll strictly be an office lie."

"And tell me what exactly this lie of yours accomplishes?"

I sit down on the edge of the bed. "It'll get Pearl off my back. She's not going to suggest you fire your girlfriend."

"My girlfriend?" His hands are on his hips. "I thought we were just fucking in this scenario of yours."

I chew on my lip as I think. "Yeah, but it'll be more effective if we're *together*-together."

I'm pacing back and forth between the bed and the dresser. I sigh at the pained expression he's wearing. Is it really that terrible to pretend to be with me? I'm not a Brazilian swimsuit model, but I'm not exactly ugly either.

"Or I could just say *no* when Woods brings it up..."

"Half the staff is friends with Pearl. She's going to use them against me. But if they think I'm your girlfriend, they'll back off."

"You want to make Woods jealous," he says.

"That too."

Satcher sighs; it's a deep, weary sigh, and I immediately feel guilty.

"Oh God. I'm doing it again. I'm sorry—"

I make for the door. Oh my God, what am I turning into? Using Satcher for my benefit.

He hooks me around the waist as I try to walk past. Warm hands graze my skin. My face is hot from embarrassment. I'm ashamed of myself, ashamed of what this is doing to my brain. I cover my face with my hands so he can't look at me, but Satcher gently pulls them away. He doesn't let go, and holding my fingers between his, he forces me to look at him.

"You're hurting."

"No," I say. "I'm fine."

"I know you, Billie…"

I want to ask him how he knows me when I don't even know myself.

"You don't," I tell him. "Whatever you think you know is wrong. I'm not the same person I used to be."

"I hope not," he says.

My head snaps up, and I search his eyes for meaning.

"We aren't meant to stay the same. Life hits us from every direction, and we build thick skin in those places … calluses. It's the way we survive."

"I don't have a callus yet," I blurt. "In that spot … where my marriage was." I look away so he can't see the saltwater pooling, ready to spill out and make me look weak.

"No, you don't."

I stare at him. He's so … together. And I am not. By comparison, he's completely different than Woods, who is big and rugged and has puppy dog eyes. Satcher is chiseled and composed and his eyes are mischievous. But there's always been an element to Satcher that puts him in a league of his own.

"I've always been intimidated by you," I tell him.

"What?" He laughs—a short, bewildered laugh—like he can't imagine why.

"You've always seemed older than the rest of us. More mature. I'm thirty years old, and I still feel like a little girl when I'm around you."

"I don't know how I feel about that." He frowns and now I laugh.

"We were getting trashed and skipping class while you were already working on your master's. By the time we moved into our first apartment, you were already buying your first company. We got married; you made your first million. I don't even know why you hung out with us, you were always on a different level."

"Come on..." His dimples are out now as he shakes his head at me.

Whenever his dimples show I have to look away or I stare.

"Remember the water park?"

I laugh. How could I forget? I'd been dating Woods a little over nine months, and things were starting to get serious. Six of us decided we needed some well-deserved fun—thus the water park. Satcher had just been accepted into his master's program and we were celebrating. The day was bright and so were our moods. Satcher smuggled in a bottle of cheap vodka that we passed around, the kind that hits you hard in the back of the throat and makes you gag. My memories are blurry: I remember having three shots to Satcher's six. I remember standing in line for the big slide, joking with him about his lack of a tan, when his eyes suddenly went blank. He'd opened his mouth, his comeback ready, when he looked at me and said: *"I don't feel right."* The next thing I knew he was falling backwards, his face white. The lifeguard called the ambulance and we all stood wide-eyed until they came for him, loading him onto a stretcher. Satcher spent a night in the hospital for dehydration and exhaustion. We had no idea there was something wrong, that he was overworked or otherwise ... because Satcher always had his shit together. It goes to show that you can never tell who's struggling or not.

"That wasn't your fault," I say. "We made you drink too much and you had a lot on your plate."

"As I recall, I was the one who brought the vodka. You're forgetting that I was just as reckless as the rest of you. I was just ambitious in my spare time."

"Understatement."

He shrugs.

"We got offtrack. You always do that—steer the conversation in a different direction when you get uncomfortable." He reaches up and holds my upper arms in his hands, squeezing a little, and I stare into his face. "You're going to figure this out."

"How do you know?" I ask.

"Because you want to be happy. You may not know it yet, but it's why you came back."

"I came back for revenge," I say flatly.

"Yes, because you think that will make you happy."

I don't have anything to say to that. I suppose he could be right. I bite my lip and squeeze my eyes shut.

"Good night, Satch. Safe travels home, yeah? Let me know how your mom is doing." I make for the door and this time he doesn't stop me.

CHAPTER EIGHTEEN

F*ck Marriage launches on the Monday after we get back. My first post is the most honest thing I've ever written, and for that reason, I lock myself in my office, turn off the lights, and drink half a bottle of wine for breakfast. I'm sitting in the dark when Loren slips into my office doing a victory twerk. I try to hide the bottle under my desk, but she points out that my teeth are stained red.

"What do you mean you haven't checked?" Her face is incredulous as she pours some of my wine into her own Solo cup.

"I'm scared," I admit.

She steps around my desk and leans over me to turn my monitor on. I can smell her shampoo, her hair still damp from her morning shower. I squeeze my eyes closed as she jiggles my mouse, summoning the screen to life.

"Look," she commands.

I open one eye and then the other.

"Three thousand comments, Billie. Three thousand."

My jaw drops.

"They. Are. Loving. It."

I shove her away so I can get a look at the screen.

"Look." I point to one of the comments.

This is unbelievably brave. Why don't we have more blogs like this? Life is not perfect and we have hurt to conquer. Thank you, Billie!

"You published under Billie!" she says, surprised.

I shift in my seat uncomfortably, remembering the fight I had with Satcher on a public street. "Yeah, I guess I'm going back to that."

Loren hugs me. "I'm so glad. Truly."

We read through the rest of the comments, and by the time she leaves my office, we both have red teeth, and I'm on a high that has nothing to do with the wine I drank. I lean over my desk burying my head in my arms. It worked. It actually worked.

I haven't seen Satcher since we got back. He sent me one text after he got home saying the lump in his mother's breast was cancer. They'd caught it in time and she'd chosen to have a double mastectomy rather than just removing the cancer.

His plan is to work from his parents' house until she is back on her feet. But he sends a huge bouquet to the office to congratulate me on the success of my new column. I'm buzzing like a pollen-high bee when Woods strolls in.

"What the fuck, Billie?" He closes the door behind him and I steel myself for a fight.

I knew Woods wouldn't like what I had to say, but the truth is the truth, after all. If he didn't want me to write about it, he shouldn't have done it. Simple as that.

I sigh. "What the fuck indeed."

"That's our personal story. How could you air our dirty

laundry like that?" He jabs a finger at the computer and then levels a particularly nasty look at me.

I can see the vein popping out on the side of his forehead. I am familiar with that vein. It used to show up when we had a bad fight.

"No, Woods, our personal story ceased to exist after you walked out of our marriage. Then it became my story. My post-divorce story. And it's mine to tell." I sit as still as I can, hands propped on the armrests of my chair. I don't want to give him any tells that he's frazzling me. Like his vein.

"Holy shit, Billie..."

"If you don't want your dirty laundry aired, live a life you're not embarrassed of," I say, standing up. I walk over to the door and hold it open for him. "Now, if you please. I have a lot of work to do."

He looks furious as he heads for the door, his eyes drilling into me like he has much more to say.

"Woods..." I call after him and he stops but doesn't turn around. "Read it again. And read it like Pearl isn't pissed and breathing down your neck." I shut the door before he can respond.

The post goes viral on Facebook, and Rhubarb's following doubles overnight. Pearl takes a sick day, and Satcher gives me a raise. Every time I leave my office, Team Pearl glares at me and Team Billie gives me high fives. Life is weird.

F*ck Marriage

I have to tell you something real. I've told you things that aren't real; in fact, I've told you blatant lies: that a certain brand of yoga pants can change your life, that the perfect recipe can make your man happy, that if you use the right moisturizer (at $94 a bottle) you'll always feel beautiful and young. I've written blogs about the necessity of

Kegels (you'll be a sexual goddess if you follow these five rules!), and I've told you in no uncertain terms about the power of positive thinking (if you want to be successful, already believe you are!). You counted on me, and I delivered snake oil; a topical salve for a deep wound. Forgive me.

My husband left me for another woman. Here's the thing: I thought it could never happen. I thought that we had a bond and our commitment was impenetrable. That somehow the vows we took were a magic spell that would ward off reality. Imagine my surprise when I realized that the yoga pants failed me, and the perfect beef tenderloin with the red wine glaze couldn't save my marriage. Even my dewy, youthful skin (at $94 dollars a bottle) couldn't keep his eyes glued to only my face.

The distance between us took a while, and it would be unfair to rest the burden of our failure solely on him. I was too busy to notice the things I was stacking between us: my success, my business, my exhaustion, my excuses. Every once in a while I'd notice it, that the little things weren't making me smile. Or that his presence made me feel guilty and annoyed rather than blissful. I used my new feelings about him and myself as a wall; it was a wall of subconscious guilt. He'd walk into a room and I'd think: What do you want from me now? Why can't you just figure this out on your own? Why do you keep giving me wounded looks?

He's a piece of shit for doing what he did. I'm not making excuses for him. But I refuse to see the downfall of my marriage through a lens of narcissism. They say that love is a battlefield, but I wasn't a warrior. I was a soft romantic; my armor was a firm ass and a full face of makeup. Silly armor for a silly girl. The war for love is fought by saying: You're the one I want, you're the one I need, you're the one I'll fight to keep.

Neither of us fought.

When you're cheated on, you build a house around yourself. You build it strong. The walls are made of Never Again. The bricks—all the things you did right, the mortar—your anger. Divorce makes you live in a tall house because you put more effort into your grieving than you ever put into your marriage. That's what we do as humans, we grieve harder than we ever tried and we build a magnificent fortress of hurt and self-righteous indignation. In front of this fortress is a garden where you grow your shortcomings. It's a magnificent garden because that's where you put all of your effort now. A garden of well-tended self-abuse. You water the shit out of your garden and it grows and grows. I grew a variety of things in my garden: bitterness, self-hate, numbness, self-pity, resentment, and defeat. I tended that garden with such detail, trimming and nurturing my personal hell until I couldn't find my way out. And let me tell you, it's a full-time job to hate yourself that much. Because once you start growing the vine of bitterness, it chokes anything healthy that begins to sprout.

I lost two years of my life in that garden. I grew it to a jungle. And somewhere in the middle of my personal jungle, I grew dehydrated. I was watering the wrong things, dying slowly. No one was coming to save me, no one knew how. And that's when I realized that if I didn't save myself, I'd not just waste two years of my life, but the whole thing. I burned it down: the house, the garden, the walls—and I came back to New York. I came back to my old job, I came back to face what made me run. I'm here; I'm different, but I'm here. And I'm here to tell you what I learned: fuck love, fuck marriage, fuck divorce, fuck walls, fuck anything that takes our ability to survive and to survive well. We will rise, and we will build a new house, not a fortress, but a house full of natural light, surrounded by a garden of forgiveness and self-love.

Welcome to F*ck Marriage. We're going to make it out alive. I promise.

CHAPTER NINETEEN

*S*atcher texts me before I leave the office for the night. He's back in the city and asks if I want to meet for drinks to celebrate. I go home to change and meet him at the address he gave me.

"Your mom?" I say as soon as I see him.

"A true warrior. She was baking two hundred cookies for a church bake sale when I left."

"But how is she in here?" I ask, tapping my head.

Satcher shrugs. "She has that silent suffering thing. I believe it comes with women of that generation."

I grunt. It's true. My generation plasters their suffering on social media, but our parents' generation is quite the opposite.

"All we can do for someone like my mother is show up, that's her love language. She will deal with what's happened privately, in her own way."

I nod.

"What is this place?" I ask, suddenly distracted.

Satcher grins. "It's a temple of beer worship."

"Named the Burp Castle?"

"Named the Burp Castle." He nods seriously while I look around.

The walls are covered in murals of monks. When I look closer, I see the dark humor in the artwork. A ship burns, sinking into the ocean in the background, while in the foreground, a surprised monk floats on a barrel of beer as several of his monk friends are drinking cheerfully on a piece of driftwood nearby.

"No loud talking allowed. Whispering only by order of the brewest monks," I read the sign and one of the bartenders looks up suddenly and shushes me. Satcher smiles at my expression.

"What the hell?" I say under my breath.

"Shh." He leans down close to my ear and his breath tickles my lobe.

I pinch the closest piece of his flesh which happens to be his pec. Hard, there's barely any skin to grab, but he yelps anyway and the bartender glares at us. If we are going to have a conversation in this place it will have to be whispered in each other's faces. For a fleeting moment I wonder if that was Satcher's plan, but then I laugh the thought away. Satcher doesn't have to do sneaky things to get close to a woman; he could have anyone he wanted without the tricks a lesser man would need.

"There's a table over there." He juts his chin toward the back of the bar where a group has just stood up to leave.

"I'll grab it," I say. "You—" I poke him in the chest "—get the drinks..."

He winks at me and heads toward the bar.

I watch him from where I sit. The self-assured way he moves through the bar, wedging his way into a spot just vacated by two college girls. He lifts one finger and the bartender spots him right away. If I'd gone up to the bar, I'd have stood there for ten minutes before the bartender noticed me. Satcher has a presence. When he walks into a room, people look up wondering if he's someone important. Within two minutes, he has our drinks and is making his way back to me. I eye the way his shirt sleeves are folded up to his elbows, exposing his tanned forearms. I take the drink he hands me, shaking my head.

"What?" he asks. "You have a *look* on your face."

I don't have to ask him what kind of look. I'm embarrassed. I was checking him out. I play with my necklace, touching the raised ring finger. His eyes move down to look at it and then it hits me.

"You got me this, didn't you?"

One corner of his mouth lifts. "You used to always wear things like that, do you remember?"

"Yes," I say. "Before I started dressing like Martha Stewart, apparently..."

We both laugh and then Satcher says, "What the fuck was that about anyway?"

I play with a napkin, folding it into a tiny square and then smoothing it out until he lays his much larger hand on top of mine to still me. I suck down some of my beer and puff out my cheeks, making my eyes big.

"When I started the blog I thought it would work in my benefit to look more mainstream."

"Mainstream?" he repeats.

"Yeah ... you know, the leather and ripped jeans were unrelatable to my audience so I toned it down a bit."

"Ugh!" I say when I see the look on his face. "Shut up, Satch. It's important to be relatable. Boring. Floral print and whatnot..."

"You certainly had the floral print thing down..."

"I hate you," I say, but there's not enough conviction in

my voice for either of us to believe it.

He laughs and it warms me right down to my toes, which I wriggle in my shoes. I shake my head, pressing back my smile.

"It wasn't just your look that changed though, was it, Billie?"

"What do you mean?" Though I know exactly what he's talking about.

He leans forward like he's going to tell me a secret, and automatically, I bend toward him too.

"Once upon a time, a girl with fishnet stockings, a leather jacket, and black fingernails got high with me and danced on my kitchen table."

"Until I broke the table ... sorry about that."

"It was a nice table." He nods, frowning. "And it died in an honorable way..."

I snicker.

"You went to parties just for the free food and booze..."

"I put on ten pounds that year."

"You got a tattoo on your inner thigh that said: *This way to paradise*."

"It cost me fifteen hundred dollars to have that removed." I shake my head.

"You stopped owning who you were and became something else."

"People evolve, Satcher. We aren't supposed to stay the same." I throw his words back at him, but he's shaking his head before I'm even finished.

"People evolve, yes. That's healthy. But they don't change everything about who they are unless they have a good reason, and Billie, you're unrecognizable."

I frown at how his words make me feel. When was it exactly that I traded my edge for a good corn chowder recipe? The blog—I'd started to change when the blog did well. I remember scouring other blogs, studying what they did that garnered the most readers. Then I reinvented myself to match the blog, instead of having the blog match me. I deflate, pressing my lips together as I stare at Satcher.

"Don't do that," he says.

"Do what?"

"Get sad about what you lost."

"You just pointed out that I lost myself and you expect me not to be sad about it?"

"Well, maybe it's time to find yourself again. Meet your old self somewhere in the middle."

"Good advice." I pick up my beer and drain it, then I shake my glass at Satcher. "Another."

I don't know how it happens, except I do. I was having a surprisingly good time: Satcher teasing me, me teasing back. At one point I jumped up to dance to a Billy Idol song that was playing while Satcher spun around in his stool to watch me. If I'd ever felt carefree it was now, in this bar, with this man. Carefree: the old me. Pre-floral print and the blog. Pre-Woods and Pearl.

Three drinks and two shots and Satcher is helping me up the stairs to Jules' apartment.

"Are there no goddamn lights in this building?" he growls.

The tip of my shoe catches on the stairs and he steadies me. We reach the front door, and I lean against the wall as Satcher searches my bag for my keys.

"You can still see it, you know?"

He puts my key in the lock and turns it. "What?"

"My tattoo. This way to paradise."

He looks startled for a moment and then his face breaks into a smile. "Fifteen hundred dollars couldn't erase who you actually are."

I shake my head. I'm not *drunk*-drunk, but I am drunk. The room sways around me as I step inside and flick the light switch. Nothing happens. I try another and the room stays dark.

"Power's out," I say.

I stand still in the middle of the room, swaying in the dark. I hate how when I'm drunk I feel everything. I thought getting drunk helped take your mind *off* of things.

"He left paradise."

Satcher comes in and closes the door. He walks to the breaker box and opens it. "Who?"

"Woods, he left paradise."

He shuts the box and turns around to look at me.

"Paradise lost. Poor Woods." I crack up, then I start crying.

"It's not the breakers," Satcher says, walking toward me. "Must be the whole building."

"I'm drunk and I'm afraid of the dark," I say. I lift my hands to the ceiling and spin around. Satcher has to catch me before I hit the ground.

"Don't forget dramatic," he adds, righting me on my feet. "We can go back to my place. I'm not leaving you here in the dark."

"Is this how it works? You lure a woman into your shiny bachelor pad with the promise of warmth and drink?"

"And dick," he says, which makes me laugh until my stomach aches. "But no drink," he finishes. "You've had enough."

"I'm probably an alcoholic," I admit.

Satcher has his back to me now as he grabs a duffel bag out of the hall closet. "Yup," he says. "Probably so."

I nod, grateful, wondering how he knew to look there. "Just let me grab some of my things." I use the flashlight on my phone to grab pajamas and clothes for the next day, tossing them into the duffel. Then I make my way to the living room where Satcher is waiting. He's scrolling through his phone and when he sees me, one corner of his mouth lifts. It's so natural that I walk right into his arms and hug him.

"What's this about?" he says into my hair.

"I don't know. It just feels like you've been saving me since I got back to New York."

"Billie, you are the very last woman who needs saving. One day you're going to realize that."

I doze in the backseat of the cab for the ten-minute drive. By the time we climb out of the elevator in his building I've sobered up and have the beginnings of a headache.

While he makes a snack, I wander into the bathroom to change into my pajamas. I laugh when I look down and see I grabbed my most grandmotherly pants and shirt combo, decked out in pink roses. I stuff them back in my bag and put on a T-shirt I brought instead. When I join Satcher in the living room, he eyes my legs and whistles low.

"I see paradise," he says.

I bend at the waist and study my thigh. "No way," I say. "You have to get really close to see it."

"That's not what I'm talking about, Billie."

I straighten up and he laughs at my blush. Then I do something so completely unlike me. I lift my T-shirt over my head until I'm standing in front of Satcher in only my panties.

"Why just look?" I say.

I'm on my stomach, the soft down comforter beneath me; my fingers grip the material, making fists. I'm nervous but without the awkwardness. I've known Satcher too long to truly be out of sorts. He's behind me. I can feel his heat on my skin. I turn my head to watch him, my hair partly obscuring my vision. He rubs warm palms down my back, putting pressure in all the right places so that I arch beneath his hands like a cat. When I feel like things can't get any more intense, he grips my buttocks between his hands, kneading. I'm wet at his touch, and I turn my face away so he can't see the desperate begging in my eyes. Gently, he takes hold of my ankle and pushes my leg up so that my knee is bent toward my chest. Then he releases himself from his pants with one hand, while a finger from the other slides inside of me. I blink hard, breathing through my nose, my chest heaving as I bite the insides of my cheeks. I'm squirming, unable to keep still as a finger works into me. He groans when he feels me, like this is the first time he's touching a woman this way. As he works one finger then two inside of me, he bends down to kiss my shoulder ... my neck. I'm panting; the sound makes me ashamed and I try to quiet it, but when I do, Satcher twists his fingers in such a way that I start up again.

He smacks me hard on the fattest part of my ass and my eyes fly open in question.

"Lift your hips," he orders.

I slide my leg straight to match the other, and with my face still pressed against the bed, I lift my hips slightly. I can feel him looking at me as he caresses my backside, running the pad of his thumb across the wetness between my legs until I want to scream, *Hurry up! Hurry up!*

I feel him position himself against me, but he doesn't push in; it's a hard pressure that opens me and promises to deliver.

I groan, wiggling my hips. "Satcher... "

As soon as I say his name, he pushes into me; a drop and a

slide so sweet and painful the rest of my words are cut from my lips and replaced by a gasp.

He drags in and out, lazy movements that rub along my throbbing muscles, making me shiver in anticipation of the next. And while he pushes and pulls—in and out, in and out—he massages my back, my shoulders ... hard when he pushes in and soft when he pulls out. I'm lost in the rhythm, the muscles in my body in ecstasy.

When I twist my head back to see him, his eyes are open and glassy, his tongue gripped between his teeth. He's making a low humming in his throat. When he catches me looking, he smiles a sleepy, closed-mouth smile.

"Turn over," he instructs me. "I want to see you when you come."

I roll my body and he's between my legs, lowering himself onto me. I close my eyes at the sheer pleasure of his weight. Running my hands along his arms and back, I wrap myself around him. In the five seconds it's taken to turn over I am desperate to feel him inside of me again. He watches my face when he sinks down and fills me once more.

"You're not wearing a condom," I say. It's not a rebuke, more of an observation. Satcher has made jokes about never being caught without a condom.

"Do you want me to put one on?" His breath catches my hair and glides along my ear.

I hesitate. "No," I say. "Do you want to put one on?"

"Not even a little bit," he breathes. "I haven't done it like this ... in a long time." I'm conscious of his hands, his fingers, pressing into the softness of my lower back as he lifts my hips to meet his thrusts.

He starts to move again and my body responds instantly, opening up for him with a trust that scares me. This is Satcher: I don't have to be scared of him. I know everything about him—good and bad. *He's been here all along*, I think. *Right in front of you and you almost missed him.*

"I'm going to come hard." His voice is raspy with pleasure, his eyes closed. "But first I want you to come ... on my dick. Can you do that, Billie?" He's barely finished his sentence when I do. It was his saying my name in that voice of his that threw me over the edge. My legs clench around his body and I scream into his shoulder, lifting my upper body off the bed to meet him where he holds himself up to watch me.

"Yeah," I breathe. "That was good."

He laughs with his face buried in my neck, and I hold onto him as he moves harder.

There is pressure, and a pain so good my eyes roll back in my head when his whole body stiffens, his muscles tensing underneath my hands. I feel him come. I've never felt a man come before; but suddenly he gets even harder and I have to adjust my legs, opening them wider to accommodate him. With me spread out beneath him whimpering, he looks at me with a strained expression on his face.

I don't hold back as I clench around his dick, lifting my hips to take all of him. I can feel his cum leaving his body and pouring into me. It's one of the most erotic moments of my life.

Later, we do something I have not done in a very long time: we lie together, our bodies curled around each other.

"The last time I was cuddled like this it was by my parents' bulldog," I say.

Satcher laughs into my hair, tightening his grip around my waist. "What's his name?"

"Gerard."

"Lucky Gerard," he says.

CHAPTER TWENTY

When I wake up, I'm sore. I bury my face in one of Satcher's pillows. How long has it been since I've done that, and with such enthusiasm? I can't imagine Keith Gus touching me the way Satcher did. He was more of a wham-bam-thank-you-ma'am kind of guy. On more than one occasion I had to walk him through getting me off. And Woods, well, he always made sure to take care of me before we had sex, that way he could focus on himself the remainder of the time.

Satcher has a latte waiting for me on the kitchen counter when I wander out of the bedroom. I peer into the mug blinking in surprise; it's the perfect milk to espresso ratio. The espresso machine is humming as he makes one for himself, flicking switches and using the frother like a professional barista.

"Are you good at everything?"

He looks up from what he's doing. There's stubble on his jaw. I get a flash of him with his eyes half closed as he pounded into me, and my stomach does an unwelcome flip.

"You tell me," he says, raising an eyebrow.

I hide my blush behind the rim of my own mug.

"Your phone's ringing."

I glance over to the counter where my phone is flashing. Woods.

"It's Woods," I announce like he can't already see that for himself.

"Why's that bastard calling my girlfriend?" Satcher leans back against the counter holding his tiny cup of espresso.

I laugh as my eyes rove over his body shamelessly. It takes a lot of work to look like that. How many hours does he spend in the gym?

"Why aren't you picking up?" He rinses the cup, lays it on the drying rack.

"Because he needs to learn his place." I smirk. "I'm with you now."

He shakes his head, amused. "Girl games."

That's fair. Women like to throw random tests out there just to see what will happen. I don't tell Satcher that the real reason I didn't pick up is because I don't want the intrusion. I like the way it feels to be here with him, just the two of us. Last night wasn't fucking. I've fucked enough men to know the difference. Maybe he fucks every girl like that. Maybe that's why women's eyes grow large when he walks into a room.

"You up for a run and some breakfast?" He sets my empty mug in the sink.

"Sure," I say. "I'd just have to stop at home for my tennis shoes."

He nods and goes to get changed. I walk around while he's in the bedroom, studying his furniture, the artwork on the walls, and the tiny pieces of him that are strewn around. He's tidy but not too tidy. I like the balance. There are books everywhere and I wonder how he finds time to read.

"You judging my book collection?" He comes up behind me and leans down to lightly kiss me on the back of my neck.

"Trashy thrillers," I say, shaking my head. "How do you find the time?"

"I can't sleep," he says. "But if I read a few chapters before bed..."

"Your mind never shuts down," I say.

"No, it doesn't. Except last night. I slept well."

I grin. I don't tell him that I had the best night's sleep of the last few years. No nightmares, no tossing and turning, no lying awake and staring at the ceiling with the dread of tomorrow heavy in my chest. Curled against his hard, warm body, I'd felt safe. It was like sleeping underneath a tin roof while it rained outside, a fire burning in the hearth. I turn around and his arms automatically circle me. Satcher's body feels different than Woods'. He's taller for one thing, harder. His hands move like a masseuse's; every time he touches me he does so with just the right pressure of fingertips and palms, that I feel drowsy. He leans down to kiss me and we end up making love one more time.

We go for our run, and on the way back, Satcher takes me to a little cafe for breakfast. We sit outside, the heat already pounding down on our heads, and order omelets. Satcher orders every vegetable imaginable in his, and when I make a face he teases me about the pound of cheddar I added to mine. We fall into a comfortable silence watching the city folk navigate the sidewalk. There's an ache between my legs that ever reminds me of the things he did to me.

It's sweet, the casual way we eat breakfast, the walk back to his place, during which he grabs my hand. Woods tries to call a few more times and I send him to voicemail, though he never leaves a message. It doesn't matter. Nothing matters today. For the first time in a very long time I remember what it's like to feel simple things and enjoy them immensely.

We stay at Satcher's place a lot. It's closer to the office. I like the way it always smells like cigars and coffee. When I ask him about the cigar smell he takes me to a drawer in the kitchen. It's one of those big drawers, twice as wide as a regular one. Inside is his own personal cigar shop. Hundreds of them—lined up and labeled.

"When do you smoke them?" I ask, rubbing my fingers over the labels.

"On cigar night," he answers.

"And that's when?"

"Mondays and Fridays."

"Why those two days?"

"Because I need something to get through the worst day of the week and to celebrate the best day of the week."

"Oh!" I say, genuinely amused. "I guess I have something like that too." I lift a cigar to my nose and inhale the chocolatey smell.

"What is it?"

I smile at Satcher, shrugging my shoulders. "I guess you'll have to hang out with me on one of those days to see."

He looks at me, amusement dancing in his eyes. It's nice to be looked at like that. Like I'm something to be intrigued by.

On one of the nights I sleep over, I wake to find Satcher in the kitchen sitting at the island and staring into an empty coffee mug.

"What's going on with you?" I ask, sliding into the seat next to him.

His smile is dim and I watch his face in concern.

"Insomnia." He shrugs. "It's always been with me."

I'm still half asleep and I process his words quietly for a moment.

"Do you want me to leave or is company okay?" I rub my arms, suddenly realizing how cold it is in here.

Satcher stands up and walks to the thermostat, raising the temperature a few degrees.

"Your company is always okay."

I walk over to where he stands and take his face between my hands. There are dark circles under his eyes. Why have I never noticed?

"Has it been worse than normal lately?"

"No, actually, it's been better."

When I look at him quizzically, he smiles. "Sex ... sex puts me to sleep."

"Oh my God!" I say. "You're a manwhore for a reason!"

The rumble of his laugh comes from deep within his chest. He pulls me against him in a tight hug and I reciprocate, my own laughter pressed up against his skin.

"Come on," I say, taking his hand and leading him toward the bedroom. "I'll help you sleep."

My intent was to lay him on his back and prove my riding skills, but as soon as we reach the bed I see that he has other plans. He pushes me down and climbs on top of me instead, spreading my legs and resting between them. I can feel his hardness pressed against the crack of my pussy and I writhe, impatient. He kisses me, taking his time. When I'm frantic, he lifts himself off of me and pulls me on top of him. Finally! But before I can lower myself onto his very hard dick, he moves me upward until I'm straddling his face.

"No," I say, blushing. "I've never—"

His mouth reaches me before my words reach him.

"Oh my fuck," I say, tensing. I stare down at him in shock and awe.

"What were you saying?" he asks, his tongue stilling.

I lace my hands in his hair. "Nothing. Please resume…"

He laughs that deep throaty laugh before his tongue flicks and rolls slow, slow circles toward my very loud end.

CHAPTER TWENTY-ONE

When I open the door, the first thing I notice are the shoes: tennis, immaculate white. Not mine. Leaving the door wide open, I take a few cautious steps inside. What type of thief takes their shoes off before robbing you? I round the corner and step into the living room, and that's when I see a suitcase. It's a practical hard shell, slick black like seal skin. I glance furtively around the apartment, my heart galloping. I hear her voice before I see her.

"Billie! Oh my God, Billie." She comes from the bedroom launching herself at me, wrapping her arms around my neck in a hug so tight it's choking.

"Jules? What are you doing here?"

When she pulls away her eyes are glossy. "I hated it there."

"But ... your job!"

"I know," she says. "But I missed New York, and I'd been seeing someone when I just up and left, and I kept wondering if I'd just walked away from the best thing that ever happened to me."

I stare at her not knowing what to say. I'm still processing the fact that Jules is back, while also trying to understand what this means for me.

"You never told me that. About a guy..."

Just like with everyone else, my friendship with Jules had taken a backseat during my divorce. But something as big as meeting the man of your dreams and then breaking up seemed worthy of an email at least.

"You've been ... busy," she says, and I immediately feel guilty. Busy with my own self-pity. Sooooo busy. I bite my lip.

"Tell me," I say.

Jules' cheeks flush when she talks about him.

"Er ... well, we were seeing each other on the down-low. We hadn't made it official yet, but we'd said I love yous and then I got the job offer..."

"Okay, okay," I say, pushing her toward the living room. "Tell me everything."

We settle on the couch after Jules insists on making us drinks.

"I can't tell you my whole sob story without alcohol." She sighs, plopping down next to me.

She tells me about the guy she's known forever through friends. They started seeing each other a year ago and things got pretty serious. Then she was offered the job and chose to leave even when he asked her to stay.

"I feel so bad," she says. "I hope he can forgive me. I came back for him, right? That means something."

I nod. Jules has never really been into the dating scene, always more career-focused than the rest of us. The fact that she actually came back—choosing a man over her career—is big. Huge.

"You're in love!" I say in surprise. For the first time since I've known her she looks vulnerable.

"Yeah. It's all new for me. Scary..."

"Ugh, Julia. Don't worry about it. He's going to be so excited you're home."

"Don't call me Julia." She laughs. "It's weird."

She is sexy, aloof, successful, and kind. Any man would jump through hoops to have her.

"What if he's already dating someone else? Or if he can't forgive me for leaving?" Her face is genuinely worried.

I reach across the couch and touch her hand.

"He won't care why you left, just that you're back." I mean to be comforting, but she bursts into tears.

"I'm sorry," she says, when I've gotten up to get her a tissue. "I'm just so emotional. And just so you know, you're welcome to stay here. I was thinking if everything goes right, I'll move in with him."

I smile. "Thank you."

Her face suddenly lights up. "Oh my God, you look great."

I look down at my much thinner figure feeling embarrassed. It's one thing to be thinner, it is another for people to be constantly pointing it out.

"Yeah, your wardrobe makes me feel like a different person. It was the confidence boost I needed coming back to the city."

"Well, don't stop now. I've always wanted a sister." She throws her arms around my neck and I hug her tight. It will be nice to have her back. Currently, she is my one and only friend. I'm about to ask her if she's hungry when the buzzer sounds.

"You expecting someone?" she asks, looking at me.

Shoot. In all the excitement, I forgot that Satcher is coming by to pick me up for lunch. Jules is already at the intercom. She buzzes him up without knowing who it is. I look down at my workout clothes wondering if I look as bad as I feel. I'd meant to take a shower, wash my hair...

The door opens and Satcher walks in, his head down as he slips off his shoes. When he looks up, Jules and I are standing side by side.

We speak at once. The same time I say, "Hi," Jules says, "How did you know I was back?" And then she rushes into his arms, jumping at the last moment, and wrapping her legs around his waist.

The look on Satcher's face is one of shock as he stares at me over Jules' shoulder. I can only imagine what my face must look like.

My mouth suddenly goes dry as the full realization hits me, and it feels like I took a sledgehammer to the stomach. Jules untangles herself from Satcher, landing on her feet but not stepping away from his side. She puts an arm possessively around his waist and turns to beam at me.

"This is him, Billie. I've been seeing Satcher."

CHAPTER TWENTY-TWO

I reach for words, but they're slippery, swimming below my ability to articulate them. Satcher is at a loss too; he reaches up to run a hand along the stubble on his chin. Jules is speaking to him, babbling happily, but he's looking at me and I can't read what's in his eyes.

I feel like I'm underwater, everything moving slowly. Even the pains in my heart feel like they're being dragged along the bottom of the ocean floor. It's all making sense, of course. He always seemed so comfortable in Jules' apartment. It had crossed my mind that he always knew where things were, but I'd attributed it to him making lucky guesses. How stupid I've been. Why hadn't he told me he'd been seeing her?

"I'm so hungry," I hear her say to him. "Want to get lunch so we can talk?" Her eyes are lit up; they're the eyes of a woman filled with hope for the future.

I don't wait to hear what he says.

"Well, I'll just leave you two to it," I say. "I need a shower." I dart from the room before either of them can respond.

I let the hot water pound down on my back until it turns cold, only then do I step out of the shower. Wrapping a towel around myself, I press my ear to the door to hear if they're still in the apartment. All is quiet. I get dressed in a hurry, grabbing my things from the various places they've been left. I don't want to be here when they get back. I won't be able to keep my expression neutral. Jules will see it all over my face. I think about texting Satcher, but I don't know what to say. He looked just as blindsided as I was, expecting to come to lunch with me and running into his former girlfriend instead. As far as I knew, Jules and Satcher had only hung out a few times in our group get-togethers. Both workaholics, it was difficult to get them both in the same room at the same time. Years ago I remember thinking they'd make a great couple, but back then Satcher was fucking his way through the Upper East Side while Jules was married to her job. I wonder how they reconnected. If it had something to do with Woods? But, no, Jules hated Woods; after he cheated on me she said she never wanted to see him again.

I take a long walk in Central Park and when it's safely been a few hours, I head back to the apartment. Jules is home when I get back. I breathe a sigh of relief when I see she's alone. She's sitting on one of the barstools in pajamas, her hair up in a messy bun. Her laptop sits open in front of her, but the screen has long gone into sleep mode.

"Hey," she says.

"Hi."

I try to read her mood. She's relaxed. Neutral. But it could be jet lag. If I ask her how it went without telling her about Satcher and me, I've deceived her. I don't want to do that. I walk toward the bedroom and then remember I don't know where I'll be sleeping.

"I cleared out the office," Jules says. "I'm going to take that until everything is worked out."

Worked out?

"No way," I say. "You should have your room. It's your apartment."

"Absolutely not. I'm the intruder. We had a deal. Besides, once I start working again I'm hardly home. I don't need the space."

I nod, but I'm embarrassed. It doesn't feel right. Jules turns back to her computer, staring at the dark screen. I should just go to bed, stay out of it, but she looks so forlorn.

I squeeze my eyes shut. "Everything okay?"

I hear her sniff; thankfully, it's not a teary sniff but more of a resolved one.

"Yeah. We're gonna figure it out. He's been seeing someone. It just makes me feel sick to know that. Some other woman touching him. What if he loves her?"

I can feel my face going pink. I walk to the fridge, grab two bottles of Perrier, and set one in front of her.

"Actually, can we have something harder? Something that will make this sick feeling in my stomach go away?"

"I think if you want the sick feeling to go away you probably shouldn't drink." I laugh. I take back the Perrier and pull out the bottle of Grey Goose instead.

"He said he needs time to think," she says. "What do you think that means?" Her face is twisted with worry.

I want to hug her, but that will make me feel like a worse person.

"Probably that he needs to think," I say.

She makes a face at me and I shrug.

"It was a shock to see you. He probably needs some time to sort out his feelings."

She nods. I pass her a vodka and soda and then proceed to make myself a double.

"I've only been gone four months. You'd think he could have waited a little before jumping into something new."

"That's not fair," I tell her. "How abstinent were you in Brazil?"

She snorts, her fingers playing with the condensation on her glass.

"He said he has to talk to her," she blurts.

I'm about to ask who *her* is when I remember it's me. Satcher needs to talk to me. The realization that the very thing that has been making me happy these past weeks is about to go away knots up my insides. I swallow my tears and smile.

"I'm going to bed," I say, kissing Jules on the forehead. "See you in the morning."

She's distracted when she nods. I carry my drink to the bedroom and shut the door quietly behind me. I check my phone and see that Satcher's called twice. There's a text from him too:

Call me when you get a minute.

I don't want to call him. I'd rather delay the inevitable. I put my phone face down on the dresser and climb into bed fully clothed, burying my face in the pillow. Not my pillow—Jules' pillow. Not my apartment—Jules' apartment. Not my Satcher—Jules' Satcher.

I am such a loser.

CHAPTER TWENTY-THREE

I don't see Satcher until work on Monday morning. He's waiting for me in my office, one coffee sitting on my desk and the other in his hand. I realize that I didn't even think to make coffee this morning or stop for one on the way; I've been dependent on his morning deliveries. It's become our ritual: lattes in my office before the rest of the staff arrives, some nineties band playing through my speakers.

"Hey," he says.

"Hey," I say back.

There's a dead silence during which I round my desk and sit in my chair. I stare at the paper cup of coffee for lack of anywhere better to look. *Rebel Grinds*, it says on the cup. A streak of brown runs down the white where the coffee must have spilled over the side. I feel numb, dangerously numb. It's the type that stays and you learn to live with it. A cruel survival tool that alters who you are, rubbing your emotions down to nubs.

"Billie, can you look at me, please..."

I lift my eyes to his face. No sign of dimples. His eyes are dark like he's hardly slept. I think about how he sleeps better after he has sex and then my mind immediately goes to Jules and I feel like throwing up.

"You knew," I say. "You knew I was living in Jules' apartment and you never mentioned that you were dating her."

"Past tense. We were seeing each other before she left. We ended things. Why would I bring that up?"

"Because I'm living in your ex-girlfriend's apartment!"

"Stop it, Billie. She's your friend."

I do stop it, because he's right. But it feels like the type of situation I need to sulk over. I pick up the coffee he brought me, take a sip. Smacking my lips together I make a decision. I won't let this get in the way of what I came back for. Satcher has sidetracked me. A small romantic reprieve that was shut down before it went too far.

"It was a bad idea anyway, Satch. Let's just forget about it, okay?"

"I'm not forgetting about it," he says. "I don't want to."

"Fine," I say, standing up. "I'll forget about it and you can remember it fondly while you fuck my roommate."

I know it's hurtful, but I want to hurt him. It seems that I can't get it right no matter what I do. There's always another woman—a better woman to take my place.

I don't know where I'm going, but I march out of my office to get away from Satcher. Loren has arrived to her desk, her bicycle helmet still on her head. She's unpacking her book bag. I watch as she unloads a can of soup, a beat-up S'well bottle, and a stack of file folders. She jumps when she sees me. "What the—"

"Sorry," I say.

Out of the corner of my eye I see Satcher leave my office. He looks my way, but I keep my eyes glued to Loren.

"Trouble in paradise?" Her eyes drift between Satcher and me.

I wave her question away, the corner of my mouth tucked in.

"Hey!" I say brightly. "Do you have the numbers ready for next quarter?"

She buys into my change of subject, unhooking the helmet from under her chin while rifling through the folders on her desk with her free hand. Once I have the budget under my arm, I circle back to my office. Empty. I shut the door behind me and hope everyone leaves me alone for a few hours.

I get home that night to find Jules pacing the hall. It looks like she hasn't bothered to shower or get dressed for the day. Her hair is in a messy braid, pieces pulling free from the rest in little tails; a day's worth of mascara is flecked and smudged beneath her eyes.

I drop the bags of groceries I carried in and go to her.

"What is it?" I ask. "Has something happened?"

"I think I made a mistake. He doesn't want me. I shouldn't have come back." A sob escapes her throat.

Career-oriented, driven Jules, crying over a man. I've never seen her like this. I falter, not sure how to comfort her. For the boy-crazy friend: *He was a douche! You'll meet someone better!* But I can guarantee Jules has never felt this way before, so the normal pep talk won't count.

"Is this the first time you've been in love?"

I see the answer in her eyes when she looks at me, and I feel a fresh wave of guilt for not telling her the truth. Most of us, by the time we are Jules' age, have weathered through several heartbreaks. We become old pros at hurt. Our breakup playlists are saved to Spotify, and we know exactly where to find our comfort ice cream in the freezer section.

"I thought I was being so romantic, coming back here like

things would just pick up where we left off..." Her nose is pink. "I'm so stupid."

"You're not stupid," I say. "You're beautiful and you did a brave thing."

"Yeah, well, lot of good it did me..."

My own feelings pushed to the side, I want to shake Satcher. How could he let a girl like Jules get away? I shake my head at her. Reaching for her braid, I pull out the hair tie and begin untangling it, running my fingers through the dirty blonde waves. I'm dabbing at her eyes with my sleeve when the intercom buzzes. Jules reaches over to press the button.

"Jules, open up. It's me." We both freeze at the sound of Satcher's voice.

"He's here? Oh my God." She jumps up from the stool, staring down in horror at her bathrobe. There is a sizeable coffee stain down the front. She looks from me to the door in panic.

"Go," I say. "I'll keep him busy."

She smiles at me gratefully then runs for the bathroom. I take a moment to steel myself before swinging the door open.

He doesn't look surprised to see me. He's wearing old Levis, ripped in the knee, and a Yankees T-shirt on top. I can make out the outline of the muscles I was fondling just days ago. I close my eyes against the memories.

"Can we talk?"

I glance over my shoulder at the bathroom door. I can hear the shower running. "You have ten minutes."

He follows me into the living room. I take the armchair. Folding my legs under me, I hug a pillow to my chest and stare at him expectantly. I might cry, huge possibility.

"I have feelings for you—" he starts.

I want to shove my hands against his mouth so he can't say any more, but I sit still, biting down so hard my jaw aches.

"—I don't want to stop seeing you, Billie."

I stare at the hair on his arms, at the bright white tennis shoes he never took off. He always takes his shoes off when he comes over.

"Before she left ... before I came back, did you think you could fall in love with her?"

My ears strain to hear the shower, but it's been replaced with the sound of the blow dryer.

"Yes..." He pauses. "But that was before. Things have changed."

"Nothing's changed," I say. "I can't hurt my friend, Satcher. She's all I have left."

"You have me."

I swallow. I can hear his hurt. He's my ex-husband's best friend; *my* best friend is in love with him. It doesn't matter what I feel.

"It's over, okay? It just ... can't happen."

He stares at me, not saying anything, his eyes dark with anger...regret...? I don't know. I stand up. I need to leave the room before he sees me cry.

"She's in there scrambling to get ready... " I pause. "I suggest you take her out for a nice dinner. She's a good person..." My voice trails off.

Satcher looks away. "I know that."

"Good. Don't hurt her."

I pass Jules in the kitchen as she walks toward the living room where I left Satcher just a moment ago. She smiles at me excitedly and does a little spin so I can check her outfit: tight jeans and a simple white top. Her hair is still a little damp, hanging in soft tendrils around her face. She's only put on a little mascara and some lip gloss, but she looks effortlessly beautiful. I give her the thumbs-up, my smile immediately dropping as soon as she can't see my face.

I hear him greet her, the deep timbre of his voice making

my heart ache. *Oh well,* I think. *It could have been good, but now we'll never know...*

In the bathroom I lean my forehead against the mirror, which is still fogged over from Jules' shower. With my eyes closed, I roll my head from side to side, my fingers pressed to the wall. I feel like I'm being dramatic but also that I have a right to be. *Five minutes of drama and then I'll sort myself out*, I promise myself.

"I'm okay, I'm okay, I'm okay... " I say to no one.

No one would believe me anyway.

CHAPTER TWENTY-FOUR

For the next two weeks I excel in avoidance. If there were trophies for dodging two people, it would belong to me. My stomach feels continuously volatile: acid and anxiety. To distract myself, I take long walks, staring up at the skyscrapers that shoot from the ground pistonlike. I stay out late after work frequenting the same dive Woods and I ended up in on our first date. After a week, the bartender raises one meaty finger in the air to acknowledge that he's seen me then brings over a lemon drop without me having to ask.

"I like your face tattoo," I say.

The only acknowledgment that he's heard me is the slight raising of his eyebrows. He walks back behind the bar without a word. I suck at making friends.

On weekends, I get up early, sneaking out before Jules can ask where I'm going. When she comments one day that she's hardly seen me, I lie and tell her that I've started dating again. The excitement on her face breaks my heart. She genuinely wants me to be happy. I'm lucky to have a friend like her, which makes the fact that I've slept with the man

F*CK MARRIAGE

she's in love with even worse. I buy pot from a guy in Central Park with four fingers on his right hand, and I smoke on Jules' fire escape, flushing the nubs of joints down the toilet.

I come home late one night after an exhausting day of work, sure that they won't be there, but when I close the door, I see his shoes parked neatly next to Jules'—tennis, which means he probably stopped here after the gym. Music is playing in the kitchen, Billie Holiday. I back up a step, planning my escape, an excuse ready on my lips if either of them catches me.

"Billie!"

I turn slowly toward the kitchen, my face neutral. Jules stands in the space between the kitchen and the small dining room, a spatula in hand. She's wearing a side pony and knee socks and I can't help but smile.

"I'm making dinner," she says. "You have to eat it or my feelings will be hurt. I won't take no for an answer. We can smoke some of your pot after dinner." She smirks.

I feel my face growing warm. She knew all along. I almost sniff my clothes to see if that's how she caught me.

"You're not the only one who enjoys the marijuana, Billie," she says, rolling her eyes.

I only hesitate for a moment before kicking off my heels and following her cautiously into the kitchen. Satcher is seated on a barstool still in his workout gear. When he sees me, he stands. *Such a gentleman*, I think. I want to roll my eyes, but my chest hurts.

He's looking at me with too much familiarity, too much softness. Are the corners of his mouth tucked in like he's forcing normalcy, or is that my imagination? I stare longingly at my bedroom door wondering what excuse I can come up with to disappear behind it.

"How've you been?" he asks this softly as Jules bangs around at the stove.

Sad. Pathetic. Mopey.

"Great."

"Good." He looks at me carefully like he's trying to uncover some truth I'm not saying.

I suppose he's right to think that.

"No one's ever gone to such great lengths to avoid me," he says.

It's not a complaint; there's some amusement in his voice.

"It's because you suck in bed," I say before I can stop myself.

Satcher chortles and Jules turns from the stove, alarmed.

"She's funny." He dips his head toward me and Jules carries on cooking.

I don't feel like bantering with him so I look away. Jules dances around the kitchen unaware. She's in an exceptionally good mood. They probably just had sex, which makes me want to vomit.

"Satcher, can you make us drinks?" Jules asks. "Anything you like. I'll even drink one of those nasty Manhattans you love."

I watch as he walks to her little bar, lifting glass bottles to examine what she has. She takes a break in cooking to go over and kiss him. Satcher tenses up at first and then bends to kiss her back. I look away.

"Soooo, you gonna tell us about this guy you've been seeing?" Jules eyes me through a haze of steam as she empties vegetables into a colander. From the corner of my eye, I see Satcher's head turn—just a fraction so that his ear faces us.

"It's nothing," I say.

Jules frowns. "It's not Woods that you're seeing, is it?"

My heart is rapid-fire behind my ribs. "Can we not do this?" I say through my teeth.

Satcher is walking toward us. Saved by the drinks. He puts a glass in front of me a little harder than normal. Some of the liquid sloshes over the side and onto the counter. I pretend not to notice.

It's a lemon drop.

"What's that?" Jules asks. Her nose is scrunched up, eyebrows cocked in confusion.

Satcher and I exchange a glance. The warmth in his eyes makes me uncomfortable.

"It's Billie's token drink," he says.

Jules shakes off the last of the water from her hands and picks up her glass, his simple explanation accepted.

"To Billie and her new beginning..." She lifts her glass.

It's a good lemon drop. I wonder where he learned how to make them and if he learned for me. *Of course he didn't*, I think. *Silly girl*. When dinner is ready, Jules seats us around her little dinette to eat. I force a few bites between my lips, staring only at my plate. Satcher stands up at some point and returns with fresh lemon drops. I see him frown every time he takes a sip and I can't decide if it's because he likes it or hates it. Jules talks enough for all three of us, babbling on, oblivious to the weird tension. She calls Satcher "babe" and touches his arm whenever she speaks to him. I watch her elegant fingers knead his arm, his neck; her skin is shockingly white against his. I feel detached from my body like I'm being forced to watch everything happen from above. I can see myself floating up near the ceiling staring down at the teal rug beneath the table, the walnut bookcases that she's color-coded rather than alphabetized. There's no way to tell what Satcher is thinking—feeling. I wonder if he's in his body or floating somewhere else too.

After dinner, I insist they sit while I clear the dishes. I need space between us even if it's only the twenty feet to the kitchen. When I look up from the dishwasher, Satcher's chair is scooted sideways and Jules is sitting on his lap.

I finish up as quickly as I can and make a dash for my

room. I crawl into bed pulling the covers over my head. Instead of going to sleep—which is probably what I need to do—I text Woods.

What are you doing?

His reply comes back two minutes later accompanied by a picture.

At a bar. They say hi.

I study the picture. Woods is in the forefront, his arm extended to hold the phone. Behind him are Desi and Xavier, two of our friends from college. Their eyes glow red like bar demons. I look longingly at their drinks, sweating on the bar in front of them, and it's like Woods reads my mind.

Come down. The guys want to see you.

He texts over the address immediately and I stare at it long and hard. Bad idea?

A burst of laughter leaks underneath my door. I hear Satcher say something and then Jules' response. I stuff my head underneath my pillow trying to block out the sound of their happiness, and then just as quickly I roll onto my back, phone held above my face.

Okay. I text back. *Be there in ten.*

The bar is typical: poorly lit, dark wood, a couple of TVs. The guys are lined up with beers in front of them, slouch-shouldered, staring at the screen. Desi spots me first.

"Well, well, well, the prodigal daughter has returned." He gets off his barstool to hug me. Xavier, who's never had much to say, gives me a fist bump. I glance at Woods, who is eyeing me up and down, a buzzed smile on his face.

"Hey," he says. He hooks an arm around my waist and pulls me in, planting a kiss on my cheek.

"You're drunk." I laugh, pulling away.

"Not yet." He turns back to the bartender. "Lemon drop for the lady."

The bartender makes eye contact with me and I shake my head. No more lemon drops tonight.

"I'll have a beer," I say.

He nods and moves away to get my drink. I bullshit with the guys for a few minutes. Desi pulls out his phone and shows me photos of his new baby. His wife and I were friends once upon a time. Woods got custody of the friendship when I left. When the game comes back on, I move down the bar and slide into the seat next to Woods. He nudges my knee with his leg.

"So," he says.

"So..." I say.

"I heard Satcher and Jules hooked up. What happened between the two of you?" He empties his glass and glances up at the TV to clock the score. He's enjoying this, I realize.

"What's it to you?" My beer arrives and I take a sip.

"Oh, you know ... my ex hooks up with my best friend and I'm interested to know what happened..."

"It doesn't seem like you two are best friends anymore," I say. "Want to tell me what happened with that?"

Woods bristles. Two spots down, Desi slams his fist down on the bar, his eyes glued to the screen above him.

"He didn't like what happened with Pearl. We got into it the day after you left town."

"Into it? Into it, how?"

No one had bothered to mention this to me, including Satcher. I'd even asked him about the tension and he'd brushed off my comments like it was all in my head.

"We fought..."

"Physically?"

"Yes, physically," he says. "He punched me and I punched back. Come on, Billie—you telling me he never mentioned this? You'd think he would since he's had a candle burning for you for years."

I can't believe what he's saying. I'm quiet for a minute processing it all.

"It wasn't like that for Satcher and me. We've only ever been friendly..."

"Maybe on your end, but I've known Satch his whole life. He's been in love with you for a very long time."

I make a face. "Come on. You're kidding me right now. Satcher, who has commitment issues and has slept with half the women in Manhattan?"

"Women overthink everything and men barely think." He shakes his head.

"So your tension with Satcher is over me?"

"Yes. That's where it started."

I lean back in my seat, incredulous.

"Well..." I pause to take a giant sip of beer. "Whatever it was, it's over now. Satcher is with Julia."

"Certainly an odd turn of events," Woods says, studying my face. "You sad about it?"

"Why weren't you this concerned with my feelings when we were together?"

One corner of his mouth tucks in. "I was, but when you're knee-deep in insecurity and denial about your role in things, it's hard to show it."

"Wow, ten years' worth of therapy in one night." I lick my lips, eyeing the bottles behind the bar. "Time for something stronger," I say.

"Hey, remember that time we actually went to therapy?"

I roll my eyes. "If you can call it that..."

"I miss you, Billie."

That cuts right through me. I glance at Desi and Xavier to see if they've heard, but both of their faces are tilted toward the TV.

The bartender steps in front of us.

"Four shots of something strong." I hold up four fingers as I say it.

"Not for me." Xavier stands up. The game has ended and he's shrugging on his jacket. "Wife needs me to pick up tampons." He smirks.

"Want to split a cab?" Desi asks.

Xavier shrugs and I wonder if he's ever committed to anything with a strong yes. Maybe his wife. The guys head out and then it's just Woods and me. We don't speak for the first few minutes and it reminds me of the comfort people grow into when they've spent years around each other. Our shots arrive and I slide two of them over to him. We touch the tiny glasses together and then both our heads tilt back at the same time.

"Ugh ... goddamn," Woods says. He wipes his mouth with the back of his hand. "I'm too old for this."

"One more, old man," I say, nudging the second shot.

He frowns, but his eyes are dancing.

The second shot goes down harder. I wince against the acid burn tickling my throat. Woods looks green. The liquor warms the dead parts of me; I feel myself revving up, coming to life. *This is how one becomes an alcoholic*, I think. Leaning back in my chair, I stretch my arms above my head. It feels good to be out of that house, away from Satcher and Jules.

I probably need to start thinking about getting my own place, but then I think of what Jules said about moving in with Satcher if everything goes right, and I feel sick.

"What?" Woods says. His eyes are hazy and there's a slight slur to his words. "Your face dropped all of a sudden."

I shake my head, pushing Satcher and Jules into a mental closet and locking the door.

"I'm good. This is fun."

"Yeah," he says.

"Do you and Pearl go out drinking?"

His eyes narrow just the slightest bit, but I know his expressions well enough to catch it.

"No ... Pearl doesn't like the calories." His voice is flat ... bored.

"Oh," I say.

When he leans over and kisses me I'm not expecting it. My eyes are open as his soft mouth presses against mine. There's no tongue, or spit, or roaming hands, just a tender kiss between two old flames.

I should have pushed him away sooner than I did.

"Why'd you have to go and do that?" I lean back to look him in the face. There's not an ounce of remorse.

"The spirit led me."

I sigh. "I better get going."

Woods grabs my hand. "Stay," he says.

I shake my head. "Another day. When you're sober."

I get home around two in the morning. Fumbling with the lock, I drop the keys. I bend to retrieve them, and when I straighten up, the door is open and Satcher is staring down at me.

I yelp, jumping back in surprise.

"What are you doing?" I can hear the defensiveness in my voice.

"Opening the door so you don't wake the entire building."

"Where's Jules?" I peer around him suspiciously.

"She's in bed. I was getting ready to leave..." His voice is low, barely a rumble.

I have a fleeting memory of our naked bodies moving together as he spoke baritone words in my ear. *"You're so wet, Billie..."*

I shiver. It had been so easy to fall open for him. Too easy.

I press a palm to my chest where it still feels raw from what happened between us.

I stumble forward, eager to get away from him, and my heel catches on Jules' rug. He catches me, bending his knees to loop an arm around my waist.

"How much have you had to drink?"

"You know. You were the one making them." I try to walk past him, but he blocks me.

"You reek of liquor. This isn't from what I made you."

"Well, last time I checked I was an adult and I don't have to answer to you about what I've been drinking."

In my mind, he's going to try to stop me from walking to my room. I make a dash for it, but the apartment is dark. My knees hit something and I'm thrown off-balance. I feel myself falling, my hands groping uselessly at air. In an attempt to help, Satcher reaches around to grab me and misses, his elbow connecting with my eye.

"Goddammit, Billie," I hear him mutter.

I'm on the floor, one leg twisted beneath me. I straighten my leg and roll onto my back, staring up at the dark ceiling.

"Shit. I'm sorry..." He sits down next to me on the floor where I'm cupping my wounded eye.

"I'm a loser," I say. "A drunk loser."

"No." Satcher pulls my hand away from my eye and examines it with the light from his phone. "You're going to have a shiner."

I sniff. We stay like that for a few minutes and then Satcher gets to his feet, holding out his hands so he can pull me up.

"I'm sad," I say tearfully.

Satcher kisses my forehead. "I know. Come on, let's get you to bed."

I allow him to lead me to my room, the warmth of his hand traveling up my arm and into the cold of my heart. I pull away from him, but he doesn't leave ... except to go grab a bag of frozen peas to hold over my eye. He sits me on the edge of my bed and kneels in front of me to pull off my shoes. Placing them next to each other on the floor, he glances up at me.

"Who were you drinking with?"

I lick my bottom lip trying to think up a good lie. We both know he has no right to ask me that, but I can't look away from his eyes. I shrug. "Woods."

"Ugh, Billie..." He leans back on his haunches, shaking his head.

The only light in my bedroom comes from the streetlight outside. I wonder why he hasn't turned the light on as I study his face in the near dark.

"Shut up," I say. "Don't lecture me."

I fall backward into the comforter and hear him laugh softly. My packet of frozen peas has fallen to the floor. I turn my head sideways and stare at it, my eye throbbing. I've hardly eaten anything today, the dinner Jules made mostly pushed around my plate. No wonder the liquor hit me this hard.

I expect him to leave after he helps with the shoe situation, but he very gently peels off my jeans and then lifts my shirt over my head. I'm lying on my back in my underwear staring up at him.

"What happened? You were in a better place. You'd moved on from the shit with Woods."

"And by shit, you mean my eight-year relationship with the love of my life?"

"Oh, come off it, Billie. The love of your life doesn't leave you for another woman."

We're both silent, me weighing his words. I'd be lying if I said they didn't hurt. It's fine for me to know that Woods hadn't really loved me, but everyone else knowing it makes me want to cry.

"He made a mistake."

"You're damn right he did. And he's the type of guy who makes those mistakes. Pearl will be no exception."

I think of our kiss, Woods' lips so soft against mine. I hardly believe he'd go home and confess to Pearl about it.

"I was in a better place because of you," I blurt.

My hand wants to reach up and cover my own mouth. I flex my fingers. No. I'll own this. This is what I feel and I have nothing to be ashamed of. Except maybe of the fact that I'm still lying in my underwear while we argue. I reach for a blanket and sit up, wrapping it around my shoulders. I don't feel quite as drunk anymore.

"I was falling for you, Satcher. But that proved to be a stupid thing to do, didn't it? I suppose I should have consulted with the graveyard of hearts you've accumulated over the years." I start to turn away, but his voice comes back at me, angry.

"That's not fair. You pushed me away. You're still in love with your ex-fucking-husband."

He's right, of course, but it's not like he saw us as serious. I was just his in-between girl; the basic bitch he fucked in-between his model girlfriends.

"Right. And you really fought back on that one!"

"Holy shit, Billie..." He slides his hand through his hair. "It's like you're setting me up to fail."

He stands, turning to leave.

"Woods told me why you fought," I blurt this when his hand is on the doorknob. "Is it true? You hit him when he cheated on me?"

"I hit him because he cheated on you," he says without turning around.

"Why didn't you tell me?"

"Why would I?"

"I don't know ... because you stood up for my honor!"

"You left. None of us saw or heard from you for two years. And don't forget what sent you to that place, Billie, where you left everything you loved and crawled into a hole for two years of your life."

"Why are you saying that?" I pull the blanket tighter around my shoulders. The room feels like it's shrinking in on us. Is this the way truth is supposed to feel—claustrophobic?

"Because I can see it all over your face. You're falling for him again."

If I try to deny it, Satcher will see right through me. I bite the insides of my cheeks to keep from lying.

"It's none of your business, Satcher. You're with Jules. Who I choose to spend my time with is not your concern."

He's in my face and I don't know how it happened. One minute he was holding onto the doorknob, the next we're virtually nose-to-nose.

"Say you want me. Say you want me and I'll leave her to be with you."

My pulse is pounding behind my ear; I can feel the flicker of it under my flesh. My mouth falls open ungracefully. I can smell his skin, his breath is lukewarm on my cheek. I'm tempted to reach out and pull his mouth toward me, but I've already made one mistake tonight by kissing Woods.

"No." I turn my face away. "I can't ... Jules..."

He's already backing up, a sad expression on his face.

"I need another drink," I say, standing up.

I make it out the door and halfway to the kitchen before I feel his hands on me. Suddenly the floor is no longer beneath my feet. I gasp as Satcher tosses me over his shoulder and carries me back to my bedroom. He tosses me on the bed and I glare up at him too angry to speak.

He points a finger at me. "No more drinking."

I open my mouth to argue, but he turns his back to me.

"Sometimes, Billie, God sends an ex back into your life to see if you're still stupid."

He's gone before I can throw something at his head. I cry myself to sleep. Sober.

CHAPTER TWENTY-FIVE

There are all kinds of reasons people get divorced: they grow apart, there is abuse, they were never in love in the first place, they want different things...

But when two people get divorced because one of them let a third person into the marriage, the person who was left behind faces years of psychological warfare they launch against themselves. Your person didn't love you enough. Do you know how devastating that is? To realize you weren't loved enough. I spent two years asking myself what I could have done better, scouring my memories for signs that he was unhappy. Why didn't he tell me? I could have changed, I could have tried harder, I could have...

Maybe I shouldn't have waited to be better. Is that the problem with all of us—we need a reminder to be a decent wife, a decent daughter, a decent mother? It doesn't matter now anyway.

. . .

On Monday morning, I head to work, my shiner hidden behind a pair of huge sunglasses I borrow from Jules' closet. I tried caking makeup over it, but that just made it more obvious. To my utter dismay, Woods is waiting for me when I open my office door.

"God, you scared me." I walk past him, tossing my things on my desk.

"I wanted to talk to you about—"

"Nothing to talk about," I say dismissively.

My stomach clenches. I don't want to hear how he regrets kissing me. Apologies of that sort make the heart hurt.

"Stop, Billie, queen of avoidance. We need to discuss what happened."

"No." For a moment, I forget about my black eye and look directly at him.

"What happened?" He's on me in a minute, pulling off my sunglasses and examining my eye.

"Nothing. It was an accident."

He has my chin between his fingers and I can feel his breath on my face.

"What type of accident?"

I pause. "I took an elbow to the face, it's nothing."

Woods' face darkens. "Whose elbow?"

"For God's sake, Woods," I say, pulling away from him. "No one beat me up if that's what you're insinuating. Aside from you, of course. But the heart is easily hidden."

I drop into my chair, but Woods stays where he is.

"Billie, what happened at the bar—"

"Stop it..." I cover my ears with my hands, and when I realize how childish I must look, I drop them. "You—we were drunk. You don't need to say anything." I wiggle my mouse and my screen jumps to life. I'm praying that's enough for him and he'll leave, but when I look up he's still standing there.

"That's just it. I wasn't that drunk."

I stare.

"I wasn't that drunk," he says again.

He walks over to the chair facing my desk, the one Satcher always sits in, and drops into it. Outside my window it starts to rain, water beading the glass and then trickling away.

"You left so quickly after ... we never got the chance to talk. I wanted to explain."

I raise my eyebrows. My mouth is dry, my heart pounding out my grief.

"You knew where I was."

"You're right. I was a coward. After what I did I was afraid to face you, especially on your turf."

I fold my hands on my lap so he can't see them shaking. Why am I like this? I need to be stronger ... harder. I came back here to prove myself and I can't even control my body's reaction to him.

"It's been a long time. It's behind us. I've moved on." I imagine Satcher would snicker at that part if he was here.

"I haven't," Woods says.

"You're getting married," I remind him.

He licks his lips, staring toward the window. "You only love the rain on your terms. Washington was too much; here is too little."

He used to say that to me all the time. He'd suggest we move to Seattle and have an adventure and I'd brush him off saying I couldn't live in constant rain.

"We should live where your eyes match the sky..."

"Why don't we live where your eyes match the sky." I'd laugh.

"The Caribbean?"

"Don't flatter yourself..."

"Despite what you think, I didn't mean for that to happen. I love—"

My door opens and both of us look up at the same time. Satcher's face is unreadable as he steps into my office. He's wearing a navy blue suit, the top buttons of his white shirt open to reveal his collarbone. As soon as he walks in his smell is everywhere. He swallows the room and for a brief moment I forget about Woods.

He walks directly to where I'm sitting, and just like Woods, takes my chin in his hand to examine my eye.

"Nasty shiner." He breaks the silence.

"You're telling me. It was like my heart wasn't beat up enough, let's give her outward bruises too."

The dimple appears. He's always appreciated my dry humor.

"Wait. You did that to her?" Woods looks from one of us to the other.

"Yes. Another thing you and I have in common," I say brightly. "Black eyes compliments of Satcher Gable."

"The fuck, Satcher?" Woods says, ignoring my comment.

Satcher barely looks at him. "A moment when you have time, Billie. I'll be in my office."

I nod, and he walks out without acknowledging Woods. *Savage.*

*A*fter lunch, I meander over to Satcher's office. I'm trying to pretend that whatever he has to say to me isn't important. When I walk in, he's sitting behind his desk working, a half-eaten container of salad in front of him.

"What are you working on?" I sit down in the green chair running my fingers over the fabric.

"Now that you're here I can invest my time into growing

my other companies. Thank you, by the way. You did me more of a favor than I did you."

I shrug. "Rhubarb feels like the only good thing I have left ... even though it's not mine."

He has a weird look on his face.

"So, what did you want to talk to me about?"

He leans back, propping his hands behind his head, and stares up at the ceiling.

"I don't want to tell you what to do," he says.

"Then why do I get the feeling that's exactly what you're going to do?"

His eyes flicker from the ceiling to my face.

"This is still my company, Billie. I care about what happens here. And if Pearl finds out that you're meeting up with Woods at bars—"

"She's not going to find out. And it's not going to happen again," I rush.

"She has a lot of loyalty with the other employees. If she left, they'd follow her. That could set us behind for months. Not to mention, Woods still has a significant share of Rhubarb; if he wanted to, he could make things very difficult for us."

"Stop," I say.

I'm agitated at myself and Satcher. He has no right.

"What I do in my spare time is none of your business." I stand up. "You don't have to protect me from Woods! I know how to handle him."

"I'm trying to protect you from you," he says.

My mouth goes dry and the tips of my ears tingle like they always do when there's too much emotion to deal with.

"We never tried to work it out. I ran and it gave him the excuse to take the easy road."

"God, you're dense." He leans back in his chair, tapping a finger on his desk absently. "He should have chased you.

None of what happened was on you, Billie. He's the one who fucked up. There is no excuse for cheating, ever. If he wanted out of your marriage, he could have done that without being a complete fucking scumbag."

"But he didn't." My voice rises. "We all make mistakes. Why do you even care, Satcher?"

I'm livid. I can't believe Manhattan's slutttiest man is lecturing me on relationships.

"Because I would have chased you."

The silence following his declaration is bloated. At first I'm too shocked to respond. When the anger finally catches up to me I stand so abruptly Satcher's eyes grow wide.

"Fuck you," I say. "You're just another man who dropped me for someone else."

I know it's awful. I shouldn't have said it, and it's definitely not fair considering I was the one who pushed him away. But despite how much of a role I had in his decision to be with Jules, despite how he argued against it—he did it. Left me for her. He has no right to judge Woods.

"I think you should leave," he says. "You're not being rational."

Trigger words. I stand so abruptly the green velvet chair topples over.

"You're an asshole," I say before marching for the door.

"But at least I'm an asshole who knows what I want," he calls after me.

I slam his office door so hard I hear Satcher curse on the other side of it. Since when does Satcher know what he wants? He's been flouncing from one model to the next for years.

CHAPTER TWENTY-SIX

On Sunday morning I go see an apartment that's for lease in Brooklyn. I take a cab since the weather has turned and I don't want to bother with the subway ... yet. The neighborhood isn't terrible, and travel to and from work will be a hassle, but the thought of having my own space outweighs every negative thought I have. Before Woods cheated on me and I ran home to Washington I'd only ever had roommates: the girls at college and then my husband. And even though I spent two years living in my parents' guest house, it still felt like I was living at home with them. This will be my very first solo apartment and I am going to be completely broke paying for it. The owner, an overenthusiastic blonde who is donning a Bride hoodie, is getting married and moving in with her husband-to-be.

"We want to start a family right away," she tells me, kicking a stray tennis ball under the bed.

I watch it roll out the other side and hit the wall. Stacked near the front door are a couple of beat-up rackets. I spot a photo of said fiancé on the nightstand; he's a standard American guy wearing a letter jacket and holding a beer. I'd bet my life his parents had a country club membership Upstate where they played tennis together.

"So anyway, we need a bigger place," she finishes.

She looks no older than twenty-three. I want to tell her to run, to avoid the marriage thing until she's lived with him a few years. But I'm familiar with this type of hopeful devotion. She babbles on about her fiancé's two bedroom walk-in, the original hardwood floors, and the extra closet space as she shows me around her tiny studio (which doesn't have a closet). There's a bathroom I can barely turn around in, a small gas stove, an olive green fridge that groans like it's in pain when she opens it, and a view of an alley with a dumpster overflowing with trash. I stare down at a cat who is ripping open a bag of garbage with its claws and say, "I'll take it."

She seems relieved, and I remember how eager I was to start my life with Woods all of those years ago. She has me fill out an application and I write her a check for first, last, and security. I can move in right after the holidays, which is perfect because Jules will be gone through Christmas to visit her family. I will have the apartment to myself until it is time to move.

When I get back to Jules', no one is home so I make myself a sandwich and itemize my belongings. I don't have much more than I arrived with. I'm going to need things: a bed, a small table, a wardrobe. I'm going to have to tell Jules tonight. I wonder if she'll sublease this place and move in with Satcher? The thought makes me lose my appetite and I throw the rest of my sandwich in the trash. I tell myself that it won't be so bad. All I have to do is get through the holidays and then I will be wonderfully free. No more bumping into them on the way home from a date night, no more seeing Satcher's shoes next to the umbrella rack, no more agonizing about whether they are having sex behind her closed bedroom door. My only consolation in this whole situation, versus the one with Woods and Pearl, is that I love Jules and genuinely want her to be happy.

My feelings for and about Satcher are confusing. He was my friend, and then he was my lover, and now we're at an impasse where I'm not sure what I'm allowed to call him other than boss. The tension between us doesn't go unnoticed. By Wednesday, we've done such a bang-up job of avoiding each other, Woods comes into my office to ask if everything is okay. I stare at him for a long time, the question hanging between us. Woods is the person who knows me most—it is an uncomfortable thing to admit, but we spent a little under a decade showing each other our best and worst. Maybe sharing my situation with someone who knows me as well as he does would ... help.

I open my mouth to say something, but nothing comes out. I can smell his Juicy Fruit from across the room and I have to work my way past the pangs of nostalgia that stir in my heart: youth, a love I thought endlessly powerful, my entire future ahead of me. I suppose the only thing to say is the truth.

"I'm confused," I admit. "Dazed and confused."

Woods grins at the movie reference and sits in the chair facing my desk.

"Spill," he commands.

"You're my ex-husband," I say. "Entirely inappropriate."

"And go!"

I can't hold back my smile at the way he ignored my excuse, because he *does* know me. I have to be pushed to share feelings. It's never been easy for me to talk about matters of the heart.

"I got my own place," I say. "In Brooklyn."

He nods slowly. "Ah. Have you let Jules know?"

I shake my head.

"You and Satcher..."

I groan. "I don't want to talk about that."

"You two were a disaster waiting to happen."

I sit up straighter, bothered by his words. "What's that supposed to mean?"

"Come on, Billie. What do you two even have in common?"

"What do you and Pearl have in common?" I shoot back.

Woods stares at me dumbstruck, which is why I don't immediately notice the door opening behind him.

"Clearly more than the two of you did."

I look up to see Pearl standing in the door to my office. She's wearing a T-shirt and jeans, her hair tied back in her signature messy knot. I hadn't heard her come in, but of course she's here. Woods isn't allowed to be alone with me without her supervision. Pearl and I have had little to no interaction since her miscarriage. She returned to work with what seemed like a new determination to pretend that I don't exist, and I have been perfectly all right with the fact that I never have to talk to her.

"Then why are you so threatened?" The words come before I can stop them. Fighting words. I didn't intend on fighting, but sometimes the fight finds you.

Woods groans, and Pearl steps deeper into my office like she's ready to deal with things head-on. Her lips are pursed, and her wide eyes gun me down with every blink. Great, I just started a girl gun fight.

"He was married to you and he didn't want to be. Now he's marrying me. What is there to be threatened about?" She feels really good about her words.

I watch as she crosses her arms over her chest. It's my turn to serve the insult, but I'm too angry to formulate words. The rage makes me lightheaded. My vision swims in and out of focus and my limbs tingle as I make an effort not to jump up from my seat. It's bad enough that she did what she did, but to be self-righteous about it?

I wonder if my true self is still there, buried underneath the various forms of myself that I've cultivated over the years: blog Billie, divorced Billie, Wendy, the Billie who came back to New York to prove to everyone that she's fine. But the Billie of old, the one Satcher has referenced on occasion, would not argue with someone she thought beneath her. Pearl believes herself to be Woods' hero. It's comical really, that she thinks she swooped in and saved him from something bad (me).

"Pearl..." It's Woods who breaks the silence, Woods who stands up and looks from one of us to the other like he's deciding how to handle the situation.

"Let's go," he says.

I shift my eyes from Pearl to Woods. The downcast movement of his eyes and his quick herding of Pearl toward the door makes me want to lash out at him, call out his weakness. Did I really expect him to defend me in front of his fiancée? No, but I didn't expect him to be with someone like Pearl either. How could he? She is a watered-down version of me. And she knows that, she knows it. Which is why my presence bothers her so much. I watch them leave and then I raise my fist and hit it hard on the desk, flinching when it makes contact. I hate them. I hate all of them. But, mostly I hate myself. I lost my husband and business—all to that insufferable creature. I don't care what I've told myself in the past about Woods bearing the burden of responsibility for cheating on me; right now I'm angry, and every ounce of that anger is directed at Pearl.

CHAPTER TWENTY-SEVEN

The annual Christmas party ... I volunteer as a party planner mostly to keep myself busy. I act like it's not a big deal, that I want to call a hundred restaurants to do things like secure a private room and set a menu. In reality, I just want to keep busy and not go home. Home is where Satcher is, and work is where Woods is. And now every inch of my life is invaded by the men I couldn't hold on to. The plus side: if I pull off the best Christmas party, I'll gain favor with the staff. Currently, half of them are Team Pearl, while the other half are with me. I choose a place called Summertime Sunday, all bohemian decor. It looks like a foreign market inside with brightly colored scarves strewn from the ceiling and jewel-toned lanterns on every table. At Christmastime they string lights everywhere and the effect leaves me breathless. It's perfect.

On the day of the party, we've wrapped up the last of our holiday posts by noon. The office is buzzing with holiday excitement. In the break room are platters of Christmas cookies and spiked eggnog. Satcher had twenty bottles of Champagne delivered this morning and people are milling about wearing Christmas sweaters and sipping on the endless supply of bubbly. Everyone is in good spirits with it being the last day of work before the office closes until after the new year. Loren has hung tinsel from desk to desk, and Pearl set up a Christmas tree the week before. Satcher comes into work wearing a Santa hat and the ladies swoon, including me.

I'm walking by the break room when one of Pearl's lackeys says, "I'd be his naughty elf..."

I roll my eyes, though I can't blame them. For the last few weeks I've tried *not* to look at him. Every single time our eyes meet I feel a sharp pang of sadness. I hate myself for feeling that way; it's not like we spent years in a relationship, though judging my hurt level, that's exactly how it feels. I remind myself that we were friends long before our forage into romance, and that we can be friends again with some effort on my part. I just need to ... forget.

I leave the office early to run home and change. The apartment is empty when I get there. Our Christmas tree sits in front of the window, the lights on. It's the first time I've been alone in the apartment for months and I soak it in, standing in the near dark and staring at blinking lights hoping for an emotional recharge. After ten minutes, I reluctantly head to the bedroom to change.

Last week while buying presents to send home to my parents, I spotted a dress hanging in the window of a boutique. It was out of my budget, my eyes bulging when I saw the price tag. Initially I'd handed it back to the salesgirl, but during the five steps it took to reach the door I changed my mind. It was Christmas, after all; I could splurge and buy myself something this one time. I marched back to where she was still standing, and taking it from her hands, I carried it to the register and pulled out my credit card before I could change my mind. Now I carefully clip off the tags before tugging it over my head. The dress is silver, the fabric so soft and slinky it runs through my fingers like water. When it drops around my body, it hugs all the right places. I borrow one of Jules' coats and head out the door. Holiday traffic knots up every intersection, and by the time I've stopped at the bakery to pick up the cake, I'm already twenty minutes late to the party. When I finally walk through the doors everyone is already standing around with a drink in their hands. When they see me they cheer. I laugh, shaking the snow out of my hair, and slip out of the coat.

I'd been too busy to wonder if Satcher would bring a date to the party. And, of course, that date would be Jules. I smooth a smile across my face, beautifully empty, and walk toward them. I'm so good at this. When did I become so good at this?

"Billie!" Jules hugs me while Satcher looks on quietly.

As soon as Jules completes her hug, she's back at Satcher's side. She twines her arm through his and clutches his bicep, looking around the room.

The throbbing bleed of emotion comes, emptying into my chest, painfully constricting, then dropping like lead to my stomach.

"Hi, Satch," I say quietly.

He's angry with me. There's no expression on his face when he looks at me, but his eyes flash. I can't stand it, his anger.

I duck my head, shameful tears rising to fill my eyes. And then I feel a hand on my back. I know that hand, I lean into it from years of practice.

"Satch. Nice to see you, Jules." Woods' smooth voice dries up my eyes.

I've never been so glad to see him. How can a person who left you to drown also have the power to make you feel okay?

"Wish I could say the same," Jules quips.

"It's been three years, Julia," Woods says. "Maybe we can play nice just for one night. Especially since Billie put the night together?"

Jules' lips tighten, but she doesn't argue.

"Where's Pearl?" Satcher asks.

"She was feeling under the weather."

"She seemed fine in the office this afternoon."

I glance at Satcher. What's he getting at? I'm frankly quite glad Pearl isn't here to ruin the night. Let her stay at home sipping her organic tea and feeling superior.

"Well, you know how it goes. This time of year there's always something sneaking up on you." Woods smiles stiffly and I notice he already has a cocktail in hand.

"Hey, do you mind getting me one of those?" I ask.

He smiles genuinely for the first time and nods at Jules and Satcher before heading to the bar.

"I think I'll get a drink too," she announces. "Something about Woods' face makes me want to drink..."

"I'll get it for you," Satcher says, touching her arm.

"No, I'm fine. This is your Christmas party, my love. You mingle."

I recoil at the pet name. She leaves and then there's just Satcher and me standing awkwardly in the middle of the room. My tongue feels caked with awkwardness, all elbows and knees.

"Didn't your mama ever tell you that you should never let an old flame burn you twice?"

"You have more dick in your personality than your pants, you know that, Satch?"

"What do you think is gonna happen, Billie? Everyone gets hurt in this scenario."

I glance at the bar. Jules and Woods are on opposite ends not looking at each other.

"What scenario, Satcher?" I say his name with the same amount of vinegar he used to say mine. "He's getting me a drink."

I feel like he's judging me for something I haven't even done. He shakes his head, disappointed. Before either of us can say another word, Woods returns with my drink. After he hands it to me he stands close, almost protectively. I wonder who he wants to protect me from and my eyes fall on Satcher. There is something happening between them even now, some silent exchange of eyes.

"Come on," Woods says, steering me away. "This is your party, you should mingle."

I allow him to lead me away from Satcher. Despite the hard dread rolling around in my stomach, the night is a smashing success. Everyone marvels about the restaurant's ambience, and when the food arrives they *ooh* and *ahh* over the presentation. Woods never leaves my side, and it almost feels like it used to when we were together. I make a joke and he laughs, looking at me like I'm the funniest person alive. He makes a joke and I joke that it's not funny at all, and then everyone else laughs. It's a thing we've always done, and it works—we're funny together. People always said we had this chemistry that you feel. I'd thought so too until the day he up and left me. During the dinner, when I look over at Jules, she's glaring at him like she wants to rip his throat out. Satcher, on the other hand, won't look at me at all. When I'm at the bar grabbing a drink and taking a second to breathe away from everyone, Loren comes up behind me. Resting her elbows on the bar, she grins at me.

"I've had too much to drink," she says.

"Me too," I admit.

"Is that why it looks like you and Woods are about to fuck?"

I give her a look, the look that says *watch it!*

"Everyone can see it. There's so much sexual energy between the two of you I think it charged my phone."

"Shut up," I say, laughing. "He's the boss, I'm the boss—we're just working the room, making sure everyone is having a good time."

"Well, Satcher's the boss too and all he's done all night is scowl at you."

I frown. "He's being a dick."

"Maybe he's just worried about you."

I pause to consider and then I decide against it. "Please—" My words falter because I don't know what else to say.

I glance over my shoulder at the long mahogany table. Jules is leaning into him, nestled like she's freezing and he's the only warmth. He has his arm slung casually around her shoulders. I feel a pang of jealousy and push it away. I'd been there, underneath his warm consideration. When he pins his attention on you he makes you feel like the only woman on the planet.

The bartender hands me my drink, and I lean my back against the bar surveying the scene. I refuse to have a headstone there. I will not let Satcher Gable have any power over me whatsoever. It was ... and then it was over and that is that.

PART II

CHAPTER TWENTY-EIGHT

SATCHER

She looks like herself, but she's somebody else. I make inventory: same legs, same voice, same facial expressions ... different words. Bitter? No. Bitterness hasn't reached her yet; she's surprisingly staved it off. Her shoulders are undoubtedly thinner, but not as rigid as they were a decade ago. Life does that to everyone, though. I make a point of standing as straight as I possibly can, if only to fool the Fates. Tonight she's wearing some type of magic garment. My thoughts go back to high school, tearing through the *Harry Potter* books in ninth grade. Except, instead of invisibility, her dress gives her visibility. The shimmering silver catches my eye every time she moves, even if it is just to pick up her wine glass. I am trying to ignore her, except once you look at the dress, you have to look at her legs ... and her tits, and then inevitably, you are back to her face, which lacks the symmetry of the model types I usually date. On more than one occasion I've heard women make comments about her. "*She's not even that pretty...*" or "*I don't get what men see in her...*"

If they'd ask me, I could tell them. Billie has sex appeal: you could plump her up, thin her down, put her in those god-awful Martha Stewart dresses she used to wear—and she still has sex appeal. Frank Sinatra knew a woman like Billie; he sang about her in "Witchcraft." Except I am trying not to look at her, goddammit. Looking at her makes me hungry. I look at Jules instead. We've been seeing each other again for two months now. Before she left for Brazil, I'd been certain I could see a future with her. It was a nice surprise to fall for Jules so easily. Maybe it was the right time to fall in love, or maybe she was the right girl; either way, the stars aligned, and for the first time in years I felt happy. Not the same type of happy that I got when I sold a company for a million dollars, or the happy that came with holding my niece for the first time—it was a private happy. A happy that confused me at first. And then when I was at my peak of fucking happiness, Jules announced she was leaving. It devastated me at first— she was the first woman who'd made me consider settling down. When she left, I put it out of my mind. That is the key to being good at anything: the ability to not be so wrapped up in something that you couldn't put it out of your mind. Be obsessed with one thing and everything else will suffer because of it. But now, as I try to put Billie and her silver dress out of my mind, I can't. I drain the last of my drink. I've had too much, we all have. From across the table, Celeste laughs her braying donkey laugh and her husband stares at her lovingly. Kudos to any man who could love a woman with a laugh like that. I kiss the top of Jules' head, and when she looks up at me her eyes are swollen with affection. It stings like salt in a wound. Several times tonight she's whispered her anger in my ear over Woods. She's a good friend and a good person. I glance at Woods, who is sitting next to Billie's empty chair. His eyes are trained on something past the table even though someone is saying something to him. I know he's watching Billie. That infuriates me. I need another drink.

"You okay, Satch?" Woods catches my eye.

He's taunting me. We were like this as boys, always trying to get underneath each other's skin. It had always been fun, amusing even. But now, there is a new tension, one that isn't fun or amusing.

"Why wouldn't I be?" I say it more for Jules' benefit than Woods'. She's looking at me with concern and I smile at her reassuringly.

"You look a little distracted," Woods says.

He's causing a scene. Everyone at the table is stopping their conversations to look at me.

"How's Pearl feeling?" I redirect the conversation and Woods suddenly looks guilty.

He hasn't even bothered to text and check up on his sick fiancée, though I doubt she's actually sick. If anything, she has a severe case of *I hate Billie*.

"She's resting," he says.

I smirk. I wonder if Pearl has any idea how bad Woods has it for his ex-wife? I wonder if Woods has any idea how bad I have it for his ex-wife? Bros before hoes. I remember the sentiment from high school and college. Dicks before chicks. Turns out, it is a fallible ideal. Billie has come right between my best friend and me, and I'd known she would the first time I laid eyes on her.

She'd walked into my house party carrying a bottle of expensive wine rather than the jumbo bottles of cheap liquor everyone else brought. I'd known it was her right away, Woods' new girlfriend. When he told me he was seeing someone seriously I'd slapped him on the back.

"The great white shark has been slayed."

He described her in great detail every time we were together, almost to the point that I was sick of hearing her name. I'd never seen him like this, enamored by one girl rather than all the girls. *"Something special,"* he'd said. *"Classy and fun as hell."*

She was nervous, I could tell by the way she shoved the bottle at me. Her leather jacket was worn at the elbows like she spent a lot of time with her head propped in her hands.

"You must be Satcher," she said.

"Right now I'd prefer to be Woods." I took the bottle from her, and her lips twitched at my blatant flirting.

"Speaking of, where is he?" Her eyes darted around the room, trying to unearth him from the clusters of people.

"He ran out for more liquor."

Her gaze traveled to the liquor table where three unopened bottles of cheap tequila sat side by side.

"I lied," I told her. "He went for pot…"

The smile reached her eyes that time. "So the first thing I learn about you is that you can't lie for shit." She grinned.

I shrugged. "Why lie when the truth is so interesting?"

"So tell me, Satcher, how much does Woods like me?"

Oh shit. She was already using my weakness against me. I'd stared at her hair, which was short and wavy around her face, one side tucked behind her ear. She was wearing handgun earrings. What type of woman wore Glock earrings? I reached for the wine opener and removed the cork while she watched me.

"He's whipped," I said. "It's a sad, sad thing to watch."

She laughed, a deep throaty laugh.

"You laugh like a villain," I said, pouring wine into two Solo cups.

"Oh, it's going to be fun getting to know you," she said, taking the wine from me.

I tilted my cup toward hers and touched it lightly in a *cheers*. "Ditto."

. . .

When I look up, Woods has joined Billie at the bar. Her hair is long, almost to her waist. She still tucks it behind one ear, but somewhere in her twenties she lost her taste for leather jackets and handgun earrings. I miss the old, reckless, unpolished Billie. The one who'd tell Woods to go fuck himself.

"Ready to go?" I ask Jules, squeezing her knee.

"So soon? Don't you need to stay a while longer?"

My eyes flicker up toward the bar. They're standing close, only a drink between them.

"No. Let's go back to my place," I say.

Jules nods. We hardly spend time at my condo, but I don't want to risk running into Billie tonight. We say our goodbyes around the table and head for the door, Jules' hand in mine. I hear Billie call my name, but I pretend not to hear.

"Bathroom," Jules says, letting go of my hand.

She veers left and I wander over to the door, hands in my pockets. It's raining, the street looks oil slick.

"Satcher..." I hear my name from behind me and I turn slowly.

"You didn't say goodbye..." Her eyes are hurt. She looks vulnerable, hands clasped at her waist, hair falling over one eye.

I don't say anything and she takes a step toward me.

"I don't know that I'll see you again ... before Christmas..." She looks over her shoulder and then in three birdlike steps she's in front of me. She takes my hand, gently unfolding my fingers from my palm.

I watch the dark splay of her eyelashes as she looks down at my hand. She lifts her fingers and places something in my palm. Then she folds my hand closed over it.

"Merry Christmas, Satcher," she says.

I watch her walk away. When she's gone I look down at

what she placed in my hand. At first, I don't know what I'm seeing: it's small, the size of a pea, and iridescent white. I think it might be a pearl, but then I see the tiny hoop on the back. It's a button. I touch it with my forefinger, pressing it into my palm. When Jules finds me, she laughs at my expression.

"What is that?" she asks, peering into my hand.

"Nothing," I say quickly. "It's raining..."

I stuff Billie's gift into my pocket as Jules directs her gaze outside.

"Let's run for it," she says.

CHAPTER TWENTY-NINE

Once we're back at my condo I can't stop thinking about *them:* Billie and Woods. How they looked at the bar, their heads bent together like the old days. In the beginning of their relationship they were like that: whispering, touching, trading inside jokes. They made the rest of us feel like outsiders anytime we were around them. But they hadn't cared, they'd existed in a heart-shaped world of their own.

I don't know when exactly their relationship went south, but I distinctly remember noticing the way they started bending away from each other, the sweet looks they used to give each other replaced with arched eyebrow annoyance. Tonight though, tonight had been a flashback of those earlier years, and that made me worry: rosy retrospection.

Jules has fallen asleep in my bed. The covers are pushed down to her waist and her hands are pressed under her cheek as if they're engaged in a prayer. She's wearing the white silk nightgown she leaves at my condo. I can't help but wonder if she chose the color to hint at the marriage she wants so desperately. The subtlety of women has always confounded me. Where men directly say what they want; women leave Easter eggs, making knowing their hearts a game. I suppose that's why I've always been drawn to Billie; while she can play the games too, before long her directness wins out.

I get up quietly and move to the living room, making myself a drink.

We are made to suffer in this life. You can't tell me otherwise. When we don't get the things we want, they get us instead, becoming an obsession, controlling our thoughts and behavior. That's what Billie is, I decided that long ago. I check my email, type up the responses. I think about texting her, but no, that wouldn't be right, not with Jules sleeping in the next room. I pace across the window, the city sluggish below me. Woods, I could try him, but he probably wouldn't answer. *It's none of your business*, I tell myself. It's the same thing I've told myself for years. And I've never been able to keep my hands out of her business: literally and figuratively. I glance at the clock: 4:49. I need to sleep. Billie is probably sleeping, having gone to bed hours ago. There is no need to worry. It's then that I remember the button she placed in my hand at the party. I find my pants in the dry-cleaning pile and rummage around in the pockets until I feel the round hardness between my fingers. Holding it up to the light I study the button, trying to understand what she meant by giving it to me.

"Satcher...?"

I squeeze my eyes closed before I turn around, the button buried in my fist.

"Why are you up? What's wrong?"

Jules leans against the doorframe. Her hair is tousled from her sleep. I watch as she props one foot on the shin of her other leg. I try to summon all the things I used to feel for her. The emotions had come so easily before ... before what?

Billie. Billie had leaned against that same doorframe months ago, and when I'd lied to her she'd seen right through me.

"Nothing," I say. "Just had some things to finish up."

Jules nods. We're both the type who think about work during all the times we shouldn't be thinking about work. She smiles faintly before going back to the bedroom. Billie would have barked at me. Sent me back to bed. A small smile touches my lips at the thought. When she first found out she'd been surprised ... understanding, but then she'd chide me for not waking her up so she could "help me sleep." I hate being powerless, especially over myself. I shake my head, trying to clear it. Regardless of what I feel, Billie made her decision. We sparked for a moment, even started to burn a little before that flame was doused out. It was a nice try, but it wasn't enough. Her feelings for me weren't enough.

I'm a businessman: I knew my odds going into it.

"Satcher ... earth to Satcher." I jar awake.

I must have fallen asleep at my desk. Billie is standing in the doorway, her arms crossed like she's not sure if she's welcome to cross the threshold. She's not dressed in one of her usual getups; instead, she's wearing jeans with rips above the knees and an old sweater that hangs off her shoulder like it's tired of hanging on. She looks exhausted and sexy, and if we were together I'd rub her shoulders and kiss my way down her alpine neck. I have a flash of memory: biting that shoulder while she writhed beneath me.

"What are you doing here?" I frown, more at the memory than her. "It's the Christmas holidays. You should be holidaying."

"Hello, pot, it's nice to meet you. I'm kettle."

She strolls in and glances at the green chair that used to be hers. Then she drags it right up to my desk and folds herself into it. I watch curiously as she leans her elbows on the desk and props her head in her hands, looking at me.

"Get real, Satch. Neither of us has anywhere to be." Her fingers drum her cheeks and I am reminded of a night in college when we went to a diner together after a night of clubbing. The others had wanted to go home, but Billie and I were hungry so we visited an all-night chain. She'd propped her elbows on the table and ordered two breakfasts just for herself.

"You could go home," I suggest.

I don't want her to go home; I like the city better with her in it.

"I've been *home* for two years and change. I've had enough rain and weird parental looks to last me a lifetime."

I laugh. "Well, it looks like we'll be working through the holidays then."

She wants to say something. I watch the struggle, her face creasing. Her fingers are splayed across her cheeks and her mouth is quirked up on one side. Her brown eyes meet mine, peat lashes blinking slowly.

"Spit it out, Billie."

The corners of her mouth tuck in and she rolls her eyes. Her next words slice through me.

"I slept with Woods last night."

I try to keep my face neutral, but she catches what's in my eyes and she visibly deflates.

"I know…" she says softly. "You don't have to say it. I know."

But she doesn't know. She doesn't know that her words have nudged my heart into a painful whine that is reverberating through my chest. Or that I want to stand up and shake her. Or that I've started pitying myself for pining. The big, bad bachelor with the broken heart.

I stay silent because I have nothing nice to say. Billie takes my quiet as a go to spew everything she's thinking and feeling.

"I didn't mean for it to happen. Or maybe I did. I don't even know. One thing just led to another, you know—"

I know about one thing leading to another: I am a thirty-three-year-old male with a big dick and great face.

"So you did to Pearl what she did to you. Does this mean the end of your vendetta, or do you plan on stealing her fiancé entirely?"

She straightens up, her back touching the back of the chair.

"She stole my husband," she says.

"So you're going to steal her fiancé. Is that why you came back?"

She doesn't confirm or deny.

"I don't like your tone." She tilts her chin up defiantly, but her bottom lip tugs out with emotion, giving her away.

"Why?" I challenge. "Is it the tone of a man speaking the truth?"

"You're supposed to be my friend, Satcher. Friends should be able to tell each other things about themselves without the fear of being stoned."

"Friends should be able to tell each other the truth when someone is being an ass," I say. Also, I don't want to be her friend.

She stands up in a huff. I can visibly see her chest rising and falling beneath her thin sweater. "This was a mistake," she says, heading for the door.

"Only the part with Woods," I call right before she slams the door.

I didn't need to be such an ass. But I want to be one. Men don't really grow up. We're mean when we hurt women; we're mean when women hurt us. It's our go-to. But as soon as she's out of the door, the guilt worms its way through the mean hurt I'm still holding up. It made her vulnerable to tell me that. She came in here possibly wanting me to help her sort through both her guilt and her feelings, and I'd told her to go to hell. I stand up and sit back down. No. I don't need to go running to apologize. I am tired of Billie's games. She has no clue what she wants, and in my experience, women like that are dangerous: flipping back and forth with decisions, having one foot in, one foot out. I turn back to the humming comfort of my three monitors and squirrel the mouse around aggressively. I'd say it was all a mistake, hiring her to run Rhubarb, but the numbers don't lie. Billie is good for business, bad for the heart. I think Woods would probably agree with that. I need to move on and focus on what is good for me. My days of pining for an emotionally unavailable woman are over.

CHAPTER THIRTY

The call comes as I'm locking up to meet Jules for dinner. At first, I think she's calling to tell me she's going to be late, but when I pick up and hear her voice, I know something terrible has happened. Her voice hits high notes of panic, warbling unsteadily across the line.

"Jules," I stick my finger in my ear to block out the cabbie who is laying on his horn. "I don't understand what you're saying. Can you slow down a bit and say it again?"

She's not the hysterical type, and that simple fact twists my insides into knots as I wait for her to calm down.

I hear Billie's name ... twice ... My stomach has climbed from its spot in my abdomen up into my throat, and as I pull the key from the lock, Jules repeats her story in a slightly less hysterical voice.

"She was crossing the street, at the intersection! A car ran the light and hit her and two other people."

"Where did they take her?" My voice is all business, but my hands are shaking.

I bound down the street dodging waves of pedestrians, as

Jules screams the name of the hospital in my ear. I tell her I'm on my way and hang up as soon as I have all of the information. The hospital where they took Billie is only twenty blocks uptown, but the holiday traffic has severely congested every street in that direction. It would take at least an hour to get there by cab. I run.

The hospital is packed, the city ripe with New York-style emergencies. There's a woman ahead of me at the desk asking asinine questions to the sole person manning the desk. I tap my foot, impatiently willing her to move on. When she finally does, I take her place.

"Billie Tarrow. She was just admitted. Hit-and-run..." The woman behind the desk glances at me over her glasses and then goes to work at the computer. After around a minute, I lean over the desk. "Have you found her...?"

"Was just finishing something. Looking now," she says.

The receptionist has large eyes behind even larger round glasses. I tap my fingers on the desk. "The woman I love is lying somewhere in this hospital while you're *just finishing something...*"

She pushes her glasses up her nose. "And do you think you're the only one here who has a loved one they want to see?"

"No, but right now I'm the one in front of you, so I'm the one who matters."

She tightens her lips, fingers moving across the keyboard. Finally she says, "She's in surgery. You can wait on the fourth floor with her family."

I head for the elevator wondering what family Billie has in New York. It's not until I'm walking into the waiting room that I see Woods is already here, a pale Pearl at his side. It's apparent that Pearl doesn't want to be here, and I don't blame her, but Woods does. That's what bothers me: the dedication on his face like he's still responsible for her in some way. I want to remove that look from his face, remove him from the hospital, but I have no more right to be here than anyone else. Woods is speaking to Jules, who has mascara smeared across her cheeks and is wringing her hands as I approach.

"Oh, thank God." Jules launches herself at me, burying her face in my chest.

"How is she?" I ask no one in particular.

"We don't know yet," Woods says.

He looks so stricken, my best friend instinct kicks in and I want to ask how he is. I turn to Jules instead, pulling her away from my chest so I can see her face.

"What happened?"

"I was on the phone with her. She was really upset ... crying. She said she was going back to Washington and then I heard this noise." Her eyes glaze over and it's as if she's remembering the noise because she shivers. "I kept saying her name and then someone picked her phone up off the ground and told me what happened."

I hold her tight as she sobs against me. "Has someone called her parents?" I direct this at Woods, who is the only person in the room who might have their number. He nods, his nose red.

"They didn't even say they were coming," he says. "They just told me to keep them updated."

I'm too worried to be angry. "What surgery? What are they doing to her?"

"There was internal bleeding..." Jules' voice trails off.

I'm frozen: my face, my heart—all of it. I don't want to think about what state Billie is in, but I can't help it. In the next hour, another family trickles into the waiting room. We learn that they're the parents and the husband of the other woman who was hit by the vehicle. She was pushing her toddler in a stroller when the green SUV came barreling around the corner. Their three-year-old son, Dakota, didn't survive the impact; his mother, like Billie, is still in surgery.

When a doctor walks in two hours later, everyone in the room stands. He's still in his scrubs, which I notice with relief, aren't covered in blood. That has to be a good sign, right?

"Billie Tarrow's family?" He looks at me when he asks this, and I nod.

"She was bleeding internally when the ambulance brought her in. We managed to stop the bleeding, but we won't know the extent of her injuries until she wakes up. She's in critical condition. Unfortunately, we can't let you see her right now."

We nod simultaneously. I glance at Woods, who looks disheveled, and I see that Pearl is watching him as well.

"We're going to get going," Pearl says. "Call us if anything changes?"

Jules looks away. She'd rather die than ever call Pearl, but I nod. I can tell Woods doesn't want to leave, but Pearl grabs his arm and steers him out. Jules and I collapse into the plastic chairs. I realize it's almost eight o'clock and neither of us have eaten.

"I'll go get something," she offers. "I can't sit here and wait anymore. I feel like I'm going out of my mind."

"All right," I say slowly. "I'll call if anything happens."

She leaves, her eyes tinged pink, and her fists curled into balls under the sleeves of her sweater. I sit back down to wait. Jules has been gone for no more than twenty minutes when a nurse comes in and informs me that I can see Billie.

"Is she awake?" I ask, following her into the hallway.

She shakes her head. "No. But touch her, talk to her. Let her know you're there. It helps."

I nod as she leads me to the door of Billie's room. She leaves me there and I hesitate a moment before stepping inside. Billie is the only color in the room, her skin pale and mottled with cuts and bruises the color of ripe fruit. I flinch when I see the oxygen tubes snaking into her swollen nose and I realize that it's broken.

"Oh my God," I say to myself.

I stand for what feels like forever, staring down at her broken body. This is my fault. I fought with her, said terrible things. She left the office upset and distracted. I pull the only chair in the room right up to her bed. I can't hold her hand because of the tubes and needles, so I touch the only piece of her arm that isn't scraped and bruised.

"Billie," I say. "It's Satch. I'm here, okay? And I'm not going anywhere. I swear."

There's no movement on the machines that read her vitals, no movement on her face. *What if she never wakes up?* I think. *I wouldn't be able to live with myself.* I text Jules to tell her I've seen Billie, but by the time she arrives with two bags of takeout, they've told me visiting hours are over.

"But I didn't get to see her," she complains.

"We'll come back first thing tomorrow," I say.

I have no plan to leave the hospital tonight, but Jules nods even though she doesn't look convinced.

"I can get out of work tomorrow. I don't want her to be alone when she wakes up."

"No. You've taken your vacation time for Christmas," I remind her.

She frowns. Jules took off two weeks to go visit her family for the holidays. She flies out the day after tomorrow.

"I'll stay. The office is closed anyway," I say.

Reluctantly, she nods.

We eat in the waiting room, though we probably could have gone home since they won't let us back in to see Billie.

When we're done eating, we clean up our mess, silently dumping the empty containers into the trash.

"I don't want to go. I feel so guilty," she says.

"She's not going to wake up tonight," I tell her. "Get some rest and you can be back right after work tomorrow."

She nods, wrapping her arms around my waist. "I'm lucky to have you," she says. "Billie and I both are."

I doubt that, especially since I am the reason Billie is laid up in that bed in the first place.

When we walk out the door, there are two cabs waiting in the line.

"Two cabs. Perfect," she says.

I put her in the first cab, bending down so I can see her.

"I'll see you tomorrow." I kiss her on the forehead.

As soon as her cab disappears, I walk back into the hospital.

I doze in the waiting room, my head tilted back and my legs stretched out in front of me until a teenage boy whose head is bent over his phone trips over my legs. I jar awake and he mumbles an apology before moving to a chair near the window. As soon as the nurse on duty will allow it, I am back in Billie's room occupying the sole visitor chair. She tells me that there has been no change since last night. I spend the next few hours rubbing my thumb across her fingers and staring at her face in case she decides to open her eyes. I'm sick with worry, and to make matters worse, not a person in this goddamn hospital will give me a straight answer. I take to the Internet, which feeds me page after page of depressing statistics about head injuries. I try to reason with her, tell her she has to wake up, but she stays stubbornly still. I memorize the veins in the thin skin of her eyelids.

Jules comes to the hospital during her lunch hour. When she sees me in the same clothes as yesterday, she frowns.

"You stayed all night?"

Before I can answer, Woods walks through the door, a bouquet of wildflowers in his hand. His eyes widen when he sees Billie.

"Great. The whole crew is here," I say.

He ignores me and steps over to her side, staring down at her. I'll give it to the guy, he looks worried.

"Probably shouldn't let Pearl see that moony look on your face," I say.

"Fuck off, Satcher."

Dust motes dance in the streaming light. I watch those instead of looking at Billie and Woods. She's in a coma, and I'm jealous that he's standing so close to her. I don't know whether to laugh at myself or be disgusted.

"Did they arrest the driver?"

"Yes," I say.

An officer came by this morning to let me know. The driver's name is Rey and he claims he had a seizure and didn't know he hit the women and child until ten minutes later when he woke up in his car a block away. The police aren't buying it. I told him I was her husband and now all of the nurses are calling me Mr. Tarrow.

"Pearl and I are leaving for Missouri tonight." He rubs a hand along his jaw while staring at Billie.

"I'll be here," I say. "I'll stay with her."

Jules grabs onto my arm and squeezes slightly. She'd suggested canceling her trip home, but I told her not to. Billie would be mortified if she knew Jules had forgone Christmas with her family to sit at the hospital.

"Somehow that doesn't comfort me," Woods says.

His eyes leave Billie and suddenly he's studying my face. I

clench my fists. The fact that he's here infuriates me. Forty-eight hours ago he was having sex with Billie while his fiancée waited at home for him. I am sick of Woods and his inability to make a choice in life and stick with it.

"Satch..." Jules, who can sense my anger, looks up at me, her eyes searching my face.

The hospital room shrinks around us. Jules is relaying a look that says *this is neither the time nor the place,* but I'm so angry I shrug her hand off my arm and take a step toward Woods.

"You have no right to be here," I tell him. "You're nothing to her. You left her."

Woods snickers. "I have more of a right than you do ... oh wait..."

He has a sick smile on his face and I know what's coming next.

"You've always wanted to be that person for her, haven't you, Satch?"

A thick silence fills the room. I feel Jules stiffen beside me, then inevitably, the heat of her eyes bores into me. But I can't look at her because Woods and I have locked eyes. For twenty years I've loved my best friend, when things got bad, when he broke Billie's heart—I loved him. But now as I look at the man I used to skateboard with, then go to keg parties with, I feel nothing but contempt. Even as a boy, Woods was fickle. Our brown bag lunches at school were a perfect example. Every day my mother packed the same lunch for me: a ham sandwich, a banana, two Capri Suns. Woods would go through phases, swearing by roast beef sandwiches and then saying he'd never eat another and switching to turkey. He could never decide what he liked or wanted. That went for his extracurricular activities too: switching from football, to baseball, to piano lessons—all in the span of four months. He'd want to be a pro athlete and then he'd decide he'd rather be a musician. I can't even imagine the amount of money his mother lost every time he decided to take up a new hobby and then drop it. Before Billie, he'd dated a hippie named Zion for nine months. Zion had dreads and wore skirts with bells sewn into the hem. During their relationship, Woods grew a beard, got his nose pierced, and joined a yoga studio. He told me that he envisioned himself buying a ranch and growing his own vegetables (he was vegan now). We'd moved to New York together because we hated the suburbs, hated the slow drawl people from Georgia spoke with, and all of a sudden, he was talking compost piles and sustainable energy. He told Zion he loved her and they'd started looking at sapphire engagement rings (no blood diamonds for Zion), only to break things off as soon as Billie stepped into the picture. I'd thought he'd finally found himself when he got together with Billie. Hippie beard-wearing Woods transformed into New Yorker bar-hopping Woods. Suddenly, he was wearing a leather jacket that he pilfered from a thrift shop and talking about living in a loft. The first time we all went out to dinner together he ordered an eighteen-ounce ribeye.

"I thought you were a vegan," I'd said.

"Was being the keyword," he'd responded, sawing at his steak with a knife.

I thought who he was with Billie would stick. He was twenty-four walking around the Upper East Side with hearts in his eyes.

Woods doesn't know who he is and he slaughters hearts in his attempt to find out. It hasn't made a difference to me ... hell, I've even found it amusing, until he hurt someone I love —more than I love him.

"You should leave," I hear Jules say to him.

I hardly acknowledge his exit, choosing to stare at Billie's still form instead.

I hear the door click closed softly and then Jules comes to stand in front of me. *I don't want to do this right now,* I think. This is about Billie, not petty jealousy and pissing on each other for ownership. I think she's going to ask me about what Woods said, but instead, she smiles weakly and tells me she's going to get going.

"Sure," I say, still a little dazed.

I lean down to kiss her cheek, which makes her look even sadder than she did a minute ago. She doesn't ask me if I'm going to stay, or offer to bring me a change of clothes, and when she leaves, I'm so relieved I feel guilty.

"Mr. Tarrow?" A nurse steps in, jarring me from my thoughts. "Your mother is here to see Billie."

"Let her in," I say.

A minute later, Denise walks through the door.

"Hello, son," she says, raising her eyebrows. "Just coming to sit with Billie and her husband..."

I stare at Denise, who was like a second mother to me growing up. We still have the type of relationship where she smacks my arm if I give her attitude, and she kisses me on the cheek affectionately every time she sees me. This time, however, I don't get a kiss.

"Hello, Denise," I say dryly.

"I saw my son in the lobby," she offers. "He was fuming."

"Yeah?" My voice is bored.

"I wonder," she walks over to Billie's bedside and frowns down at her, "if he's mad at you or himself?"

I don't answer. This is how Denise communicates, with observations and statements. You are meant to deduct your own meaning and comment if you feel up to it; otherwise, she just keeps going.

She reaches out a hand to smooth Billie's hair, and suddenly, I wish someone would touch me, tell me everything's going to be all right.

"Woods is a lot like his father. He always comes back to his truth."

I want to tell her that she's giving Woods way too much credit ... he has no idea what his truth is.

"A person can't be your truth," I say.

Denise looks at me in surprise. I don't know if she's feigning it or if she's genuinely surprised by my statement. "Can't they?"

I falter and then say, "No," firmly.

She purses her lips nodding slowly. "So Billie isn't your truth?"

It feels like I just stuck my finger into a light socket; a current of electricity surges through my body.

"She isn't the one you've been holding everyone else against?"

I say nothing. How does she know that? Woods' mother is a witch.

"Our truth is something we know about ourselves without a doubt. It's woven into our DNA."

"Loving someone can't be in your DNA," I say.

"Really? Then why can't you get it out? Get Billie out?"

I'm breathing hard now. If she comes close, she'll be able to see my nostrils flaring with the effort it's taking to keep my emotions under wrap.

"You've dated everyone under the sun, and you keep coming back to Billie. Am I right?"

I don't answer.

"She's there now. All the time. Part of who you are. What you hold love against."

I don't understand why she's saying all of this until she makes her next statement.

"That's who Woods is to Billie. And who Billie is to Woods."

Everything in me goes cold and stiff. I feel like I've just turned to wood, and not in the good way.

"If you'll excuse me," I say to Denise. "I'm going to head home for a few hours if you'll be with her."

She waves me away, her eyes already on Billie. I can't get out of there fast enough.

CHAPTER THIRTY-ONE

When I get back to the hospital several hours later, showered and in clean clothes, Denise has been replaced by a woman I don't immediately recognize. She's slight with a short, neat haircut that doesn't quite reach her shoulders. Her cardigan is purple and so are her shoes. When she hears me come in, she turns her head without standing up. There's something about her profile, the aquiline nose and pouty lips...

"Mrs. Bolster?"

Billie's mother stands and I see that she's clutching a purple purse in both her hands.

"I'm Satcher," I say. "One of Billie's friends."

She smiles faintly. "I remember," she says. "From the wedding..."

That's right. How had I forgotten? It had been the one time I'd met Billie's parents.

"Has she...?"

She shakes her head. "No change," she says.

I walk over to the bed and stare down at Billie, wanting to touch her but also not wanting to freak her mom out.

"I'm so glad you're here," I say, and I mean it. Billie may claim that she has no close family ties, but in light of the accident, support is important.

"I saw Denise." Her eyes are glassy and I feel like she's just looking for something to say.

"Yeah. She was here before I left. She really cares about Billie."

"That's nice," she says. "That things could stay so civil after..."

"After...?"

"After Billie wanted a divorce."

"Right," I say.

So Billie had lied to her parents. I don't exactly blame her. It makes things easier for sure. When you are the one left in the relationship, you experience a level of pity and coddling from your loved ones that makes the whole situation feel worse. If she is the one who supposedly left Woods, she can shut down the questions, be aloof. Billie hates to be pitied, hates undue attention. The divorce equals a level of personal hell that is separate from the actual heartbreak.

"Has Woods been to see her?"

The question is fairly mild. It's her tone that's heartbreaking: hopeful. I wonder what type of relationship Woods had with her parents. Knowing him, he probably charmed the shit out of them.

"Yes," I say.

Her face lights up and I wonder how hard that part is for Billie, taking the fall for the end of the marriage, being the bad guy to her parents.

"That's nice," she says again.

Her voice sounds far away, like it's not part of this room, or Billie, or even New York. *She's here because she has to be*, I think. This is what Billie grew up with, this person ... this parent. I think about my own childhood, my own parents.

Jennifer and Jeff Gable, who have an abundance of emotion, especially when it comes to their children. We are a talk-it-out family, and I can guarantee that if I were the one lying in the hospital bed, my entire family would have flown in the first night, including all six of my sisters. They'd all be fighting, but they'd be here.

"Is Mr. Bolster here?" I ask.

She shakes her head. "He had to stay behind to take care of the house." Her voice is airy, barely there.

The house. Weak. Not a dog, or an ailing parent, or even a job—none of which are worthy of not being here for your daughter. The house. Something that doesn't need taking care of. I glance at Billie and my gut twists into a knot.

I have a dozen more questions for her, but I can tell she's already checking out of the conversation. I want to stay with Billie, but I feel awkward being here ... especially since I've just discovered how much I dislike her mother.

"Are you staying nearby?" I ask finally.

She shakes her head. "I have a red-eye flight tonight. I'll stay here with her for a few more hours."

"Tonight? But Billie hasn't even woken up..."

She frowns at my proclamation like she doesn't care to hear it.

"I can't stay away for much longer ... Steven..." Her voice trails off at the end of her excuse, too weak to verbalize.

I say the only thing I'm thinking, the only thing that matters. "Billie needs you."

She looks at Billie then and I notice that she's still clutching her purse, the knuckles of her fingers white like she's afraid someone is going to rip it from her grasp right here in the hospital. Big, bad New York. Always the villain to outsiders.

"I'm sorry," she says, shaking her head.

And I don't know if she's saying sorry to me, or Billie, or

the room in general. I glance at my watch, a ploy to leave the room before I tell this woman what I think of her.

"I have to go," I say with a brief nod.

And then I leave before she can respond. *It's the holidays*, I tell myself. She probably doesn't want to be away from home for the holidays. But even as I try to smooth over Mrs. Bolster's transgression, I can't. Billie is her family.

I decide to go back to my condo and wait it out. The fact that Billie hasn't woken up yet is a heavy weight around my heart. I want to be there when she does wake up. A couple of hours after I leave Mrs. Bolster at the hospital, I meet Jules for dinner. I didn't want to come, but with Jules leaving for home in the morning, I feel obligated to see her one last time. I'm so distracted I can't focus on anything she says to me.

"Satch, did you hear me?"

I set down my fork, which I've been holding without actually eating anything.

"No. I'm sorry," I say.

"You're worried about Billie, aren't you?"

I don't answer. It seems fairly obvious. We have plans to go to the hospital after our meal, but I'm dreading it.

I've become accustomed to holding back my feelings about Billie—careful constraint, an aloof tone when I speak to or about her, the way I've trained my eyes to only spill over her slightly so that no one notices. With her lying bruised in a hospital bed, it's harder to remain neutral. The only way I know how to deal with her question is to ask one of my own.

"Aren't you?"

"Of course," she says.

I tell her about seeing Billie's mother at the hospital, how she said she had to get back home instead of staying with her daughter who is in a coma.

"Maybe there's something we don't know," she suggests. "A

family sickness, or Billie's dad may not know how to use the microwave."

She's trying to lighten the mood, but I flinch anyway.

"You're probably right about the microwave," I say. I've drunk more than I've eaten. "Fuck," I say, rubbing my eyes. "I'm drunk."

Jules looks nonplussed. She looks at her phone. "Satcher..."

"Yup..."

"She's awake."

I stand up so suddenly the table wobbles, spilling my full glass of water. I toss bills on the table ... forty ... sixty ... eighty. Our dinner didn't cost that much, but I don't want to wait for the check. Jules grabs her jacket and scarf, and we're out the door less than four minutes later.

When we get to the hospital, Woods is already there waiting outside Billie's room. I tense up. I shouldn't have drunk as much as I did. I peer through the glass and see several nurses around her bed. I can't see anything but Billie's feet, a lump underneath the sheet. My mouth carries the bitter aftertaste of bourbon.

"What are they doing?" I ask gruffly. And then—"Where's her mother?"

"They're checking her vitals. The doctor is supposed to be here in a minute. And she left for the airport an hour ago. I texted her."

He texted her. Like he's still her husband. I'm being irrational. I try to shrug it off, wishing for the dozenth time that I hadn't had that last drink. I'm not an angry drunk exactly, but I'm irritable ... less tolerant. In college, Billie told me that I'm too controlled in my normal life, and when I drink I lose some of that. I want to fucking lose it on Woods.

The doctor nods at us on his way into Billie's room. He looks like a mad scientist: wiry, white hair poking up at odd angles, and a droopy face that looks like it's melting off his skull. We stand in the hall, tense and impatient. Woods glances down at his phone every few minutes. I want to ask him if Billie's mother is coming back, but I know I'll only be disappointed by his answer. Finally, the room clears out and we're allowed to see her. The doctor steps into the hall.

"Mr. Tarrow?" He looks at me.

"I'm Woods Tarrow." Woods steps toward the doctor with an air of importance.

"Billie's husband?" he asks.

Woods' face colors. "No ... I'm her ex-husband..."

The doctor frowns. "I'm afraid I can only release information to her husband."

"That's me," I say.

"She married brothers?" He doesn't wait for me to answer; instead, he launches into Billie's diagnosis. Concussion, sprained wrist, broken ankle, three cracked ribs, and severe bruising to her face. "She's going to need to take it easy. No stairs. We're going to keep her for another day to monitor her concussion."

"Thank you," I say when he finishes his spiel. "Can I see her?"

"You can," he says, eyeing Jules and Woods. "One at a time."

I nod. I ignore the stares Jules and Woods give me and push through the door. Billie is sitting up, but her eyes are closed. When she hears the door, she cracks open an eye.

"Hey," I say.

"Hi." Her voice is raspy. She licks her lips as I approach the bed. "They think you're my husband," she says.

"Yeah," I say, ducking my head. "I may have told them that."

She starts to laugh then immediately flinches. "Ow…"

"Lucky for you I'm not really that funny, so that was a one-time thing." I pull the chair up next to her and sit on the edge of it, leaning toward her.

"I can't believe I married a guy with such a sucky sense of humor."

I can't hide my smile. Here she is lying in a hospital bed cracked and bruised and she's making jokes.

"We were really worried about you," I say. "Took you a while to wake up."

"It takes me a while to do everything," she says. "I'm a slow learner."

"Apparently. Anyone ever teach you how to cross a street?"

Her chest heaves. "Stop being funny," she says. "It hurts."

"Your mom was here," I say. "She left to go home before she knew you woke up."

"Ah," is all she says.

"Listen, Billie, before they come in here I need to say sorry…"

"For what?"

"Well, I don't like your mom. But also for the argument we had. I was out of line."

This time she holds her ribs while she laughs. "It's fine, Satch. Honestly, I don't know what I was thinking. You were right to be pissed."

"No. It's none of my business."

"Okay," she breathes, "so let's just forget about it. Fighting isn't good for our marriage."

"Speaking of marriage," I say. "Woods is outside."

The smile drops off her face. "Oh…"

I perk up immediately. "Do you not want to see him? I can tell him to—"

"No, it's fine, Satcher," she says. "I suppose I need to put an end to all of this."

"Jules is here too."

"Okay. Maybe send Jules in first. Buy me some time so I can figure out what I'm going to say to Woods."

"I have a notebook. I can write something out for you."

"Shut up," she says, a grin on her face. And even with the black eyes, and the yellow bruises grazing her cheekbones and jaw—she's alarmingly beautiful.

I'm on my way toward the door when the words burn a path from my heart to my mouth. "Billie..."

She looks up from her lap, the smile still on her lips.

"I was scared. Scared I'd lose you forever. I don't know that I've ever been truly scared before this."

I can't tell if her eyes fill with tears or if it's a trick of the light.

"You're a good friend, Satcher," she says.

I force a smile. I don't want to be her friend.

The next day is the first day I feel like I can finally breathe in weeks. Jules leaves early for the airport. I see her off outside of my building, still wearing my pajama pants as I tuck her into a cab. She texts me from the airport to say she spotted Woods and Pearl heading to their gate.

I thought they left last night, I text back.

Jules' text comes back quickly and it's just one word: *delayed*.

It's a week till Christmas and the city has emptied out as New Yorkers make their pilgrimages home for the holidays. They're letting Billie go home tomorrow, but she will have to have surgery on her ankle right after Christmas. She grumbles at that news and I have to make jokes about the doctor's ear hair before she smiles again. I get my condo ready for her even though she doesn't know she'll be staying with me. The doctor gave me strict instructions that she's to take it easy to allow her ribs to heal. No stairs. Since my building has an elevator and hers doesn't, I made the executive decision to take her home with me. When I pick her up from the hospital the following afternoon, she's wearing a pink Adidas hoodie and sweatpants. I toss my beanie at her and she gently pulls it over her hair, flinching when her fingers graze the cuts on her forehead.

"How do I look?" she asks jokingly. She still has two bruised eyes and a split lip, but her smile is bright and beautiful.

I answer her honestly. "Like beautiful hell," I say.

Her laugh rings out in the hospital lobby, and heads swivel to find the source of joy.

Once in the cab, Billie stares out the window, her head propped on her fist, breath frosting the glass. Last-minute shoppers stream up and down the sidewalk, jackets pulled up around their faces as their gloved fingers grip shopping bags. When we stop outside of my building, she frowns.

"Why are we at your place?"

"This is where you're staying for a few weeks," I say, ignoring her sour look.

"Why? What's wrong with my place?"

I list off the reasons she can't go home yet and her frown only deepens.

"Doctor's orders," I say. "Besides, we're both here for the holidays, so we might as well make the best of it."

That seems to appease her. I carry her small bag into my building, walking slowly as she navigates her crutches over the cracks in the sidewalk. Her face is pinched in concentration and possibly pain, but when I ask her if she's hurting she shrugs it off like it's no big deal. My apartment is ready for her. I'd spent every moment I wasn't at the hospital doing things like stocking the fridge and changing the sheets on my bed. When I lead her into my bedroom, she stops abruptly in the doorway, shaking her head.

"No way. I'm not sleeping in your bed."

"Why not?" I ask.

Her face flushes and she mumbles something about Jules.

"You're injured," I argue. "Sleeping on the couch isn't an option."

She hesitates. "I can go home."

"Not an option either," I say. "Until you're walking without crutches."

She licks her lips, eyes darting around. She's trying to think up another excuse, but I've already beat her out, anticipating her bullshit excuses. There is no other option unless she wants to rent a hotel room for a few weeks. I tell her so.

We both know how hotels jack up their prices around the holidays. The resignation settles in her eyes, and I can visibly see her shoulders rise and fall in a sigh.

"Does Jules know?"

"Yes," I lie.

I haven't told Jules yet, but I plan on doing that tonight when she calls. It's a temporary win. Billie hobbles over to the couch and carefully lowers herself down.

*J*ules doesn't take the news as well as I expected.

"Satcher, you're my boyfriend. I know Billie is our friend, but you refused to come home with me for Christmas and now you're spending the holidays with a woman who isn't me."

I'm making a run to the liquor store, and as Jules' words hit my ears, I dart across the street to beat a cab.

"I didn't go home to see my own family," I say. "Billie has nothing to do with my staying in the city."

"I didn't say she did. I guess I'm just a little jealous," Jules admits.

I soften even though I'm still annoyed. "Jules," I say. "She's just had a terrible accident..."

Despite the loud noises of the city I hear her sigh on the other end of the line.

"I get it, okay. Like I said, I'm just a little jealous my boyfriend is spending Christmas with my gorgeous friend."

I see the liquor store up ahead and I don't want to be having this conversation anymore. I picture myself tearing off the lid of a bottle of vodka and taking a long swig, the powdery burn crawling slowly down my throat. *That can't be a good sign.* Wanting to chug liquor like a college kid when I talk to my girlfriend on the phone. I probably need to have a couple of deep thoughts about this very disturbing reality. The problem with thinking deeply about your behavior is that it has to be followed by personal accountability. Once you acknowledge you're being an ass, you either have to stop being an ass, or you have to embrace being an ass, and both options are uncomfortable.

I tell Jules I have to go. I can hear the hurt in her voice, the wavering like she's not sure what to say. Instead of feeling guilty, I feel irritated. My friends would say that I've been single for too long, and when someone comes along and tries to tell me what to do, I buck against it. But I don't believe that's the case at all. No, when you're with the right person, they can tell you to dance like a duck in Central Park while wearing a tutu and singing Liza Minnelli and you'll consider doing it. Love is a compelling drug.

By the time I am exiting the liquor store, my plastic shopping bags full of ingredients to make Billie her favorite drink, a rough idea is forming.

CHAPTER THIRTY-TWO

"Satcher..." Billie's arm is frozen midair, her fingers still clutching her phone when she looks at me. She's just hung up with Jules and I'm assuming Jules has told her.

"Satcher," she says again, and this time her tone edges on impatience, "you broke up with Jules five days before Christmas ... over the *phone?*"

"Yes."

She slams her phone down on the table and hobbles over. The bruises on her face have mostly faded; the color painting the underside of her eyes is a dull yellow. I watch the anger dance in her eyes as she glares up at me like a defiant child.

"What the hell were you thinking, you insensitive prick? You can't just treat people like that!" She's tossing things around, lifting jackets and the stack of paper bags I set aside for recycling. I want to ask her what she's looking for, but I'm too amused watching her. Finally, she finds it, a box wrapped with candy cane paper. The smile drops from my face as I watch Billie frown down at it. Jules had left the present before I set up the tree and made me promise to wait until she got back to open it. She said it was our present together. I'd meant to put it under the tree, but then I got preoccupied with Billie staying with me and forgot about it.

"What are you doing?"

Billie is rolling the package around in her hands thoughtfully.

"Nothing. Jules just wanted me to retrieve this for her."

"Retrieve? Did Jules say the word *retrieve*?"

"Yes," Billie says without looking up.

So I am a transaction now. Jules has reverted to business speak, her way of being cold. The knife slices through the lemon skin, spraying a mist of vinegar. I can feel Billie's eyes on me again, hot and angry.

"What, Billie? Spit it out."

"I don't know if I want to," she says. "This is awkward and I'm in the middle of two friends..."

"Drink."

"What?" Her eyes are glazed over as she stares at me in confusion.

"I made you a drink."

Her face contorts like she's not sure she wants to take my drink. In the end, she reaches out to grasp the stem looking disgusted with herself. Billie can't say no to alcohol. It's her vice.

"Only because it's a lemon drop," she says.

She takes a sip and I can tell she's half expecting it to be disappointing because her face is surprised after her first swallow. I raise my eyebrows in question and she blinks in annoyance.

"What? It's good, okay?"

"You're so angry about it," I say, turning away to hide my smile.

"Because I'm annoyed with you, Satcher ... because you're ... annoying."

"Have you ever thought there's a reason you find me so annoying?" I lean my forearms on the counter in front of her and she does good work avoiding eye contact. I watch as she toys with some stray granules of sugar on the counter, picking them up with the pad of her finger and then rolling them around.

"All of a sudden?" She rolls her eyes. "And no. Some people just *are* annoying."

"Is that right?" I straighten up, propping my hands on my hips as I stare at her. "You've never complained before..."

"What are you saying?"

I can't keep the grin off of my lips and she's avoiding looking at me because of it. I want to tell her that I know her so well. That when she likes something she pretends she doesn't just to test her own self-control. That the fact that I've just made her the world's greatest lemon drop makes her angry because she's looking for reasons to be mad at me.

"I don't want to put words in your mouth, Billie, but I once heard you say that you're turned on by men who can mix a great drink."

"I was drunk when I said that. I didn't mean it. And stop using my own words against me."

She slides off the barstool, testing her ankle cautiously on the ground before taking a step. She's halfway to the living room when she swivels back around, having forgotten her glass.

"Just because I don't want to waste," she says, hobbling back over. "Men who have girlfriends shouldn't make other women drinks."

I laugh louder than I intended. "I didn't know that was a thing," I say. "You're so spiteful on pain meds."

. . .

*H*er mood only gets worse when I make dinner. By the time I'm clearing the dishes away she's despondent and glaring at everything but me. I shouldn't be enjoying this, but I am.

"Go to bed," I say.

"Don't tell me what to do," she snaps. "I'm an adult."

I raise my eyebrows as I finish emptying the dishwasher. "Well, it was a suggestion, but if you'd rather stay up all night, be my guest." I slam the dishwasher shut and head to the living room, but she calls me back.

"Satcher!"

"What?"

She shakes her empty glass at me.

"No more," I tell her. "That was a treat. You're on too many pain meds."

"Ugh!" She storms off to the bedroom and slams the door. An adult temper tantrum.

I smile, remembering the perils of growing up with six sisters, the constant yelling and slamming of doors. The more ridiculous she is, the more I'm endeared. The realization makes me shifty ... uncomfortable.

Two hours later, I am sitting with my legs propped on the ottoman getting ready to start a movie when I hear the bedroom door open. She appears in the doorway and I keep my eyes averted to the TV. My chest is bare since I was anticipating bed—the only thing I'm wearing are the flannel Christmas pajama bottoms my mother faithfully sends every year. Without looking up, I pat the seat next to me. She only hesitates for a moment before coming over. I'm surprised when she curls next to me, more surprised when she places her head in my lap. When she starts to cry, my hands automatically find her hair, her face, her back. I stroke and rub as she weeps and weeps.

"I'm sorry," she says finally. Her voice is tear-clogged. "For being an ass."

I don't say anything. I rub her back as Will Ferrell pours syrup over his spaghetti.

"Satcher," she says.

"Yeah..."

"You're a really good man. Thank you."

I get up to make her another lemon drop.

CHAPTER THIRTY-THREE

The next morning I find Billie already sitting at the island, staring into a cup of coffee. It's three days until Christmas and I want to propose an outing that could potentially cheer her up.

"Will you let me put a smile on your face today?" I ask, stepping around her to the coffee pot.

She looks up slowly and I see her eyes are still puffy from last night. It only adds to her beauty unfortunately, and I look away to avoid obvious staring.

"Satcher..."

"Don't," I say, holding up a hand. "Whatever excuse you're going to shoot at me, just let it go, and let me put a smile on your face today."

Her face contorts as she struggles with her answer. I hold my breath—that's a thing—I actually hold my breath waiting for her answer.

"But, there's something you should know—"

"I don't want to know anything. I just want to do Christmas shit and see you smile."

"That's so cheesy." She sighs.

"Good idea. We should do fondue for dinner. I know a place..."

"Satcher!"

"Shut up," I say. "Get ready."

For whatever reason, she obeys, shuffling off to my bedroom to get ready. When she emerges twenty minutes later, she's wearing a floor-length black dress that's long enough to cover the boot on her left foot. She has her leather jacket thrown over one arm, and in the other, she's holding a scarf and hat. To hide the bruises around her eyes, she's put on dark smoky makeup and bright red lipstick.

"Wow, you look like college Billie," I say.

She grins. "Emo Billie then?"

I fist bump her in response and suddenly, I feel scruffy and underdressed.

"Ten minutes," I say. "I have to go change."

She settles on a stool at the island in the kitchen, propping her good foot on the stiles of the stool and planting her boot flat on the floor. My bedroom smells like Billie: her perfume, her skin, her lotions. I step over her duffel bag, which is lying next to my closet doors, clothes piling out of it like spilled organs. I text my doorman instructions and make quick work of changing and putting on cologne, and we're out the door in under ten minutes. I managed to smuggle my heated blanket under my coat, and when we emerge on the street in front of my building, I slip Fred a twenty and take Billie's arm to steer her across the icy sidewalk.

"I'm regretting this already." She frowns. "It's cold. Why are we even leaving your nice warm apartment?"

"Because you're turning witchy. You need fresh air and Christmas cheer."

"Fuck that," she says. "I need a drink."

"And a drink you shall have," I say, leading her to the curb where our ride is waiting.

Billie looks past it at first, no doubt searching for a cab. When I step up to the horse-drawn carriage, her laugh rings out, making me warm all over.

"No. Seriously? Are you for real?"

She's pulling off her gloves to fondle the horse's nose. He charmingly dips his head, licorice-colored lips searching her palm for a treat. The driver (who introduces himself as Phil) gives her a sugar cube and she feeds it to the horse, giggling when he nips her palm searching for more.

"What's his name?" I hear her ask. "Oh my God, Peppermint? Are you for real?" she says to the driver. "His name is Peppermint!" she calls out to me.

Once I've helped her into the carriage, I climb in after her and spread the heated blanket around us. The driver shows us where we can find more blankets and hands us a thermos and two cups of hot buttered rum.

"Oh my God, oh my God!" Billie wriggles in her seat like a little girl, eyes lit up in excitement. "Where are we going? Will he take us to see Rockefeller Center?"

"He'll take us wherever we want," I say.

"No shit." Her eyes are large and excited. "I'm going to get so drunk! This is great!"

The carriage lurches forward. I blink rapidly when Billie finds my hand under the blankets and squeezes softly, her tiny little fingers tangling with mine.

"Thank you. I forgot what excitement feels like." Her eyes are misty when I look at her.

For the next fifteen minutes, Peppermint trots confidently forward while we sip our hot buttered rum and stare at the magic of the city under her Christmas spell. When we pull up to the first pub, Billie's tossing off her blankets and hiking up her dress so our driver can help her down.

"You have twenty minutes at each place," he says, winking at me. "Enough for a quick nip and some kissing." He has a heavy Irish brogue and even heavier white eyebrows that are collecting snow even as he wags them at me.

"It's snowing," Billie calls from the doorway of the pub.

I run to catch up to her and we push inside the warm interior of The Dog and the Drink, the smell of stale beer and wood polish replacing the city smells. I watch Billie's face lit by the lights from the bar and her enjoyment. My father always said that there was nothing more beautiful than my mother's face when she was excited. He was the type of man who, for my entire childhood, went out of his way to get a favorable reaction from his wife, his newest stunt always outdoing his last. Over the years, I've watched him build her a greenhouse, a gazebo, a fire pit with swings around it, a koi pond, and finally, an art studio when she said the spare bedroom didn't have the right light or enough space.

Seeing Billie's face transform over a carriage ride and some beer does something nostalgic and important to my heart. I understand my father in a way I never have before, always discrediting romance as a ploy rather than something pure from the heart. And yet here I am—many women would call me a dick, a prick, a philanderer—baking up ways to make my best friend's ex-wife swoon. Pathetic.

We order two pints and stand at the bar drinking our beer out of old-fashioned steins, listening to the eighties music playing over the speakers. When our time is up, we make our way back to Peppermint. Phil is smoking with his back leaning against the horse, watching the front of the pub. Billie asks if she can hold his cigarette. He pulls out his pack to give her one, but she shakes her head.

"I just need to hold it," she says.

He hands it over and she closes her eyes as the smoke wafts toward her face. Phil and I exchange a look, but then she's handing it back and holding out her arm for help into the carriage.

"Where to next?" she asks, pulling the blankets to her chin. "Do you think Phil washes these?" she whispers.

"I do not," I reply, giving her warning eyes.

She pulls my blanket up around us and then lays Phil's questionable ones over the top of it so they're not touching us. Under the blankets, her hand reaches for mine.

"Is that your cigarette hand?" I tease.

"Shut up." She smiles. "I miss it, you know? I just want to pretend sometimes."

"Pretend you're on your way to lung cancer! Excellent idea."

"God, when did you become such a goody two-shoes?" she asks. "As far as I can remember you used to smoke them with me."

"I was just trying to hang," I say.

Billie leans forward and calls out to Phil. "I need two fags, Phillip."

He looks at her, confused.

"Cigarettes," she reiterates, rolling her eyes.

Phil hands her two Marlboros and his lighter.

"No, Billie, absolutely not," I say as she lights one up.

"For old times' sake, Sasquatch."

She puffs until the cherry glows bright red and turns to stick the remaining cigarette in my mouth. I don't protest when she leans toward me, allowing her cigarette to light the one propped between my lips. My mouth has no trouble remembering what to do. Billie watches me through slightly narrowed eyes as my cheeks concave to pull the acrid smoke into my lungs. She doesn't cough at all, but I heave as if this is my first time.

"Out of practice, old man." She grins.

She blows smoke through lips so candy-apple red I want to lean over and taste them. Her lipstick would get all over my face and I would love every second of it. I have more inappropriate thoughts about her lipstick on other parts of my body as we turn a corner and she leans into me. Goddamn. I rub a hand over my face trying to ignore my dick, which is swelling.

Our cigarettes are stubs now; we pinch them between our fingers as we smile at each other.

"Just two old people trying too hard," I tell her, flicking the butt into a grate as we drive by.

"What? No!" She feigns offense. "We've totally still got it!"

The carriage jerks to a stop, and Billie breaks eye contact with me to look around.

"Are we going shopping?"

Peppermint has come to a stop outside of a crowded department store. A steady stream of shoppers pushes through a revolving door, their faces alternating between blissful and murderous. I help Billie down and she wobbles awkwardly on her boot as she waits for me to speak to Phil.

"We have thirty minutes," I say, grabbing her hand.

"Okay. What are we shopping for?"

"Each other," I tell her. "Twenty-dollar limit."

She stops dead, forcing me to backtrack or get run over by the determined pedestrians.

"Where do you think this is? Target? You can't buy a shoelace in Barneys for twenty dollars," she says.

"Fifty," I counter. "And we have thirty minutes to choose wisely."

We fist bump and separate once we're inside. Billie hobbles right toward the elevators, and I take a left through the makeup and perfume. I have no idea what I'm looking for and I already bought Billie a Christmas present. Slightly buzzed from the beer and hot buttered rum in Phil's flask, I wander aimlessly, hoping something catches my eye before Phil and Peppermint get a ticket for loitering. I spot something in the home department I think she'd like. It's a hundred and twenty dollars, but I grab it anyway and carry it to a register. The button Billie gave me sits at the bottom of my coat pocket. My fingers brush it as I search for my phone. I think about asking Billie about it, but there's something about that night when she handed it to me that feels sacred. If I ask and she tells me, the spell will be broken. I don't even know what the fuck that means, but it feels true. Billie is already waiting in the carriage with a broad smile on her face, when I emerge. I hop in and she automatically snuggles closer to me, hungry for warmth.

"Well...?" she says. "Do we do this now or later?"

She's bouncing in her seat, a little sparking livewire. I kiss her nose because we're that close and her eyes crease in a smile.

"Stop being cute," she says. She rolls her eyes, but it doesn't matter because they're dancing with a light I haven't seen in a while.

"Okay," I say. "You first."

She grabs a bag from her feet just as Peppermint lurches forward and proffers it at me with an alcohol-induced enthusiasm. We bump heads and then laugh as we rub the sore spots.

As I dig around the tissue paper, my mind once again goes to the button. Billie is watching me anxiously. My fingers brush against something hard at the bottom of the bag. She chews on her lip, her face somewhere between excitement and nervousness. When I pull my hand out I'm not exactly sure what I'm looking at.

"What is it?" I turn it over in my hand. It looks like a very bright, very knobby doll made entirely of ... wait for it ... buttons. Buttons of every color and size make up its face, limbs, and torso. I stare into its black button eyes, confused.

"It's a button baby," she says sweetly.

"A button baby?" I repeat.

She nods, taking it from me. "The idea is that if you need a button—say if you lost one on your coat—you'd find a replacement on this guy. Also, you know all those extra buttons that come with shirts and pants and whatnot?"

I nod. She turns over the button baby and shows me a zipper. "You put them in here for when you need them."

"Hmmmm." I reach into my pocket, deciding it's the right time to bring up the white button she gave me the night of the Rhubarb Christmas party. I hold it out to her and her face lights up. She carefully takes it from my palm and deposits it inside of the button baby, zipping it closed to keep the button safe.

"Sooo ... about that button..."

"You don't remember, do you?"

I can see the disappointment on her face and it makes me feel like crap. I almost suggest that she has the wrong person, the real owner of the button memory can't possibly be me.

"I—I don't."

Her laugh fills my ears. "Well ... maybe you will someday. And then my Christmas present won't seem stupid."

"Why can't you just tell me?"

Billie shakes her head, a coy smile teasing her lips. "Not today. You'll remember one day."

I frown at her.

"Now me." She holds out her hand, wiggling her fingers.

I pull my less confusing gift from between my feet and hold the bag out to her. "I'm afraid my gift has no deep, forgotten meaning."

"Oh, hush..."

She reaches into the bag just as Peppermint guides us over a pothole and whatever she's holding drops from her fingers before she can see it. She swears colorfully before plunging her hand inside again, and when it emerges, much to my relief she starts to laugh. I can't help but join her. Just past the makeup I'd found a jewelry station where using tiny letters you could build your own bracelet to say anything you wanted. I'd chosen a silver bracelet for Billie and then spelled out the words: *Fuck Wendy*.

"My God, Satcher. What did you have against Wendy anyway?"

"She wasn't you," I say. "She was a modified version."

"True that." Billie sighs, slipping the bracelet over her wrist. "Well, I'm back. Full force."

I don't have time to respond; we've arrived at the next pub.

"Shall we?" I hop down from the carriage and hold out my hand.

Phil gives us a little more time for dinner since all we've had sloshing around in our stomachs for four hours is alcohol.

"Eat!" he calls as we walk toward the restaurant. "Or you will drown from the inside out."

Billie is sleepy-eyed when we slide into the tiny corner table. She tucks her hair behind her ears then rests her hands flat on the table while she waits for me to shrug out of my coat and sit. She's beautiful—a little windblown, the tip of her nose kissed pink. There is a deep recess in my heart, a place I keep shut up, that aches whenever I look at Billie. For that reason I look away, at anything but her.

"Can I ask you a personal question?"

She glances up from her menu, eyebrows raised.

"I suppose so," she says, setting it down. "Will it make me cry?"

"Oh God," I say. "Please don't. I don't do well with crying women."

"I highly doubt that, Satcher. With the trail of broken hearts you leave, I bet you're good at comfort."

I grin. She's right, of course.

We pause to give our orders to the server. Once he's gone, Billie turns to me. "Shoot," she says.

"Why did you tell your parents you were the one who left Woods?"

Her lips disappear as she folds them in and looks away.

"How do you know about that?"

"The hospital ... your mother..."

"Ah," she says. "Did you tell her the truth?"

I shake my head.

"Thanks." Her voice is soft, and my heart feels her sadness in such a way that I'm compelled to touch her, as if I can soak some of it up.

"They'd have blamed me. No matter what—" she says quickly when she sees the expression on my face. "If Woods cheated on me it would mean I was failing him in some way. I guess I didn't want to hear it, you know?"

"Understandable."

She fidgets with the strap of her bag, one side of her mouth screwed into her cheek.

"Does it make you think of me differently?"

"No. Of course not. God, I've told my mom the reason I'm not married is because I have a small dick and no one will have me," I tell her.

"Ah well, what a lie that is," she sings, and her eyes dance with mischief.

"She knows that. She changed my diapers for three years."

We're laughing when the server delivers our drinks. High on penis jokes at my expense. I love it. I love that she doesn't censor herself for anyone, and I love that she teases me mercilessly. When you date as many women as I have, you learn that everyone has a construct they want to portray.

Personalities become like outfits: carefully curated, a smokescreen for the brokenness inside. It's hard to tell what's underneath the layers everyone is wearing. Billie is the first woman I've met who comes at you naked. She admits when she's wrong, isn't afraid of telling you the terrible truth about what she's done, and doesn't have a secret agenda. She is what she is and that's exactly what I fell in love with.

"Sláinte," I say, raising my glass.

"Sláinte," she says, meeting my eyes.

We click glasses.

CHAPTER THIRTY-FOUR

We spend the next day in my apartment lying on the couch, recovering from our exuberant drinking efforts from the day before. Billie chooses the movies, and to my surprise, she picks entirely non-romantic storylines instead of the holiday films I thought she'd go for. We spread cream cheese on crackers and sip at our huge tumblers of water, reminding each other to hydrate. For lack of a better word, I find the afternoon sweet in its simplicity—easy. But that's the way it's always been with Billie. At one point, I find myself lying with my head in her lap. Casually, Billie plays with my hair as Liam Neeson issues his famous *"I'll find you"* into the phone. My eyes drift closed and I wake up to the credits as Billie lifts her arms over her head in a stretch. Between movies, we take turns complaining about how sick we feel, and around six, Billie offers to make breakfast for dinner. It's snowing outside when I join her in the kitchen, the lights from the Christmas tree casting lazy reflections on the window.

"This is kind of fun, you know." She cracks the last egg into the bowl and tosses the shells. "Like a sleepover…"

I grin over the top of her head and hand her the bowl of onions she asked me to dice. "Does that mean I get to share the bed with you tonight?"

Her laugh is halfhearted.

"My mother told me she still feels like she's having a sleepover with my dad after thirty-six years," I tell her.

My parents largely grossed their children out for much of our adolescence. As adults, we've learned to appreciate their love fest, but we all still look away when they make out like two teenagers.

"That's sweet," she says, avoiding my eyes. "My parents don't talk to each other unless it's to comment on the weather."

"That's depressing." I pop a cherry tomato in my mouth as I try not to let on how closely I'm watching her reactions.

"Yeah. I wanted the opposite of their marriage. And look at me now. Marriageless. An old divorcée with no prospects."

I snigger. "Oh, please. You'd have plenty of prospects if you were ready."

She pretends not to hear me as she searches through the silverware drawer. I listen to the clatter of metal and frown.

"Spatula?" I dig it out of a different drawer and hand it to her.

Our fingers brush and she pulls her hand away like I've shocked her.

"Were you truly happy with Woods?" I think about her blog post. I'd read it on my parents' couch—three times, four—wondering if it was the idea of love she'd been in love with rather than Woods.

"I don't know. I was ignorant, I guess. So in a way ... yeah. He fulfilled my idea of marriage and I enjoyed that."

"And the person you are now, the woman you've become—would she be happy in a marriage with Woods?"

I'm surprised when she laughs.

"No," she says. "This person is much more complicated."

"Then why do you still want to be with him?"

Her hands still. She sets everything down and turns around to face me, leaning her back against the counter as she dries her hands on a dish towel.

"Because we made a commitment. We were supposed to fight through it. I was willing."

"Then why did you leave? Why didn't you stay and fight?"

Her lips move, but the words stay trapped in her throat.

She withdraws completely after that, her smile disappearing from her face. I should ask why, but I'm partially amused by the way she keeps glancing at me when she thinks I'm not looking. After we eat, she's frowning down at her empty plate when I finally ask what's bothering her.

"I have to tell you something," she says. "I don't know if I should. But I'm in a tough position and I've honestly lost sight of who I'm betraying at this point."

I lean back in my seat having already pushed my plate away.

"Jules?"

She nods slowly.

"Okay..." I crack my knuckles, surveying the kitchen.

Billie's tongue is locked in her promise to Jules. I'll have to guess if I want to find out.

"I need to know where to start," I say.

She turns her head to look at the counter and I follow her eyes. The present Jules wrapped and left at my house sits next to the knife block. It wasn't there before so I assume Billie put it where I could see it.

"Do you want me to open it?"

She shrugs casually, though her eyes are wild.

"Billie...?"

She shrugs again, her eyes blinking slowly like she's trying to convey the importance of Jules' gift.

"Okay. All right. I'm going to open it. It's my fault, not yours…"

I retrieve the package, hoping its placement by the knife block isn't an omen, and turn it over in my hand. Billie stares at it like she's afraid.

"You're freaking me out, Billie."

"I'm freaking out," she says. "Bad."

I stare from her to the package in my hand in confusion.

"Give me a clue," I say.

Without a word, she stands up and walks into the kitchen. I watch as she gets two shot glasses from the cabinet and then retrieves a bottle of tequila from my bar.

"That's sipping tequila," I tell her. "Very expensive."

"Good, then it'll go down smooth and work fast."

I don't argue as she pours us each a shot and slides mine across the counter. I pick it up, never removing my eyes from her face.

"What would Jules give you that she'd want you both to open together?"

"I have no clue."

She bites her lip and holds up her shot glass, motioning for me to do the same. Our heads tilt back at the same time.

"If you were a happy couple who planned on being together for the rest of your lives…" Her voice breaks.

I watch as she chews on the inside of her cheek, clearly at odds with her loyalty. Her eyebrows are arched over her eyes and she seems to be urging me toward the answer by raising them higher.

I suddenly feel cold all over. "Billie … no … are you…? Is she…?"

She doesn't answer me. My hands shake as I unwrap the box, the tequila curdling in my stomach like sour milk. Underneath the cheerful wrapping of bows and candy canes is a simple white cardboard box. I lift the lid, my hands shaking.

"Fuck." I drop everything on the counter.

"I'm assuming you know what that is," Billie says dryly.

I rub a hand across my face. "You've known about this and you didn't say anything? Goddammit, Billie."

"She asked me not to."

I bend down to retrieve the slender white stick lying between my feet. Before flipping it over, I turn to Billie who is looking at everything except me.

"Is this a positive pregnancy test?"

She nods. I breathe through my nose trying to calm myself. In my often scandalous years of being a bachelor I've never once had a pregnancy scare. I turn the foreign white stick over in my hand and stare down at the single word in the tiny rectangular box: PREGNANT. Everything freezes when I see that word. How many days has she been gone? I count in my mind. I ended our relationship what—three ... four days ago?

I turn to Billie. "Is she still pregnant?"

"I don't know. I've texted her, but she hasn't answered me. I think she's angry with me too?"

I run a hand through my hair wishing I'd insisted on seeing what was in that box sooner. But how could I have known? Jules and I have never spoken about children. She brought marriage up on several occasions, and though I hadn't engaged with the idea, I'd not discouraged it either. It must have been nerve-racking for her to put that test in a box and wrap it without knowing what my reaction would be. In a blur, I search for my phone. I need to call Jules. Billie is pacing back and forth across the kitchen, eyeing the liquor cabinet.

I point at her and say, "No." Firmly.

"Why not?" she fusses. "This is stressful."

"You drink too much. And if I have to do this sober, so do you."

She throws her hands up in the air. "Who said you had to be sober?"

I find my phone under a pile of our discarded blankets in the living room and dial Jules' number. I sit on the couch waiting for her to pick up; Billie leans on the doorway looking like she's about to throw up. Jules' voice is sleepy when she answers.

"Hey," I say.

"Hey back."

I scratch the back of my head wondering why I didn't think some words through before I made this call.

"So, I opened the present you left..."

There's silence on the other end of the line.

"Are you still—"

"Yes," she says quickly.

I breathe a sigh of relief, massaging my forehead where I'm starting to feel the prickle of a headache.

"Are you okay?"

I can hear her breathing on the other end of the line, slow methodical breaths pressing back tears.

"I'm okay," she says finally.

"Have you told anyone?"

"No. Why would I? Look, you broke up with me. I get it. You don't want to be with me, and I don't expect anything from you. I'll deal with it."

"I don't want you to have an abortion—I mean, unless you want to have one." I wait for her to say something. "I'll support you through whatever you decide," I finish.

I feel like an ass. Here she is trying to have Christmas with her family, and not only did she find out she was pregnant, but I broke up with her before she could even tell me.

I hear the sound of sniffling and I press the phone tighter to my face, my heart wrenching in my chest.

"Jules..." I say softly.

"Yeah."

She's crying. Oh God, she's heartbroken and it's my fault. I smell Billie before I see her; the mellow scent of woman muddled with her perfume that always makes me think of the jasmine bush outside my parents' kitchen window. It's intoxicating. My head swims. She touches my shoulder, her warmth seeping past my shirt and warming my skin. It's comforting and disconcerting at the same time. The woman I love consoling me after I got her best friend pregnant.

"It's going to be all right. Okay?"

"Okay," she says.

We hang up after that and neither Billie nor I say anything about the call. She dutifully does the dishes while I clean up the living room of the tossed blankets and candy wrappers. After that we go to bed. Tomorrow is Christmas, though neither of us feels like celebrating.

CHAPTER THIRTY-FIVE

I wake up to pounding on my front door. It's cold. I wrap a blanket around my shoulders and stumble to the front door, almost tripping over Billie's abandoned shoes. I kick them aside and when I open the door, my elderly neighbor, Mrs. Chartuss, is standing there in her robe, a strange hat on her head. Upon closer inspection, I realize it's not a hat, but fat foam rollers. I've never seen her anything but styled and ready in one of her various fur coats.

"Mrs. Chartuss," I say, pulling the blanket tighter around my shoulders. "Merry Christmas."

She frowns at me like I'm the one knocking on her door at the crack of dawn on Christmas morning.

"I'm Jewish," she says curtly.

"Happy Holidays then," I correct. "What can I do for you?" Behind me I hear the bedroom door open and Billie's footfalls.

"Power's out," she says. "Whole building. I loaned you a flashlight two years ago..."

"Yes, you did," I say. "Let me grab it for you." I leave her at the door looking disgruntled while I get the flashlight from the hall closet. No wonder it was so cold. Just for good measure, I flick the light switch in the hall. The light stays stubbornly off. Great. When I hand it to her, she mumbles a comment about it having fresh batteries and shuffles back to her own front door.

"Well," I say, closing the door behind her and turning to Billie. "Christmas is canceled."

"It's always been canceled." Billie yawns.

"No. Nope. Get dressed. We can't stay here. We'll freeze."

"I'm sure they'll get it on soon," she says. "Don't panic."

"It's Christmas and it's snowing. There's no way. The owner of this building can barely be reached for emergencies."

"Okay. So where are we going?" She lifts her hands to rub at her arms, which are scattered with goose bumps like she's just figuring out it's cold.

"Somewhere warm," I tell her.

"Mmm, Florida," she says dreamily.

Surprisingly, she doesn't argue; instead, she disappears into the bedroom to get dressed. An hour later, we're on the road. Billie turns her seat warmer to maximum heat and burrows into the leather like an animal in its nest.

The drive Upstate takes less time than I planned, the highways mercifully empty. We don't talk much. We listen to Christmas music with an occasional anti-holiday comment from Billie.

"Why are you such a Scrooge anyway?" I say. "From what I recall, you used to love the holidays."

"You mean when I had a husband and a home and I could cook those stupid meals, and decorate that stupid tree, and pretend I was living in a 1950s sitcom?"

I flinch.

"Point taken," I say. "But today ... today we celebrate.

Consider it your first year back from your Christmas sabbatical."

"But I don't want to," she grumbles.

"Too bad." I reach over and lower the heat. It's starting to feel like Florida in here.

"Where are we going anyway?" She sips on the paper cup of coffee she made me stop for before we got on the freeway.

"You'll see."

"Why can't you just tell me?" she gripes.

"Because I don't want to hear your complaints."

She grunts like she's too tired to argue, and I don't try to stifle my smile. Even when she's playing the part of the Grinch she's cute. I immediately toss that thought from my head. I've just found out I am going to be a father. I don't need to be mentally listing all of Billie's charms.

I park my car against the curb exactly an hour later and glance up at the expansive snow-covered lawn. To the rear of the property sits an impressive Victorian with a wraparound porch. A curl of smoke lifts into the sky from the fireplace, and it seems that all the windows (and there are a lot of windows) are lit by flickering yellow light that I know from experience are tiny faux candles my mother uses to decorate. I hop out of the car and walk around Billie's side to open her door.

"You didn't," she says, eyes large. She studies the house, a look of trepidation on her face.

"I didn't what?"

"Bring me to your home for Christmas..." she hisses. "Oh my God, oh my God—who is that?"

I look over my shoulder to see my mother standing in the doorway, arms crossed as she waits for us.

Billie slides down in her seat so that her head is resting where her lower back should go. "Is that your *mother*?" she whispers.

"Yes," I say, glancing at the door again. "Looks like she's waiting for us..."

"I didn't even put makeup on," she says miserably. "I look like a joke."

"Well, yes, you do," I say, eyeing the way she's slouched down in her seat. "You look like my niece when she's throwing a tantrum."

"Ugh!" She scrunches up her nose as I offer my hand to help her out of the car.

I notice as we walk up the path toward the front door that she stops complaining and a look of interest fills her face. There are noises coming from the house: squeals of joy from my nieces and nephews, my eldest sister's bellowing laugh. They are happy sounds, the kind that fill me with a grateful warmness. We are greeted with the type of enthusiasm saved for holidays. My mother, an elegant woman of fifty-nine, greets Billie with a hug and then holds her at arm's length, declaring that she's the prettiest girl I've ever brought home. My mother, who is beautiful herself with thick auburn hair she wears in a twist and bright blue eyes, looks like she could be Billie's mother. Billie blushes furiously at the compliment before it's my turn to be greeted. I note Mom's cherry-print apron with fondness as she embraces me, Billie waiting just past her shoulder in the foyer. She's worn the same apron since I was a child; my sisters ride her for it constantly, but my mother doesn't care. It's her apron and she loves it. The real question is how she's managed to keep it in such good condition for so long. The thing looks brand new.

"I'm about to put breakfast on the table," she says, leading us into the living room, which looks like a warzone of paper, and toys, and tiny screaming humans that resemble my sisters.

In a flash, I'm a human jungle gym as eleven of my nieces and nephews run at me screaming excitedly. The oldest is ten and the youngest has just spat up on my shirt. I kiss both their heads as everyone looks curiously at Billie.

I introduce her around the room to the various spouses, and aunts and uncles, and by the time I'm done she looks thoroughly overwhelmed.

"Come on." My mother grabs her by the arm. "I need help in the kitchen ... and I have mimosas..." I hear her whisper.

I watch as Billie gratefully allows herself to be led in the direction of the kitchen. When she's gone the questions start.

"Is that your girlfriend?" my niece asks. "She's really pretty."

"Just a friend." I tug on her ponytail as my sisters round on me.

"But who—?"

"Where did you—?"

"What does she—?"

"Whoa, whoa!" I hold up my hands to silence them. "Merry Christmas to you too. And stop being so damn nosy."

"You haven't brought a girl home since 2014," my sister Heidi says. "What was her name—?" She snaps her fingers looking around the room for help.

"Gladys!" my grandmother calls out. She jabs her bent finger into the air in triumph.

"Gladys was your sister's name, Nana," my sister Beatrice says, patting her knee.

"Oh."

"Glenda!" my father calls from the carpet where he's assembling a toy for one of my nephews.

"Noooo, it was Gloria," someone else says.

"It was Gillian," I say mildly. "But you were all too drunk to remember that—especially you, Nana," I say, kissing her on the forehead.

She reaches up to pat my cheek. "Your mother spikes the eggnog," she complains. "It wasn't my fault."

I look past her to the kitchen doors wondering what my mother is up to in there. I hear a burst of laughter that I identify as Billie's and immediately relax. They emerge five minutes later carrying dishes toward the table.

At breakfast, we pass the food around while discussing my mother's apron at great length.

"It shouldn't still look brand new," Heidi says. "It's witchcraft."

"She's had that thing since we were kids..." Beatrice explains to Billie. "We talk about this every time we're together."

"Because she won't tell us how it is that she wears the damn thing every day and it looks new." Nora spoons eggs onto her plate. She's in her last trimester of pregnancy and her belly is so large she can't scoot close to the table.

My mother grins like the Cheshire cat and winks at Billie, who in return beams back at her. How often had I imagined bringing Billie home to meet my family? I'd probably be ashamed to admit. And here she is, just like I imagined, fitting right in with the Gable crowd.

"So Billie, you're the brain behind Rhubarb," Nora says. "You know I read that thing before my brother ever bought it from you. I was quite surprised when he told us."

"And how do you think he's done with it?" Billie leans forward in her seat. "Being a longtime reader..."

Nora smiles at me. "Well, I may be partial, but my brother has the Midas touch. And if anything, his smartest move was bringing you back on."

Billie blushes furiously. If she were sitting next to me I'd reach out to squeeze her knee. My mother, ever being the proactive hostess, seated her between Beatrice and herself. I know the seating arrangement is for the purpose of grilling Billie.

I'm seated between my uncle and father. We make small talk about work while I sneak glances at Billie. Her hair is wild; without the use of her straightener the curls have made themselves known. I want to tell her that I prefer her hair this way—but I know she'll just dismiss my comment. My father, who has been a detective in New York's precinct for twenty years, catches on and raises his eyebrows at me. I shrug. Later, we switch roles; the men are in the kitchen cleaning while the women relax in the living room. My father packs the dishwasher while I rinse.

"You in love with her?" He doesn't look at me when he asks this.

I glance at him out of the corner of my eye. "Yeah," I say, handing him a frying pan.

"She's your boy Woods' girl, ain't she?"

"Ex," I say.

"Same thing. You don't touch what's belonged to another man."

I set down the bowl I'm holding and face my father. Our relationship can best be described as...a lake. Sometimes everything is clear and warm: you can see right down to the floor beneath the water—our issues lay along the bottom like an old shipwreck—undisturbed; other times, it's like something lifts the silt and makes the water murky. The temperature drops and the shipwreck rises to the surface to stare us in the face. I can already tell that today will be one of those days. *Merry Christmas to me*, I think wryly.

"Women are not property. They were in a relationship. That relationship ended."

"She was married to your best friend, son. Bros before h—"

I hold up a hand to stop him before he finishes.

Across the kitchen, Julian, Beatrice's husband, pauses in his conversation with my uncle. He catches my eye and shakes his head slightly. He's telling me to let it go. To bite my tongue and be a good son. Julian, who has witnessed firsthand the explosive arguments I've had with my father, is the family peacemaker, but something about my father using the word *ho* in reference to Billie pushes me over the edge.

"Why'd they get a divorce, irreconcilable differences? She couldn't take it when he left his socks next to the hamper?" He laughs as he closes the dishwasher.

Ever since I was a child he mocked irreconcilable differences as a reason for divorce. He's old school: divorce isn't an option. Women should forfeit careers to be housewives, and men who cry are "fucking pussies."

"He was having an affair with one of my employees."

We all turn at the same time to see Billie standing in the doorway, a casserole dish in her hand. "You forgot this one on the table," she says, ignoring all the stares and looking directly at me.

A smile presses at the corners of my mouth like it always does when I look at her. "Thanks," I say, taking it from her.

Instead of turning around and leaving, she walks deeper into the kitchen. "So, do you guys need any help or would you like to clean and practice misogyny in private?" She looks directly at my dad when she says this, her eyes wide and innocent.

"Ahh, don't take anything I say to heart, Billie. I'm just kidding around."

"Oh, I didn't take it to heart. I don't even have a heart, Woods got that in the divorce."

There's a moment of silence before my father's face cracks into a smile, and then he laughs his famous belly laugh, holding onto the counter for balance. I glance around the room and see that everyone's smiles are painfully relieved. Billie just did what most of us are incapable of doing: working her way into my father's heart. I can already tell he's besotted.

"Let's go, Billie," he says, swinging his arm around her shoulders. "I can tell you some shit about our Satcher here, really good shit—embarrassing."

She winks at me as she allows herself to be led out of the kitchen.

"Who would have thought...?" Julian dries his hands on one of my mother's dish towels. "All we had to do was insult him back and he'd accept us."

"Bro, no—" Nora's husband, Chris, emerges from the fridge holding a beer. "I tried that once and he threatened to kill me."

We all laugh and then things get quiet. I can hear Billie's voice from the living room and then my father's booming reply. They're quipping back and forth.

"You know she's not there yet..." Julian is a shrink. He says shrinky things and I want to punch him in the face.

"I'm not in this for her to be *there*," I say. "Not everyone does things with expectations."

"No, man, no. I know you're not like that. Beatrice said—"

I cut him off. "I don't care what Beatrice said. She's a meddlesome first child. Hands off Billie. She's not up for discussion."

"Damn," I hear Chris say as I leave the kitchen. "He's really in love with this one."

I grit my teeth. Isn't that the truth?

. . .

We leave late, after my mother has piled our arms with Tupperware containers of food. The containers are still warm to the touch as I stack them on the backseat.

"They're going to fall over," Billie says, coming up behind me.

I stand back to let her arrange them. When she straightens up, she gives me a look that says she's amused with me.

"Can arrange websites, business modules, and—" I smack her on the butt before she can finish and she yelps playfully. Once we're on the highway she swivels in her seat to face me and says, "Okay, let's discuss..."

I glance at her and see that she's grinning.

"What would you like to discuss?"

"So, I love them," she says, and suddenly my heart feels huge and warm like someone poured gasoline on it and lit a match. "What? Why do you have that look on your face?" She reaches over and sticks a finger in my dimple.

Instead of pulling her finger away, she keeps it there in the recess of my cheek.

"Heartburn..." I hit my chest with my fist like it's especially painful.

She reaches into her purse as she speaks the names of my family members, each one sounding like a different key on a piano. As she speaks, she pulls out a bottle of Tums and shakes two of the pastel circles into her palm. I expect her to hand them to me, but she reaches over and puts them between my lips instead. I close my eyes when her fingers touch my mouth, fighting the urge to put them between my lips so I can taste her. She's babbling on, giving me a rundown of each person in my family.

She ends her little speech with: "And no one agrees with

anyone else, but it doesn't matter. Everyone says their piece and there is so much love. So much."

I recall her mother in the hospital sitting at her bedside, quiet and stiff. If that's what she grew up with, my family would definitely be a culture shock: loud, abrasive ... and like she said—full of love.

When I pull into the parking garage underneath my building, Billie is slumped in the passenger seat, asleep, her full lips pursed like she's asking for a kiss. I watch her for a minute, her breathing steady, her eyelids still. I've never been in love, not until her, and I never want to be again—it hurts. Love hurts in the way a toothache hurts: you can't ignore it, and it's always there throbbing and aching, reminding you ... *of what?* I think desperately. *What is it reminding you of?*

That you're human. That you have weakness. That your weakness is another person.

Goddammit. I run my hands over my eyes, my cheeks, my chin. This is bad. This is very bad. My ex-girlfriend is having my baby, and I'm in love with a woman who isn't available. Life has many flaws, but the most prominent of them is the unpredictability. *Plot twist!* I think as I reach over to wake Billie up. I touch her hand, running my fingers over the puckered skin of her knuckles and saying her name. She breathes deeply and opens her eyes, focusing on me.

"We're home," I say.

She smiles faintly, stretching.

"Home," she says softly. "Where is that anyway?"

"The place that makes you feel peace," I answer.

She stares at me through her lashes, looking momentarily confused, her body angled toward me, palms pressed between her knees for warmth. She seems to be considering what I said because the next minute she reaches for me. Her movement is slow, like she's underwater. I watch as her hand floats toward me; it hooks around the back of my neck, the warmth of her touch sparking a rush of gooseflesh across my arms.

"Satcher..." she says.

It sounds like she's asking me a question, so I answer her. I reach out to grab her behind the head, pulling her toward me. With my fingers gripping her hair, we kiss. Our ragged breathing is amplified in the stillness of the car, the almost empty parking garage an even wider emptiness beyond that. It feels like we're floating in our own world. Without the car on, the cold seeps in and soon the only warmth is coming from our bodies. It makes us hungrier for touch. Billie is halfway across her seat and into mine. Her hands are inside my shirt, held against my skin like she's trying to warm herself as our lips move slowly together.

"You feel so good," I say into her hair. My hands are under her sweater, on her breasts, which are hot to the touch.

"It's just because it's so cold." She buries her face against my chest so that her voice is muffled. I cup her head with my free hand, not relinquishing my hold on her breast, and dip down to kiss her crown.

"Billie," I say, and I swear I can see my breath. "Everything about you feels good: your body, your mind, your company. The cold is convenient, but it has nothing to do with you and how you make me feel."

She sits very still even though I know she must be uncomfortable stretched halfway across the armrest. I think of something then, and letting go of her head, I reach into my pocket awkwardly, pulling the tiny white button she gave me that night we were at Summertime Sunday. I hold it toward her in the center of my palm.

"What's—" Her face registers recognition. "Oh..." Her voice is quiet, dropping to a whisper. "You still don't remember," she says.

She sounds disappointed which makes me feel guilty.

"You were drunk ... I guess I just thought..." She trails off and stares out of the passenger side window.

I'm losing her. I grab her chin and pivot her face back toward me, looking her in the eye.

"Remind me," I say.

It's so cold. We should probably head up to the apartment, but I'm afraid if we leave the car the spell will be broken.

"It was at the wedding—Woods and mine. Halfway through the reception I snuck out to the balcony to take a breather, just to get away from everyone for five minutes and collect my thoughts, you know?"

I nod, urging her to continue.

"You were already out there—" she says.

And then I remember, faintly. I was drunk, Billie was right. I'd gone outside to do something similar while the DJ's music pounded rhythmically from inside. I'd been staring out over the city, a city that I saw every day but never tired of. That was the way Billie and I were the same—we both loved New York.

I heard the door open, the blast of music from inside, and then it was abruptly cut off as the door closed again. I knew it was her before I turned around. I've always known when she's in a room, I can feel her. Setting my drink down on the ledge overlooking the west side of the city, I'd turned around. Her white dress was framed against the dark backdrop of the doors that led inside. Led to everyone who wasn't us. She walked toward me without a word and leaned her elbows on the railing, her eyes trailing the lights of the city.

"I want this to be over already," she said.

When I looked at her, the space around her head wobbled like the air was moving. Too much to drink. I rubbed my eyes. I thought about telling her the truth right then and there, that I shared her sentiment and couldn't wait for the night to be over. That my heart was throbbing in my chest like someone had squeezed it until it was tender. Before I could say anything, she'd turned to me.

"My hair is stuck."

"What?"

She turned so that her back was to me and lifted her hair off her neck. In my haze of alcohol and self-pity I saw a strand of brown snagged onto her dress. I reached out, tugging on the hair, and Billie yelped.

"Sorry," I said, shamefaced. "Hold on..."

She waited patiently, her arms still holding her hair up, her neck exposed. Spread out in front of her was the whole city we loved, and I had the urge to tilt my head down and kiss the graceful slant of her neck. But she wasn't my bride.

I struggled with the hair for what seemed like five minutes, but it wouldn't unsnag from what it was caught on.

"Are you happy?" It was a spontaneous question that should've received a fairly typical answer. I realized too late that I didn't want to hear her answer, and that with the current state of my heart, it was a stupid thing to ask.

When she said, "I don't know," in that smoky voice of hers, my hand stilled.

"Well, you will be," I said it with confidence because I believed she would be.

She sighed deeply. "And if I'm not?"

One last tug and to my dismay, the top button of her dress popped off and bounced off the concrete floor. I bent to retrieve it as Billie turned around to see what happened.

"I'm sorry."

She laughed at the dismayed look on my face. "It's just a button."

"Okay," I said, still holding it, still staring down at it in horror.

"And if I'm not?" she asked again.

I glanced up at her face and saw that she was serious. There was apprehension in her eyes, maybe the wedding jitters. Her brow was furrowed and in that moment I knew she needed something from me—not what I wanted to give her—but something.

"Then give me this button and I'll come rescue you." I placed it in her now open palm, closing her fingers over it. Her face swam in front of me. I was so drunk, so drunk and so hurt. She'd smiled and it had reached all the way to her eyes.

"I believe you," she said.

And then the door opened, and the noise of the party reached between us, breaking the spell. I watched her run back inside, almost in slow motion, one of her bridesmaids holding the door open for her.

"Billie..." I say. My words get stuck. How could I forget that?

She remembered. *She remembered.*

"Let's go upstairs," she says.

PART III

CHAPTER THIRTY-SIX

BILLIE

The rain hasn't let up and the bar at Summertime Sunday is closing. The Christmas party ended hours ago, the last of the employees floating out of the door shortly after. Woods and I have been sitting in a booth near the window for the last three hours. Through the rain-dotted windows, the city is a blur of neon signs and brake lights. His suit jacket is slung around my shoulders and my feet rest in his lap. Every few minutes he'll be saying something to me and his hands will start rubbing my arches. Several times I've thought to stop him, but the sentiment is so familiar I don't have the mental strength.

"I read it again, you know?"

"What?" I'm distracted. His hands are so warm.

"Your blog post."

"Really?" I perk up. I'd sit up straighter if it didn't mean pulling my feet out of his lap.

"Yes. You asked me to."

"What does that mean? Since when do you do things I ask you to do?"

"You don't always have to be so hard on me, you know." His eyes crinkle at the corners when he says this.

He's teasing me. I like it. I tighten my lips and pretend I'm put out.

"You were right. I saw that once I took a step back and read it with my own eyes."

"Thank you," I say.

"I—I knew I hurt you. That's not exactly rocket science. But reading the details..."

This is it. I've wanted Woods to read that post—in a way, I'd written it to him. I don't have the courage to ask him what I really want to know, so I settle for this.

"Don't you need to get home?" I ask him.

Woods glances at his watch. "No. It's still early."

"Woods..."

"Stop it, Billie. Stop overthinking everything."

Am I guilty of that? Overthinking? No more than Woods is guilty of underthinking. I smirk at the defiant look on his face ... the wrinkles on his forehead that didn't used to be there. He used to get that look with me and it infuriated me. Now Pearl is the target of his defiance and I don't mind. Not at all.

"Should we get out of here?"

His suggestion doesn't surprise me. It surprises me when I stand up and follow him out. It surprises me when we walk hand in hand through the rain toward Jules' apartment. It surprises me when I invite him in.

I tell Satcher that Woods and I slept together. I don't know why, I think it's the suspicious way he looks at me ... or maybe because of my weak moment in giving him the button. The lie uncurls from my tongue in a moment of recklessness, and I'm not sure who's more shocked by my confession: me or Satcher. The worst part is I'm not even ashamed. I do it for the coldness that filters into his eyes. I know he's struggling with his feelings for Jules, the lingering effects of what we had together still clouding his thinking. Jules confided her suspicions about being pregnant a week before the Christmas party. Two nights before we all met at the restaurant she took a test and came into my room to show me the results.

Satcher is angry with me. He thinks I'm better than sleeping with my ex-husband who is currently engaged to my nemesis. I'm not sure I am, but the night I claimed I slept with Woods went completely different than the story I told.

*A*fter Woods and I got to Jules' apartment, all of our rapidly building chemistry extinguished. It was as if the walk from the restaurant to the apartment (a mere five blocks) had cooled the attraction, leaving us tired and emotionally tense. I made drinks anyway, feeling a growing heaviness in my chest. What would I have done if things kept going like they were in the restaurant? Would I have slept with him? My mother always said that our intentions represented our depravity, while our actual behavior showed who we chose to be. Currently, I was choosing to be a lukewarm hostess, not meeting Woods' eyes. I made drinks that were too strong and when I caught sight of my reflection in the kettle my eyeliner had bled and my mascara was smudged. That's what I got for buying the cheap stuff. I looked like a back-alley hooker. I excused myself to the bathroom as soon as I handed Woods his drink and washed my face with scalding hot water. I emerged pink-faced and wearing my fluffy winter robe. There was nothing about my current look that said I was trying to seduce someone.

"You look beautiful," Woods said as soon as I exited the bathroom.

"What? No," I said, stopping dead in my tracks.

He laughed. "You put on your granny robe to send a message, didn't you?"

I eyed him warily as I made my way around the island putting three feet of space between us.

"How did you know that?"

"You used to put on that robe when you didn't want to have sex."

I laughed not just because he was right, but because he knew me so well.

I toyed with the belt of my robe while I stared at him. He watched me so closely, I felt a fleet of goose bumps skitter over my arms.

"Why did you really come back?"

His question jarred me. I was too drunk to lie though, so when I answered it was with the insecure, ugly truth.

"I wanted to know why I wasn't enough."

He dropped his head just as suddenly as he asked the question, and I stared at him earnestly. *Please, please, I'm so close to answers.*

When Woods looked up, his expression was one I'd only seen on his face twice before: once when his grandfather died, and the other when I broke down and sobbed after he told me he wanted a divorce.

"Billie," his voice was strained. "You were enough. It was me who was never enough. Every day I tried to meet your expectations and every day I failed."

A cry escaped my throat. How could he say that? I'd adored him. In a flash he'd gone from adoring me to treating me like a stranger. It was shocking. I'd never been able to figure it out—why men were given that internal switch and women were not. One little flick and they could turn their feelings on and off—so in control. *I used to love this one and now I love that one.* Men were more loyal to football teams than they were to women. They never cheated on those.

"I never asked you for anything. How can you say that?"

"That's exactly right, Billie. Because you didn't need me. I've never felt more like a useless fuck in my life."

I was shocked into silence. In the eight years we were together, three of them married, Woods never once mentioned anything like this.

"You were the brains, the talent, the ambition. Anything I offered was a dull knife to your sharp one."

"That's not true," I argued. "What did I do to make you feel like that?"

"I made myself feel that way. In the beginning it was what drew me to you, how you were so sure of yourself. So capable and bright. Your brain reminded me of a big city, always lit up and spinning around and around. I was just always a small-town boy trying to make it in the big city."

"Goddammit, Woods."

"Just shush and listen, Billie."

I closed my mouth. He held his sweating glass between his hands, but I hadn't seen him drink anything.

He shook his head, curls falling all over. Woods and his big hands, and his big eyes, and his big curls. I always loved being underneath those hands.

"It was easy with Pearl. She thought I was the beginning and the end."

His words were like an icy hand around my heart, fingers digging, digging. "So you left me for Pearl because she fed your ego? Bravo." I was already turning away, finished with this conversation. The thief of love was ego. How weak was love that it could not sustain insecurity? Wasn't it supposed to do the opposite?

"It wasn't love..."

I stopped.

"Hear me out," he said.

"I'm listening."

He walked around to face me.

"What I felt for you was love. The poets, the philosophers—they say things about perfect love. How it heals, how it behaves, how it braves all things. But they're idealizing it. Best-case scenario: love saves the day. But I was the worst-case scenario. Love is sometimes powerful enough to self-destruct. Because when an imperfect person wields the most powerful weapon in the universe, they're bound to trip over their own feet."

"How can you say this to me now?" My voice lifted and warped like old linoleum. Words that could have saved me before—saved us before—given too late.

"I'm just a stupid man, Billie. You always had too much faith in me."

It was true ... maybe. But it wasn't Woods I put my faith in, it was love. I believed it to be the ultimate redeemer, never considering that when something so perfect was handed to the imperfect, it was misused.

"I meant it when I said forever. But I overshot my ability to fulfill that promise. And I'm sorry."

My heart swelled with hurt and flowed into my chest. I let myself feel it rather than pushing it away like I normally did.

"Do you love her?" I asked.

"Yes."

"Good," I said. "Treat her better."

This time my feet didn't drag when they walked away.

CHAPTER THIRTY-SEVEN

That's how we left it and that's how I think it is going to stay.

I spend a magical and unexpected Christmas with Satcher, during which my heart swells to three times its size. I barely remember that I'm an emotional cripple, that I have abandonment issues, or that I'm in New York for revenge. I'm just Billie, happy Billie ... fun Billie ... witty Billie. Some people have a way about them. They make you feel like ... an unencumbered version of yourself. An alternate reality Billie.

Two days after Christmas, I'm on Satcher's couch in my pajamas working on some last-minute things for the blog. Satcher left before I was awake, so I'm alone with my foot propped up when the knock sounds on his door. I frown at the disturbance, wondering if I should get up or just pretend no one's home. Since no one buzzed up, it's probably a neighbor. I decide to ignore it, settling back into the couch, but then the knock comes again, harder this time.

Cursing, I struggle off the couch and hobble over, just as the intensity of the knocking increases. Whoever is on the other side of that door is about to get a mouthful from me. I fling open the door without looking through the peephole and find myself face-to-face with Woods. I gasp, and it's sort of funny. Who gasps in real life? He has about four days' worth of stubble along his jaw and he's wearing glasses instead of his contacts. I think back to the last time I saw Woods wear glasses, college maybe.

"What are you doing here?" It sounds more aggressive than I intended, but I square my jaw and stare him down.

My place in New York is changing, my feet finally finding solid ground. I may have moved back for the wrong reasons, but I am going to make a life here for the right ones.

"We need to talk," he says.

My stomach drops. The very words he said to me the night he told me about Pearl.

"We've already done that. We're supposed to be moving forward with our lives."

"Five minutes," he says.

There's something on his face that makes me step aside and let him in. He wanders into Satcher's place and looks around like he's seeing it for the first time. His eyes sweep the room, lingering on my nightgown, which is tossed across the back of a barstool.

"Where do you sleep?" he asks.

"In the bed."

I pretend not to notice the look on his face. He clears his throat and then reaches up to take off his glasses.

"I ended things with Pearl." Woods rubs his eyes.

I stare at him, frozen in disbelief. "What?"

One stubby little sentence and my insides are churning. I drift toward the window, my fist clutching the neck of my shirt, and stare out at the passing traffic.

I feel like I need time to process, but Woods is waiting for me to say something.

"Why?"

He takes a step toward me. "After our conversation—"

I hold his gaze waiting for him to finish.

"After our conversation, I did a lot of thinking ... about myself ... you."

Thinking? Now you're thinking? Years too late.

"Okay..."

I picture him skulking around Pearl and her parents on Christmas day, merely picking at his food. It's a sad thing to imagine until you include the fact that he was thinking about me, maybe even wanting to be with me rather than his soon-to-be family. This news is still settling over me when Woods says his next words. I brace myself because the look in his eyes tells me something is coming.

"I'm still in love with you, Billie."

His words hit me like cold water over the head. My shoulders jar with the impact of them.

"Don't freak out on me, okay, Billie?"

He's watching my face carefully, looking for approval. He's still scared of me, I realize. His jaw used to lock up like that when he was afraid of my reaction. I let nothing show, and it's not like I really have to try not to—my body has seized up in anticipation.

"Okay," Woods says. "This is..." He rubs a hand along his face, his mouth dropping open when his fingers reach his chin. "I tried to replace you with a woman who wouldn't question me, challenge me, fight with me. Because it made me feel," he looks away while he searches for the word and then comes back with, "—bigger."

Everything feels cold: my hands, my face, my heart. I don't say anything because I don't trust myself to speak.

"I was just looking for an easier version of you. But that's not what I want. I want the full version, the version that scared the shit out of me before."

TARRYN FISHER

"Woods..." I sound breathless. I *am* breathless. "I think," I say slowly, "that our time has come and gone."

I don't know why I say it. Didn't I come back to New York hoping for this very thing to happen? Wasn't it my plan to come between him and Pearl? So why do I feel such trepidation?

"No." He takes a step toward me.

I'm shocked to see his tears, the determination on his face.

"Billie, forgive me. I want to make things right. We belong together."

I don't have time to respond. Woods drops to his knees in what I can only interpret as supplication and wraps his arms around my waist, pressing his cheek to my abdomen. I have nowhere to put my hands so I drop them gently to his head.

*A*nd that's how Satcher finds us: me standing in his foyer cradling Woods' head against my belly, my face slack with shock. He fills up the doorway, his expression moving from surprise to anger. Our eyes meet and I hold them. I hold them not knowing what to say or do ... begging him mentally to see the situation for what it is. But no, how could he? He sees what is clearly in front of him: two old flames embracing in an intimate and emotionally charged way. As Woods sobs into my belly, Satcher first rests a hand on the doorframe like he's trying to hold himself up. He closes his eyes and I'm frozen to the spot, my heart aching, my reason tangling with my emotions. And just as suddenly, he's gone. He doesn't bother to look at me again, or close the door to his own home. His absence is startling. It feels permanent.

. . .

I don't see him again for a very long time.

CHAPTER THIRTY-EIGHT

It's four o'clock in the afternoon. My eyes are closed and someone is touching my face. Her voice is soothing, and I've been drifting in and out of sleep for the last twenty minutes. It's the day before my wedding and my husband-to-be bought me a spa package. I know I'm supposed to be relaxing, but I'm wound so tight, a few minutes ago she had to tell me to relax and stop clenching my fists.

"So let me get this straight. You came back to steal your ex-husband from the woman he cheated on you with, so you enlist his best friend to pretend to be in a relationship with you. Then you actually fall for each other, only to be thwarted by the woman he used to be in a relationship with who is also your friend."

"Yes," I say weakly. "That about sums it up."

"Dang, girl. That's messed up."

"Right," I say.

"And are you happy?"

"Yes ... I don't know. I'm confused."

"I'd say. This might be cold..."

She slathers a thick, muddy substance across my cheeks that smells like grapefruit. She doesn't speak for several minutes as the cold brush touches my skin again and again, her swipes brisk and experienced. When she's finished, I hear her get up from her stool and move around the room. I don't open my eyes; instead, I pretend I didn't just share with a complete stranger all of my life woes.

"So, tomorrow you're going to marry your ex-husband. That's something. You don't hear a story like that every day."

"I know," I say quietly.

"I hope you don't mind me asking this, but how do you know he won't cheat on you again?"

Of course her words hit me where I'm sore. Haven't I thought that a thousand times? Once a cheater, always a cheater ... a leopard never changes its spots...

"I don't, I guess. He's done a good job of explaining why it happened, but there's always that worry in the back of your mind."

I have to bite my lip to keep from crying. She works in silence for a while, and I'm grateful for the chance to pull myself together. When she's finished with her treatment, she touches me lightly on the shoulder to let me know she's done.

"I'm all finished. I hope everything works out for you, Billie."

Such simple words, but they sink deep. Me too, me too.

Since the facial was the last treatment of the day, I dress and head to the front desk where the receptionist grins sleepy-eyed while she checks me out. Tomorrow I will marry the man I've loved since I was a girl in college. And sure, we've devastated each other, tossed our lives around like a salad, and dragged other less than innocent people into our mess. But, we're older now, wiser ... more ready for the commitment ahead of us. I sign my receipt and slip my credit card back in my bag.

"Don't forget the ice," she says.

My head, which was bent over my purse, snaps up. She's not looking at me. I swipe my hair behind my ear and look at her cautiously, my heart pounding.

"What did you say?"

She looks surprised to still see me standing there.

"Oh, I wasn't talking to you..." She jabs her finger toward the door where a girl in scrubs and a heavy jacket is exiting the salon. "Christmas party tonight. She has to get the ice."

"Oh." I sound dumb even to my own ears. "Happy holidays," I say meekly.

I'm in my car heading back to my apartment when I notice that my shirt is on inside out. I burst into tears without really knowing why. I'm not crying because of the shirt; it's a barely obvious faux pas. I'm crying because ... *why?* Because the last eleven months have been something like a summer snowstorm. Because I let everything happen as if I were a mere observer of my life instead of an active participant. There has been a lot of scrambling, outbursts of emotion, and tears—bucketfuls of tears. I flew home to Washington right after Woods made his confession. Another example of me fleeing when I'm scared. God, I'm like the fucking cowardly lion.

He followed me there in true Woods' style, showing up at my parents' house in the middle of the night, soaked to the bone, and valiant in his effort. Just the sound of his voice sent me into a panic. I hid behind the living room door while my father spoke with him and inevitably sent him away. My parents were disapproving of me. They loved Woods and here he was, chasing *me,* their wayward daughter.

Woods, not to be deterred, drove into town and got a room at the Palace. It was my parents who convinced me to talk to him two days later, my parents who'd always loved Woods and didn't know what he'd done. When I finally sat down with him (after swallowing my mother's Xanax), I was stiff and milky-eyed from days of crying.

"If you want to move here, I'll come," he said. He was sitting across from me in my father's favorite armchair, leaning forward, hands clasped between his knees. "I'll sell everything and come be with you."

I believed him. I snorted. The very last thing I wanted to do was live in Washington again: miserable, weepy Washington.

"Billie, anything. I'm a changed man. I'll do anything."

It took him another week to convince me to come back to New York with him, and I have a feeling it was his last *hurrah* before he left to go back himself. He'd come to sit on my porch, which was really just four feet of concrete with two rickety old chairs I'd found at a thrift store. I'd been sitting in one sipping tea when he'd walked the path from the main house, his head bowed against the drizzle.

"Billie," he'd said in greeting.

"Woods," I mimicked back.

"Is there any alcohol in that?" he'd asked.

I handed him the mug because there was. He took a few appreciative sips before passing it back to me.

"Just give me one month," he said. "You can come right back if you don't want to stay—I'll pay for everything..."

I'd looked at the water dripping off his hair and made my decision. I couldn't stay here. I could choose somewhere else or go back to New York, but I couldn't stay here. I agreed, partly because I wanted to believe him, and partly because my old habits were settling in. Just that morning I'd been on Craigslist searching for a used treadmill. I needed to get away from the rain and the trees—a forest of trees pressing in on me until I felt like I couldn't breathe. Give me skyscrapers any day, but trees were the thing that made me feel claustrophobic. My parents were starting to look at me in that dubious way that said they didn't understand me. And I hated that—hated the feeling of not being understood. And so, I'd packed up my things on a Monday and by Tuesday I was sitting in the back of a cab speeding through the Midtown Tunnel with Woods holding my hand. *You should be happy.* The thought played itself over and over in my head as I tried to grasp this elusive happiness. Happy ... happy ... what was happy? Getting what you wanted?

I stayed with Loren, refusing to go anywhere near the apartment Woods and Pearl had shared. Pearl vacated his life and home the day he left New York to retrieve me from Washington. He said he'd come home from work and confessed that he was still in love with me. She'd slapped him across the face and stormed out, taking his car. But Woods hadn't cared about the car. He'd booked a one-way ticket to Seattle and caught a cab to the airport. By the time we arrived back in New York together, the only thing left of their relationship was the $10,000 credit card bill she'd left on the counter. Woods grimaced when he picked it up.

"She went on a little post-breakup shopping spree," he'd said.

Since Woods' lease wasn't up for another few months, he stayed there until we found our own place.

*J*ules, who has not spoken to me since Satcher told her about us, is still in her apartment. I imagine she turned her office into a nursery. I heard from Woods that she called me a snake and said she never wanted to lay eyes on me again. Though she had never wanted to lay eyes on Woods again after he cheated on me, and yet, she was divulging her feelings about me to him. Jules, who had been my friend when no one else was; I hadn't meant to hurt her. I tried to reach out to her, but she sent my calls to voicemail, and eventually I was forced to write her an email. Even though I hadn't known they were together before Satcher and I were, she didn't want to talk to me. I was the reason they weren't together; she blamed me for her lack of happiness. Their baby, born in September, was a boy. I saw a picture of him online, a tiny version of Satcher that they named Clive.

I haven't seen Satcher, not since that night he saw Woods and me embracing in his foyer. I'd sent him an email handing in my resignation for Rhubarb and apologizing for ... everything. My heart had dropped when instead of Satcher, Bilbo had been the one to answer my email, asking for an address where he could forward my things. The slight hurt, the fact that he'd rather Bilbo deal with me than talk to me himself. I didn't know how he was, or where he was. Every time Woods and I were out together I looked for him: in restaurants, at bars, at the post office. I looked for his shoulders, his side part, his dimple. I looked with an aching heart, but the city I loved seemed to have taken his side and was hiding him from me. There'd been two occasions where I'd smelled his cologne: once had been in a restaurant, and the other in a bar. I'd spun around both times to search for him, but there had always been a stranger there instead.

Don't forget the ice.

Woods brought home a puppy after three months of us being officially back together. He's a Saint Bernard and already the size of a small suitcase. I balked when I saw him, which made Woods upset.

"We talked about this," he'd said. "I thought you were ready—"

"I was ready for a ... Chihuahua," I said, stroking the puppy's silky head. "Not a dog giant. We live in an apartment in the city."

"I was walking past a pet shop." Woods looked pained, like he desperately needed my approval. "He looked so sad in his cage," he finished.

Typical Woods. He liked sad women and sad animals. I'd summed it up to a savior complex. I didn't mention the fact that this apartment was going to feel like a cage when the puppy was full-grown. I'd been out of work since I left Rhubarb, and despite my hesitation about being a pet owner, I currently had all the time in the world to adjust to it.

"Okay," I said. "What are we naming him?" He was already growing on me because he did indeed have sad eyes.

Woods looked relieved as he sat down next to me on the couch.

"Percy," he said.

I picked Percy up and stared into his eyes.

"I'm sorry in advance for being a terrible dog owner,

Percy." He whined and licked my face and I was instantly in love.

Percy, as it turned out, was a one-person dog. I was the chosen one and he rarely left my side, skidding around corners to keep up with me, and sleeping on my feet while I cooked. It was hard not to laugh at the wounded looks Woods gave the dog, like he'd been betrayed in the worst way. Woods whined about it too: *"I'm the one who wanted a dog. I'm the one who saved him. And all he does is follow you around."*

Three months into our dog ownership, Woods suggested getting another dog. His excuse was that Percy needed company, but I knew that his real reason was his need for favoritism. I spiraled into one of the worst depressions I'd ever experienced. Woods was temporarily silenced by my very poignant emotional plummet. This was who Woods was—it wasn't even his fault. People were capable of changing small things in their behavior: being neat, eating healthier, and controlling their tempers. But there were core things like Woods' propensity to look elsewhere for attention. That was not a behavior, but rather an innate flaw that led to the demise of our marriage. It was a much larger issue than remembering to put socks in the hamper, and it put my heart at risk. When I finally emerged from a three-week darkness, Woods proposed to me. Again.

He took me to the Bahamas, a vacation he said I desperately needed. We drank, we ate, we swam until our fingers wrinkled like raisins and our skin tanned dark. I felt ... better. And then one night after dinner, he got down on his knee in the restaurant and presented me with a blue box. Everyone was looking, everyone was cheering when I felt obligated to say yes. That night when Woods snored softly beside me I mentally berated myself for being too concerned with what people thought to voice my fear. Fear of marrying someone again after they hurt me so deeply, fear of never being enough to keep Woods tethered to our relationship, fear that I was trying to save something that died a long time ago.

You wanted this, I remind myself. *You came back for this*. And then we got back to New York and everyone was so happy that we worked it out. They'd always thought we belonged together, they said. And so I was swept into this belonging, because I was convinced of it myself not that long ago. The wedding date was set. I got what I wanted.

CHAPTER THIRTY-NINE

I'm locking up the apartment when a delivery guy steps out of the elevator. He has his tongue curled around his upper lip, and his head is bent as he studies the address on an envelope.

"Oh shit," he says when he almost runs into me. "Sorry."

He has one bud still in his ear, while the other is draped across his shoulder. I can hear the music playing faintly as his head moves up and down to the beat. He glances at the door behind me and then back at the envelope.

"Billie Tarrow?" he asks.

"That's me."

He hands me the envelope. "Sign here and here," he says, indicating the lines.

I'm about to ask for a pen when he buffers one at me.

"Thanks." I scribble my signature on the lines, and he rips off the receipt before handing it back to me.

"Nice day," he mumbles.

I lift my hand in a goodbye even though his back is to me.

I glance at the return address. It's an attorney's office; I don't recognize the name. My phone rings. It's Woods. I'm late. I stick the envelope in my bag and run for the stairs so I won't have to wait for the elevator.

I'm rifling around in my bag looking for the tiny box I packed with my earrings when my fingers touch the envelope. I'd forgotten about it. I hesitate, eyeing the return address. I don't really have time, but what if it's something important?

I rip it open, tenting the cardboard. Inside is a smaller brown envelope. There's a bright pink sticky note stuck to the front of it, Satcher's bold handwriting filling most of the tiny square. I blink hard, a sudden whirlwind in my chest. There is pain, and nostalgia, and regret ... so much regret. My eyes blur as I read. Even his handwriting is beautiful. How can handwriting make you miss someone this much?

*B*illie,
This was always yours. I was just taking care of it in your absence.

My heart wants only good and beautiful things for you. Forgive me for not reading between the lines.

*L*ove,
Satcher

I take longer to open the next envelope, my hands shaking. Inside is a single sheet of paper signed by both Satcher and his attorney. It takes a moment to process what I'm seeing. There is a blank line where my signature goes. He signed his share of Rhubarb over to me. I lift a hand to cover my mouth, tears stinging my eyes. Had this always been his plan? I say his name out loud.

"Satcher ... oh my God, Satcher."

There's a knock.

"Billie," my mother calls through the door. "Are you ready?"

I'm not.

"Just another minute, Mom." I have to work to keep my voice steady, but even if she heard me crying she wouldn't have come in without an invitation. The reality of this doesn't bother me anymore; trying to pretend the situation is different doesn't change the situation, it just puts you in a slumber deep enough to never learn acceptance. My family is detached, and because of that, I attached myself to Woods so fiercely, hoping to find what I'd been missing my whole life. My heart is topsy-turvy as I walk to the window and stare down at the parking lot. I see Woods locking up his car. He bends his knees to check his reflection in the window. He looks so handsome in his suit. I've loved Woods for so long. I left my home and my family in search of adventure, New York being the epicenter of excitement and power in my mind. I'd found Woods along the way. He'd been so into me, in the way twenty-year-old men were into their twenty-year-old girlfriends. But like most women in their twenties, I'd changed ... evolved. Woods hadn't liked the changes. In retrospect, he hadn't been mature enough to deal with them, especially when I went from a sleepy, wholesome PNW girl to a career-obsessed New Yorker.

I move away from the window and sit in the only chair in the room.

Satcher always liked who I was—even when I was wearing the Martha Stewart dresses, even when I was a bitter bitch. How had I not seen what was right in front of me? It's because I was obsessed with what was behind me, my future always clouded by my stiff-knuckled inability to let go.

I walk to the door, resting my palm on the rich mahogany. "Mom?" I breathe.

I hear the shuffling of feet, the swish of fabric as she comes to stand on the other side of the door. She's been waiting this whole time, not saying anything, but there. I open the door. At first she looks surprised, but when she sees me in my dress, tears spring to her eyes. She lifts her hands and crisscrosses her palms over her heart. It's something I've seen her do since I was a little girl, the emotion she cannot express verbally, suppressed into that one action. I grab her wrists and drag her into the room, kicking the door closed behind us.

"Billie, what are you doing? I think they're ready to—"

"Shh, Mom," I say firmly.

She falls silent, and I begin pacing the small space between the window and the mirror, wringing my hands. I tell her everything I should have told her before: about Woods cheating, about Angus and the accident ... about Satcher, and Pearl, and Jules. When I'm done, she steers me to the chair I was sitting in earlier and sits me down.

"I'm not good with words, Billie."

It's the first time she's ever said something so candid to me and I'm not sure what to say so I wait for her to go on.

"But you're my daughter and I want to be there for you. We don't understand each other. We don't. But I want to try."

I start to cry and she doesn't know what to do, so then I start to laugh.

She doesn't laugh with me; instead, she pulls her lips into a tight line and pats me on the shoulder.

"He didn't want to leave you," she says.

"Woods?" I ask through my laughing tears.

"No," she says slowly. "Satcher. When you were in the

hospital, he was by your side the whole time. He got really agitated with me when I told him I wasn't staying."

For some reason I can't meet her eyes. Talking about Satcher makes me feel ashamed.

"Yeah," I say softly, thinking of the deed to Rhubarb. "He's always been really good to me."

"Well, there you have your answer, don't you?"

I look her in the eyes this time, trying to understand what she's saying.

"Mom...?"

"I didn't know," she says, not meeting my eyes. "About what Woods did ... if I'd known..."

I hold up my hand to stop her. "It's not your fault. I didn't tell you guys because I thought you'd side with him anyway ... tell me that it was my fault..."

"Well," she says slowly. "It wasn't. And you deserve better than to always be wondering if he's going to do it again."

The tears that I was holding back spill.

"I think that you're more in love with Satcher than you're willing to admit. And I think that marrying someone you compare to someone else is a very, very big mistake."

I hadn't ever thought about it like that, but how many times had I compared them over the years? Satcher spoke Spanish fluently, he started and sold companies, becoming a millionaire at the age of twenty-seven. Satcher worked with a charity that sent him to Africa two weeks out of every year. When you spoke, he really, really, listened; he wasn't just waiting to speak. I'd been intimidated by him, I'd gone to him for business advice ... and more recently, personal advice. And when I asked him to do stupid, ridiculous things like pretend to be my boyfriend—he'd done it ... for me. He wasn't confused by the way I changed over the years; he'd been supportive of every new personality and style I'd tried to fit myself into.

When I look up, my mother is watching my face carefully.

"I'll send Woods in so you can talk to him," she says.

I nod. I watch her ramrod straight back disappear out the door before she closes it gently, the latch clicking like an angry tongue. Now is the time for me to think. I need to have something to say to Woods, who is unsuspecting, dressed in his suit and ready to get married to me ... again. *This is so ridiculous*, I think. This is exactly what I moved back here for. I got everything I wanted, and now...

There's a light knock on the door, Woods' unsure voice asking if he can come in. I head for the floor-length mirror feeling like there are a hundred rocks clanking around in my gut.

"Come in," I call through clenched teeth.

When I turn around he's frozen to the spot, his smile sincere and sweet. My heart beats a little faster, and in the five seconds it takes for him to walk over to me I doubt everything: him, Satcher, myself...

"Billie," he says softly. "Wow. You're even more beautiful than the first time we did this."

A strangled sound issues from my throat and I'm tempted to cover my face with my hands.

"Oh no," he says, seeing the look on my face.

I sit. I sink into the chair, my legs trapped by my dress which is tight around my thighs. If I was compelled to run, runaway bride style, I'd fall flat on my face as soon as I stood up.

"Woods..." I begin. "Why do you want to marry me ... again?" The hastily added *again* makes him smile.

"Because we shouldn't have gotten divorced in the first place."

That prickles. I push out my bottom lip, blinking at him hard. "You cheated on me," I say.

Woods looks momentarily flustered and then his face relaxes, but not without effort.

"Yes. Let me rephrase. I should have been faithful to you and then we never would have needed to get divorced."

"You cheated on me because you were unhappy. You didn't like the person I was."

"That's true," he says. "But I like the person you are now."

I blow air through my pursed lips. "That's the thing, Woods, I don't know if I'll stay the same. I can't promise that. I feel as if the person who can love me best is one who doesn't mind when I try something new."

"I can be that," he says quickly.

I look at him doubtfully.

"Woods, you've been chewing Juicy Fruit for the last twenty years. You don't like your world shaken."

"What are you saying, Billie?"

"I'm asking if you really think we should be doing this?"

"Yes," he says without pause. "Absolutely."

I look up at him curiously. "Why?"

"Because we are each other's first loves."

I mull over his words. Nice words. Reassuring words ... and yet they do nothing to reassure me. People work their way back from cheating, it is entirely plausible that we *were* supposed to be together. But we detoured, and now...

"It doesn't feel right, Woods." It's the most honest thing I can say. I expect him to protest, but he just looks at me, waiting. "I'm not soft, and worshipful, and sweet. And I'm afraid that's what you need. That's what you've always needed. I don't have confidence in myself to be that for you."

"I'll take you as you are, Billie. That's what love is."

"At what price?" I ask him. "How soon will I make you miserable again? How soon until you—"

"No. I'd never do that to you again."

I sniff because I don't know what to say—what to believe.

How long until he makes *me* miserable? When we were together I was always stuck between trying to make him happy and trying to make myself happy. Maybe it is selfish to think that way, but maybe the type of relationship exists where you could both be yourselves and make each other happy.

"Woods," I say calmly. "I can't marry you."

He doesn't look as surprised as I thought he would. It's a relief to know that I haven't caught him off guard and that he might have been feeling the same way.

He walks over and kneels in front of me, taking my hands in his. "You're it for me. I messed up and now this is where we are. I take responsibility for that. But I know you, Billie. You're going to regret this the minute you walk out of here."

I pull my hands out of his grasp.

"You don't know me," I say.

I expect to see hurt, but Woods looks angry.

"Come off of it, Billie. I know you better than anyone."

I think of our last months together. Everything that led up to his recent proposal. The effort was there, Woods had been eager to show me that he was a different person. But even as we did all of the things that would have saved our marriage in the first place, a heavy weight has hung over me. I tried to tell myself that I was hung up on past hurts; Woods had done nothing to make me doubt him ... this time. But that's just it, isn't it? One can't be hung up on the past when trying to move forward.

I look him in the eyes when I say my next words. "I'm even further from what I was when you cheated on me, Woods. I'm more of everything bad and less of everything good." My throat is burning while my eyes brim with tears. I don't want to cry. I want to evaporate: disappear.

"It'll take time ... healing," Woods assures me. "You just need to see that I'm here to stay. Things will be different."

"No." I shake my head. "I think what's different is me. I spent years wanting to rewind time and fix things between us. I was so fixated on that that I missed something important. That—I'm not that girl anymore. The one who wanted to be with you. I've wanted to be her again because I liked her better than who I am now."

He laughs. It's a bitter sound in this peaceful place. I can't blame him really. I got us into this mess by coming back to New York with him. By saying yes when he asked me to marry him for the second time. By ignoring the voice in my own mind that has never ever steered me wrong.

"And who do you want to be with, Billie? Satcher? Does he fit who you are now?" There's so much anger in his words I look away.

"I'm so sorry, Woods," I say, the tears moving sluggishly down my cheeks. I reach up to wipe them away.

"You're kidding me." He takes a step away from me, looking out the window.

I flinch at his tone. I think of Satcher then and I have to use all of my restraint not to break down and sob. I'm not okay without Satcher. The thought of never seeing him again, never being able to hear his voice, or see the dimples appear in his cheeks makes me want to double over in pain.

"He doesn't love you. Satcher only loves himself."

"You should go," I say.

I don't have to ask him twice. Woods storms out of the room, slamming the door behind him.

"You're going to be okay," I tell myself.

I'm still sitting in the chair, trapped by my dress, when there's a knock on the door. She doesn't wait for me to invite her in this time; my mother walks directly over to where I'm sitting and helps me to my feet.

"There's a cab waiting downstairs for you," she says. "You can leave out the back."

"What about everyone who came? I owe them—"

"Nothing," she interrupts. "You don't owe anyone an explanation about your choices."

"Wow, Mom."

She looks flustered. "I care too much." Her voice is barely above a whisper, but her words come out so forcefully I startle. "And just because I torture myself by caring too much doesn't mean you should too."

I grab her then and hug her so tight it's her turn to be startled. After a few seconds of shock, I feel her hands lift to my back in our first reciprocated hug in a decade.

"I'm so sorry, Mom. I love you."

"I love you too. You better go."

I nod, letting her go and grabbing the last of my things.

"I'll call you," I say. "To let you know where I am."

"Are you going to find Satcher?"

My hands still on the zipper of my bag. "Yeah. I don't know if he'll..." I mean to say *Forgive me,* but I can't get the words out.

"He will," she says. "He has it bad."

I smile.

CHAPTER FORTY

The cab takes me home where I drop off my bag and grab my coat. I walk the twenty blocks to his building even though it's snowing, and even though I'm still in my wedding dress. I need some time to formulate words ... words to express how sorry I am. My hands are numb and my lungs ache from the cold air, but I feel alive, and that's what counts. If he's not there I don't know what I'll do. Huge mounds of dirty snow are banked against curbs. I walk up the path to his building, and the doorman greets me with a smile.

"He in?" I ask.

"No. He left for the airport." He eyes my dress, which can't be hidden even behind a heavy winter coat.

"The airport? Where's he going?"

"Didn't say."

"When did he leave?"

"Early this morning. He asked me to get him a cab."

"Shit," I say. "Shit. Shit. Shit."

I pull out my phone to call him, but it goes straight to voicemail. He's probably already in the air.

"Try his mom."

I'm still studying my phone trying to decide my next plan of action so I'm not sure if I've heard him right.

"What?"

"His mom. Moms always know where their kids are. Even if their kids are forty. Mine is a huge pain in the ass. She makes me text her every night when I get home so she knows I'm safe."

"Oh my God, are you forty? You look like you're twenty."

"I am." He grins. "But my older sister is thirty-seven and my mom makes her call too."

I laugh and then say, "I—I don't really know her that well. It would be weird to call her."

He shrugs. "If you want to know where he is that's the way to go..."

I thank him and move away from the door. I bite my lip, staring down at the ground. The bottom of my dress is grey, the dirt ground into the silk like a tattoo. I suppose now is the time to stop being such a coward. I almost remarried my ex-husband because I was too much of a coward to move on with my life. I take a deep breath and hit dial.

Jennifer Gable answers on the first ring, and her tone is cheerful but businesslike.

"Gable residence."

There's a long pause after I say my name.

"How can I help you, Billie?" she asks.

"I—I was supposed to get married today," I tell her.

To which she responds, "I know."

"Well, I didn't. And I'm in love with your son. And he left for the airport this morning. And I was hoping you'd tell me where he went."

There's another long pause and then she sighs.

"He's hurting a whole lot, Billie. As his mother, I want to tell you to stay away from him..."

I hang my head in shame.

"I understand," I say. And then I add, "I also don't blame you."

"Hold on a minute, Bille, my husband wants to talk to you." I hear the phone exchange hands and then Mr. Gable's gruff voice comes on the line.

I'm preparing for the worst, a real tongue-lashing, when he says— "He went to Tulum. I told him to barge in on the wedding and object, but you know what a gentleman Satcher is."

"Yeah," I say weakly. "I do."

"You better hurry. If I were him I'd be hitting up the strip clubs and whores..."

I hear Jennifer's sharp rebuke and then Mr. Gable yelps. "I'm in trouble now, Billie. I guess I shouldn't tell her that I gave him money for a decent whore ... OUCH!"

Jennifer's voice comes back on the line as she confiscates the phone from her husband.

"Billie," she says. "Don't go after him unless you mean it."

"Mrs. Gable..."

"Yes."

"I mean it."

"Okay. You better hurry. He's going to be very drunk in a few hours."

She gives me the rest of the information I'll need to find him and I hang up after a tearful thank you. Then I book a flight to Mexico. I don't have time to change, or to pack. If I want to make the flight I have to leave now.

CHAPTER FORTY-ONE

SATCHER

Mexico has run out of sun but thankfully still has an abundance of tequila. The thunderstorms, which the weather channel says will continue throughout the week, match my mood. I drop my bags at the rental and head out to find liquor. On my way out, I drop the button baby Billie gave me in a grate closest to the street and twist off the cap to an airline bottle of vodka. I tip it over the garishly colored Christmas present and then light a match, dropping it ceremoniously. I watch it burn through narrowed eyes, the plastic popping and melting underneath the flames.

I don't want to think about Billie, but she married Woods and the pain is hard to avoid. My heart has been sick for eleven years. I don't remember what it's like not to love her. I'd rather have physical pain than this aching of the heart.

By the time the flames have died there is a rainbow of melted plastic covering the grate like melted crayons.

"Fuck you," I tell it.

I step over the grate where the button baby lies face up, charred but still colorful enough to mock me. In minutes, the rain has soaked through my T-shirt. I find a mini mart and fill a basket with the essentials, stopping on my way out to buy tamales from a taqueria. When I get back to the house I change my shirt and unpack my purchases. I'm about to make myself lunch when there's a knock on the door.

When I open the door, Billie is standing on the threshold. Her hair is dripping water onto her shoulders and her arms are wrapped protectively around her waist. I blink in shock, wondering how a fourth of whiskey got me drunk enough to imagine my heartbreaker on my doorstep. Upon closer look, I see the dark that rings her eyes, and how her bottom lip, fuller than the top, is chapped. This is no fantasy Billie. She looks anxious—one fist clenched against her stomach, her eyes blinking rapidly, the way they do when her mind is going a mile a minute. A quick glance shows a discarded duffel bag lying on the path behind her where she dropped it to knock. We stare at each other for an awkward minute before I finally speak.

"You're supposed to be on your honeymoon."

"Yeah," she says with a shrug.

The shrug could be seen as dismissive, but I notice the way her shoulders curve toward me. She's in pain.

"So why are you here?"

Her little chin juts out. I've seen her do that a million times and it never gets old.

"I called off my wedding," her voice trembles, "because I'm in love with you. I've felt this way for a long time, I just never wanted to admit it. So if you love me, let me in. Otherwise, just slam this door in my face and I'll be on my way—" Her voice drops off, leaving room for the possibility. I consider the slam, I do. A man can only take so much. But she looks so devastated standing there in the rain, dripping on my doormat, that I don't slam the door.

I lean against the doorframe, crossing my arms over my chest and narrowing my eyes at her. She squirms and I enjoy it in the way a burned man enjoys such things.

"So let me get this straight. If I love you, I let you in, and if I don't love you, I slam the door in your face and I never have to see you again?"

She nods.

"Ever, ever again...?" I reiterate.

She presses her lips together and I think she might cry.

"Ever, ever."

I step aside. Relief floods her face. She grabs onto me, wrapping her arms around my torso and pressing her face into my chest. I kiss the top of her head. Billie cries against me for a long time, her tears soaking through my shirt. I figure she has years of tears to let out and she's allowed to take her time. Tears for a lost marriage, tears for fear, and sadness, and relief. When she's exhausted her saltwater supply, I lift her chin with my thumbs and study her face.

"I've loved you for a very long time, Billie."

"Why didn't you tell me?"

"I tried."

"I guess I've never really been good at listening," she says.

"Well, I love you."

"What have you been doing with all those girls then?"

The corner of my mouth pinches up in a smile, but Billie is frowning at me. I put on a serious face and clear my throat.

"Looking for you. In every one of them."

Her bottom lip disappears under her teeth as she blinks at me, and I can tell she has something she needs to say.

"I don't think I ever want to get married again, Satcher," she says seriously.

"Fuck marriage, Billie. I only want you. I don't care what form that comes in."

"Okay," she says.

She hugs me again and I breathe her in. It's hard to describe what I'm feeling. I'm scared. She has hurt me, and she has the power to hurt me more. To keep hurting me. But apparently that is the nature of love, a big fucking risk. I hold my risk close, stroking her back.

"I have tamales," I tell her when we finally separate.

"Real ones?"

"We're in Mexico, of course they're real ones." I lead her over to the little wicker table and chairs and open the container, handing her a fork.

Billie eats like she hasn't eaten in a month. I open a beer and sit back and watch her.

"How did you find me?"

"Your mom."

"No, she would never..."

"Fine, it was your dad. And he got in a lot of trouble for telling me where you were."

She wipes her palms on the leg of her jeans and looks at me squarely.

"Satch, I never slept with Woods the time I told you I did. I was trying to make you hate me."

"Good job."

Her smile is pained. "I'm sorry."

I study her face, her posture. She looks like a woman who desperately needs to be believed.

"I broke up with Willa the night you walked me to the bar."

"You pretended to date her for weeks after that."

"Yes." I take another sip of beer and then Billie takes the bottle from my hand and finishes it off.

"Why did you break up with her?" She licks her lips and goes to the fridge, grabbing two more beers. Setting one in front of me, she slides back into her seat.

"Because I saw the two of you next to each other and she

paled in comparison."

Her face registers surprise. She stares at me for a few beats like she's expecting me to yell *Gotcha!*

"A supermodel paled in comparison next to me?" She laughs, but I don't.

"Yes, Wendy," I say. "Everyone pales in comparison to you."

She sets down her beer. "Are you being for real?"

"I'm being for real."

She stands up and straddles me. Now it's my turn to be surprised.

"Don't ever call me that again, Sasquatch," she says, lowering herself onto my legs.

I wrap my hands around her waist and kiss her nose. "Okay, Wendy."

I think she's going to kiss me but then she rests her head on my shoulder instead.

"Satcher, did you burn the button baby?"

"Yes."

She sighs. "That was special."

"That's why it needed to go."

I run my hands up her back, palms pressing, fingers kneading. It feels good to have her close. She breathes deeply and after a few minutes I realize that she's asleep. I laugh into her shoulder.

"Guess what, Billie?" I say into her hair. She doesn't even stir, just keeps breathing deeply.

"I lied earlier. We are going to get married. And we're going to have a couple of babies. Don't overthink it. I'm just letting you know."

She murmurs in her sleep, and I stand up and carry her to the bedroom. When I lay her down on the bed she rolls onto her side and curls up into a little ball. I'm going to have to go back to the store so I can cook her a proper dinner. Draping a blanket over her sleeping form, I kiss her softly.

"Satcher..." she says as I'm closing the door. I open it a crack and peer in just in case she's talking in her sleep. "Don't forget the ice."

ACKNOWLEDGMENTS

Christine Estevez, Erica Russikoff, Serena Knautz and Amy Holloway for your input and work. Lori Sabin for being the first and last person to see every one of my books. Kim Holden for that amazing e-mail. Claire and Colleen for always going above and beyond. Mom and Jeff for all the babysitting and meals. Maripili, Traci Finlay, and Josh for the details. The readers who stick with me through every genre and season of life. And as always, thanks to the PLNs.

TARRYN FISHER

www.tarrynfisher.com

- facebook.com/authortarrynfisher
- twitter.com/DarkMarkTarryn
- instagram.com/tarrynfisher

Printed in Great Britain
by Amazon